invisible girl

BOOKS BY JILL CHILDS

Gracie's Secret
Jessica's Promise

invisible girl

JILL CHILDS

bookouture

Published by Bookouture in 2019

An imprint of StoryFire Ltd.

Carmelite House
50 Victoria Embankment
London EC4Y 0DZ

www.bookouture.com

ISBN: 978-1-78681-961-1
eBook ISBN: 978-1-78681-960-4

For Dawn

MADDY

I know you. I know you in a way you can't even imagine.

I know you by the times you keep, the places you go. You don't know I'm here. I'm invisible to you. Here, curled in the corner of this shop doorway, with my knees drawn up. I lower my head as you approach, click-clacking on those heels, off to work, and you walk by without even a glance. No idea you're being studied, watched, followed.

This morning, you're running late and your little girl, tugged by the hand, scurries to keep up with you as you stride down the road towards school. She's well turned out: hair scraped back, uniform clean and pressed. She's a little scrawny. Maybe that's because you struggle with the bills; maybe she's just made that way. You turn right at the corner and disappear from sight. Gone now, for the day.

I shuffle to my feet, gather together my bags and slowly move off again, back into motion, down towards the park. There's a chance of breakfast there, at the corner café, round the back. Mick might come. They let him charge his phone. They're kind folk. I see it in their eyes. They understand. They seem to know what it's like to go hungry.

That man visited you again last night, didn't he? I saw you come to the door of the block of flats to greet him, saw his arms reach for you as he stepped inside, out of the darkness, out of the cold. You didn't feel that I was watching, crouched in the doorway of the electrical shop across the road, hiding in the shadows.

Why do you let him come to you, time after time? Do you love him? He doesn't pay you, I hope. Please, no. I couldn't bear that. That smart man in the cashmere coat. Late, as always, long after your daughter was asleep in bed. I want to understand. I want to know you.

I kept watch until the coffee shops closed. Even the Thai restaurant on the corner went dark. I waited for him to leave again. Why does he sneak to and from your door in the darkness, like an alley cat? Why have I never seen you together in daylight? Is he already married? You deserve better.

I want to ask you, one day. You don't know how much I long to ask. I want to be a real person to you, visible at last. I long for it but I fear it, too, fear it most of all. What would you say? Could you ever forgive me? I never forgot, you see. I never stopped searching for you. It was only the hope of finding you that kept me tethered to this world.

So, I hesitate. I bide my time, for now. That's one thing I'm good at now. Waiting. And watching.

BECCA

I don't know when I first saw her – I mean, really noticed her. It was only because of Rosie.

I know it sounds callous but there are so many homeless people on the high street now. They sort of mushroom in dark places. Hunched shapes in corners and doorways, sitting slumped against shop fronts, their legs invisible in grubby sleeping bags and tatty plastic carriers of belongings clustered around them.

It isn't that I'm not aware of them. I am. Painfully aware. I feel guilty every time I walk past someone and pretend not to see them. It's inhumane. I'm embarrassed that I have enough to eat and a roof over my head, and they don't. But how much can I really do to help? A pound here, fifty pence there. It feels so inadequate and I end up doing nothing at all.

I used to argue with Mark about it. He was always cross if I stopped to give coins to a beggar. He called me naïve, as if kindness was something I needed to grow out of.

'They'll only spend it on drink or drugs,' he scoffed. 'You're not doing them a favour, not really.'

For a while, I bought a cup of coffee every day for the man outside the supermarket but he went a bit strange, started complaining that it didn't have enough milk and sugar and started shouting at me, and I avoided him after that. Mental health problems, clearly. Even so, no one should sleep rough nowadays, not in our society. Even if there are deeper problems.

There are other ways of helping and I do give what I can to charities. The local church runs a shelter over the winter – well, it's the church hall and homeless people can go in and sleep there on Monday nights and volunteers cook them supper and breakfast the next morning. I know because when Rosie was smaller, before she started school, we used to go to playgroup on Tuesday mornings and, oh dear, the smell when you walked in at half past nine. Poor souls. We had to open all the windows, however cold it was, and then watch like hawks to make sure none of the toddlers tried to climb up onto the cupboards and fall out.

But Maddy? Well, she was probably there in one of the doorways for a while before I really noticed her.

It's Rosie who sees her first. I mean, actually sees her.

We're just about to cross the main road, coming back from school. I've got a bag of shopping and Rosie's book bag in one hand, and I'm trying to hang onto her with the other. She and her big brother, Alex, move at different speeds when they're out with me. He's the impatient teenager, eye-rolling, embarrassed, hurrying me home. She tends to drag, like a dog on a lead. She's in a world of her own: typical five-year-old. Anyway, the lights change and the crossing starts beeping and I make to step forward into the road and she's like a dead weight, dragging me back. And you never get long at that junction.

'Rosie. Come on.'

She twists around, staring back at the bundle of person on the pavement there, near the crossing. A good place to beg. Somewhere people have to stop. I glance at her. She's sitting on the far side of the pavement, back against the brickwork, with her legs drawn up and a dirty duvet or blanket tucked around her knees. She's wearing a stained, blue padded jacket with a rip at the top of the sleeve which bleeds white stuffing. Her hair's matted and her face is ingrained with dirt, all along the creases of her mouth and nose, black as if someone had drawn her in charcoal.

Her eyes are startling. Very blue, like the jacket. Intense. And she's looking right at us. Still and appraising, as if she's reading us. A bit spooky.

I look down at Rosie. She's looking right back at the woman, with a funny expression on her face. Not repulsed, which is what I'd expect, to be honest, just thoughtful.

She tugs at my hand. She doesn't take her eyes off the woman.

'That lady hasn't got a home.'

I stoop down to her to keep my voice low. Embarrassing. The woman probably heard.

'I know, sweetheart. But we need to go.' I tug on Rosie's hand to get her attention and move her forward into the road.

She digs her heels in. 'But why?'

The crossing switches from the green man to the hurry-up countdown. *Ten. Nine. Eight.* Missed it. I sigh. I've bought frozen peas; they're probably melting. The cars rev up again and start to stream past us.

'How about spaghetti carbonara for dinner?' Alex is going to a friend's house after school so it's just the two of us.

Still, Rosie and the woman stare at each other, eyes locked as if they're reading each other's souls.

I keep a tight hold of her hand. 'And garlic bread?'

Rosie tips her face up to me and says in a low voice, as if she's settled something: 'She could live with us.'

'No, my love. She couldn't.' I try to keep my tone casual, willing the lights to change again.

Rosie frowns. 'Why not?'

'We haven't got room.' It's the first reason that comes into my head and it's true – we're cramped as it is.

Rosie frowns as she considers. 'She could have the sofa bed. In the sitting room.'

Mercifully, the lights turn amber and I get ready to move. 'Let's go.'

I practically drag her across the road. Her head is still turned back, her eyes on that woman. She's a funny kid, Rosie. She's confident and a bit overbearing sometimes, but she's thoughtful, too.

When we reach the other side, she finally faces front again. I take a quick look back over my shoulder at the corner. The homeless woman is looking after us and she has a smile on her lips and a faraway look in her eyes. I wonder how much she'd heard. Probably nothing. Probably she's just on drugs.

I think, *Well, that's that.*

I have no idea.

MADDY

Time's the thing. It warps. It slows, slows, then it stops. Traffic lights changing; people walking; hurry scurry; shop shutters up, shop shutters down – it's all one.

Out of joint.

And if it is moving, how can I tell? No watch. No clock. *Stop the clocks*. Is that Shakespeare? Maybe, maybe not. Church bells on Sunday. That's an anchor – marks out the morning. Calling the faithful. *Ding, dong, the witch is dead*. The sun, of course. That's the first of it: clotted grey light seeping into the blackness, waking me up. Splitting my head open when I want it to go away, leave me alone. No need, waking me up. For what?

It's all gone, always, by morning – whatever liquid lubrication came to hand the night before. Mouth parched, head screeching, feet frozen. Nothing left to take the edge off. Empty arms, empty bottles – story of my life. I take a moment, coming to, working out where I am. For a moment, floundering to the surface through the mud, the darkness, I'm a child, in that boxy army-issue bed in Cyprus, Mum and Dad in the next room. The ceiling fan going whop, whop overhead, stirring the heat. The distant murmur of waves cracking the shore and rattling the stones like fistfuls of dice as they scrape back.

Then I'm a young woman again, sleeping beside John, sex-drunk, wine-drunk, long-limbed and lazy. Then the cramps hit me and life drags me back here. Muscle aches. Bones aches. Feet, legs, back, shoulders. Old woman aches, too soon. Before their time. And I shift my weight and taste the sourness in my mouth, feel the crustiness in my eyes and here I am, still alive, still kicking, against all odds, and so it begins.

I've found a new spot at the back of the small park, down by the river. Children's playground at one end and a tennis court, but trees and thick bushes at the other. You have to time it just right. They lock the gate at dusk. But it's not impossible. Those are good nights.

I go for the rhododendron bushes. Hollow in the middle and pretty dry. You crawl in low and pop up, inside the canopy. We used them as dens when we were kids – not here, back in Yorkshire. Hide and seek. And for spelling tests, later. *Rhododendron. Onomatopoeia.* Words like those sort the wheat from the chaff. The sheep from the goats.

The smells take me back. Damp earth. Splitting sap. Blossom. Yorkshire, at the campsite. Always bloody raining. And earlier, playing with that neighbour girl in Cyprus, bright, bright sunlight and the smell of fresh sweat and pine needles. What was her name? Daphne? Where's Daphne now?

I peer out now, through bleary eyes, at the thick mist rising from the river, cupping the trees. The grit and grey of winter – I try to think of spring. Will I even see it? *Out, out, brief candle! Life's but a walking shadow.* Downright morbid, the Scottish play. Self-obsessed. And look at me now, more weird sister than Lady Macbeth. Old hag. *Fifty-four. Knock at the door.* Death's door, if I'm not careful.

The light finds me, even here, long fingers poking in between the leaves, a greenish tinge. That's the worst part of the day, out here: the start. The cold freezes your bones. Bone chill. No roof. No toilet. No sink. No kettle. No other person, even. Another warm, breathing human being to say good morning and look me in the face as if they can actually see me, a mirror to tell me I'm still alive. Creaking joints. Backache. Hot steam rising as I pee in the bushes and crawl out. Hello, new bloody day, like it or not. Still here then, Maddy, old girl. Off we go.

A young man bought me a cup of tea and a cheese and pickle sandwich yesterday. The kindness of strangers never ceases to amaze. Chicken would be more my thing but mustn't grumble.

And that little girl on the corner. She saw me. I *am* still here. The memory of her comes bursting through the headache and the pains. That was the lightness in my head when I fell into sleep, that was it. That little girl. I stand and stretch slowly and feel the weak sun on my face, watery through the cloud but there, still there. Maybe she's the way, my God-given chance. Because I've seen them together – the girl from the corner and the other little girl – skipping down the high street on either side of that woman. Saturdays. And coming home together after school once, too, holding hands. Friends.

I gather together the jumble of bulging plastic bags with their torn handles and heavy damp and start to walk towards the back of the park, towards the café, opening soon. One foot in front of the other, that's the way.

There's another line, there in my head. *Something the ocean and sweep up the wood.* But that's not Shakespeare, that one. *Think, Maddy. Come on, you know this one.* A modern poet, I used to teach him, too, born up in the north somewhere. Auden! Yes! Old W.H. Auden, wasn't it?

Stop all the clocks... Sweep up the wood. For nothing now can ever come to any good.

BECCA

It's all because of the money. I get paid on the fifteenth of each month and it's always a stretch, at the best of times, making it through. I love working at the wine bar but it's only part-time work and cooking never pays well, even with a share of the tips; but I can't complain, I'm lucky with the hours. The lunch shift fits perfectly with school and Jane is very good. If customers sit late over coffee, she always lets me out on time.

But December's been tough. I really shop around and do my best to find bargains but Alex is set on some computer game that costs a small fortune and he's canny enough now, at fourteen, to know the difference between the real thing and a market stall knock-off. And Rosie deserves some decent Christmas presents, too.

And then there's food and everything. If I've got to host Christmas lunch and include Mark and his mother, I want to put on a good show and do it properly. I'm still angry about it. Mark bullied me and I wish I'd never caved in.

I told him I'd send the children over in the morning so he could do gifts with them. But he didn't want that – he wanted us all together, as if nothing had ever happened between us. He argued that he only wanted what's best for the children. It wasn't about him, it was all about them. As if I didn't spend my whole life trying to put Alex and Rosie first.

Then it became pleading. 'Just one day of the year, Becca.' His face was pathetic with need. 'Please, let me have that, I'm begging you.'

Finally, when I tried to stand firm and said I needed time to think about it, he turned nasty and started saying I was selfish and spiteful and who knows what else. He wrote one of his childish letters about it, full of crude insults and threats.

I've kept all his venomous letters, all locked away in an old suitcase so Alex can't come across them by accident. I feel I need evidence, in case anyone turns around in the future and says I was wrong to leave him, that he's a lovely man. Well, he can be, on the surface. No one else saw how subtly controlling he became over the years, how manipulative. Maybe I need evidence for myself, too, on the days I can't quite believe I really left him and how vindictive he became once I did.

Anyway, he wore me down, in the end, about Christmas Day, and I agreed to let him and his mother come for one last Christmas lunch together as a family. And then never again.

So I'd already drained the bank account when the gas bill came in – a big one; how can you switch the heating off when it's so damn cold? – so I was hanging on by my fingernails until the fifteenth and praying the kids didn't suddenly demand money for this or that. There's always something at school – presents for teachers, collections, sponsoring them for one thing or another.

On the fifteenth, I don't make it to the cash machine before school pick-up: it's too busy at the wine bar. But on the way home, I tell Alex and Rosie to just wait a minute while I check the account and draw out a lump of cash to last me through the rest of the shopping. It's a habit of mine. I've got cards but I'm more conscious of the cost of things if I have the money in my bag and count out notes. It puts me off spending too much.

It's icy – a real cold snap – and just starting to rain. My fingers go numb in the few minutes it takes me to work the cash machine. I'm nearly done when Alex pulls at my arm.

'Mum. Stop her. Please.'

He looks crippled with embarrassment. They're such different kids, those two. Chalk and cheese. And he's at an awkward age anyway, fourteen.

Rosie, of course. I told her to stand where she was, just for two minutes, but she's wandered off, and she's leaning over that homeless woman who's tucked out of the rain in the doorway of a residential block a few doors further down.

'Rosie!'

She doesn't turn. She's bending forward, her arms resting on the top of her legs, peering down at the woman as if she's examining an interesting insect. It makes my skin crawl, just watching. I don't mean to be rude but she must smell awful, that woman, and I don't want Rosie anywhere near her.

'Rosie!' No response. Whatever they're talking about – and they are talking, I can tell – Rosie is absorbed. I glance down at Alex. He's grimacing, his face showing the disgust I feel but am trying not to show.

'Just get her, would you, Alex?'

He hunches his shoulders and strides off towards her. I turn back to the machine and pull out the printed statement. My money's gone in. Thank God. I key in a request for £250 and unzip the middle pocket in my bag, ready to hide it away at once.

'Let GO!'

A high-pitched scream. I twist around, cursing under my breath. Alex is gripping Rosie's shoulder and trying to drag her away while she struggles and flails. Her hand catches him and a slap splatters across Alex's cheek. The woman, a shapeless mass of old clothes, rises to her feet in the shadows and reaches for them, trying to intervene. Her hands are curled, like claws. Grasping for my children.

'Stop!' I run down to them, shoes slapping on the pavement, and pull the two of them apart, turn them smartly, my hands gripping their arms, to march them away.

'Sorry.' I call over my shoulder to the woman without looking her in the face. Too close – she was too close to them. I want distance. The rain flies in our faces, heavier now. We just need to get home, to get warm.

After a few steps, I turn to my son. 'For heaven's sake. What's the matter with you?'

Alex says at once: 'It wasn't me. It was—'

I propel them forward. 'That's enough. I don't want to hear it.'

Alex goes into a sulk and drags himself along by my side, eyes on the ground. I can sense the glower without seeing it.

Rosie twists her head to look at me. She doesn't look cowed, she looks pert and confident as if she's certain she's in the right and I'm just over-reacting.

'What, Mummy? I was just talking to that lady.'

'Two minutes.' The rain thickens, strikes my nose and dribbles down my chin. 'Really? You can't do what you're told for two minutes?'

She shrugs, her face composed. For a few minutes, we struggle forward in a line, fighting the wind. I relax my grip on them as we near the corner and turn into our road.

'I know something you don't know.' Rosie tries to look around me to Alex to see if he's rising to the bait. He shoots her an evil glance. 'Maddy. She's called Maddy.' Rosie smiles up at me, triumphant. I can almost hear her, stooping low over the heap of homeless woman, saying in her chirpy, beguiling voice: 'Hello. I'm Rosie. What's your name?'

'You know what else?'

We're at the front door of the block now and I'm scrabbling to reach through my coat to fish the keys out of my zipped pocket. My hands are so numb, it's a struggle to get the keys in the lock, then to turn them. Alex pushes his way past me as soon as the door opens and stomps up the stairs towards our flat on the top floor.

I close the door and feel the relief of being inside in the stillness, safe, out of the wind and rain. I coax Rosie up the stairs and we pile inside. Alex disappears to their room. I take Rosie's coat from her, then draw her after me into the kitchen to give her wet hair a rub.

She's still talking. 'She's got the same name as a cake. She said.'

I'm only half listening. 'A cake?'

She nods emphatically and chuckles to herself. 'She's funny.'

I set her up at the kitchen table with some colouring and put the kettle on, then started to unpack the shopping and start on tea. My feet ache and my head is throbbing and I'm shivery. The rain has seeped through my coat and spilled wet patches across my shoulders and upper arms. I ought to go and change but it's already half past four and I want dinner on the table for five or we'll never get through homework and baths and everything else by bedtime.

It isn't until eight, when Rosie is already asleep in bed and Alex has finished his school work and lies sprawled on the floor, lost in a computer game, his thumbs flashing at a ridiculous speed, that I go to find my handbag to retrieve the money and put it away. My stomach falls to the floor as I scrabble through hair clips and crumpled tissues and sweet wrappers and stray coins and my fingers close on lining and emptiness and no cash at all.

I sit heavily on the kitchen chair and stare out of the window at the darkness and my own pale face reflected there in the glass, my stooped shoulders. Shocked. Defeated. I feel sick. I can see it. The printed-off statement. Then the steady whirr and churn and the wad of money, the stash of two hundred and fifty pounds, sitting there in the mouth of the machine, waiting to be taken.

I look down at my fingers, grasping each other there on the table, my knuckles whitening. Rosie's scream. The looming homeless woman. My mouth trembles. I know exactly what I've done. I've left it there. Two hundred and fifty pounds, sitting pretty for the next person to take. It isn't just money. It's their presents. It's food. It's Christmas.

Somehow, I manage to shake myself into motion.

'Alex. Five minutes. Please. Just don't move. OK?'

He doesn't even lift his eyes, miles away in his game. He won't budge. I can get away with it as long as Rosie doesn't wake up.

I run down the stairs and out into the street in my still-sodden coat, hair flying. Rain, thick and heavy now, freezes my cheeks. *Please God, please let it be still there. Please. I need that money. I really do. Not for me, for them.*

It won't be. I know that, even as I run. My breathing is hard and jagged with panic. Hours have passed. Dozens of people will have used that machine since then. I'm sure there was someone right behind me who could have taken it. But I must try. I must look. Already I'm thinking: *Maybe if I called the bank first thing, they could check their security cameras, see who took it, and trace them, somehow.*

The wind hits me as soon as I round the corner and turn into the high street. The pavement gleams wet, reflecting the garish colours of Christmas lights and decorations in pubs and bars and restaurants. Smokers huddle in doorways with their collars up against the weather. Dark ranks of commuters walk quickly with their heads down, heading home from the station, their hands deep in pockets, blocking the way. I dodge through them in panic, bumping shoulders, as if another minute might be decisive, as if I might catch someone in the act, their hand closing around our money.

I grow nearer and catch glimpses of the cashpoint through the crowd as I rush towards it. Someone's there. A dark, low shape, silent in the rain, sitting with its back pressed against the wall, right by the ATM. The squat figure of a woman.

I break suddenly free of the crowd and run the last stretch. It's her. Rounded not by fat but by multiple layers of old clothes. I reach the cashpoint and stare at it, touch the empty space where the cash must have been. I knew it. That it's gone. I just need to see it with my own eyes.

Beside me, she hauls herself to her feet and draws towards me. I feel like saying: *If you're going to ask me for money, you can forget it, I'm broke now, too.* She just nods at me, her face unsurprised. The smell of grease and stale sweat hits me. Too close.

'You took your time.'

She pulls a hand from her pocket and brings out a neat stack of notes, pushes them at me. I grab them and count. £250. My money. *Is it?* I look at her, confused.

Her lips purse as she watches me. 'It's all there.'

I feel chastened. 'I wasn't—'

She lifts a hand and cuts me off, impatient. Her face is pinched with cold. Her hair hangs in soaking rats' tails round her cheeks. She must be a block of ice. I shake my head, trying to make sense of it.

'How did you know?'

'I didn't.' She cocks her head. 'I was just keeping an eye, watching you walk away. You were in such a rush.'

Of course I was. I was busy hurrying them away from her, from her smell.

She goes on: 'And a young man came, right after you. He was all set to take it. If he hadn't been so pleased with himself, I might not have seen.' She gives a short, sharp laugh. 'I frightened him off. Did the mad thing. You know.' She raises her hands and waggles them, wailing.

I stare at her in disbelief. She certainly looks mad.

'And you've been waiting here ever since?' I add it up. Four hours. In a biting wind and heavy winter rain. Keeping guard for me, holding the world at bay.

'I didn't want to walk off with it.' She hesitates as if it's hard to explain. 'Imagine if I had and someone had seen. What they'd say.' She swallows and I see the worry in her face. 'I knew you'd come back. Sooner or later.' She gives another low snort of laughter. 'Later, in your case.'

She sets off back towards her doorway where her carrier bags are still heaped, out of the worst of the rain. I look down at the money in my hand and peel off a £10 note, hesitate and add a second, then run after her and try to press it on her.

'I'm so grateful.'

She tuts, pushes the money away. 'It's all right.' She smiles and her blue eyes flash. 'Buy something for Rosie.'

It's a shock to hear her say Rosie's name. As if she knows us, as if she's a friend. I don't like it. I want to take it back from her but it isn't my name to give, it's Rosie's.

'Maddy, isn't it?' I remember the way Rosie chuckled. 'Something about a cake?'

She laughs. Sudden and surprising. 'Did she say? That tickled her, didn't it?' She smiles to herself, remembering. I see in a flash that it was the highlight of her day, that one-minute chat with my little girl. The chat I stopped so abruptly. I wonder how many other people she's talked to today. Perhaps no one.

'Look. I've got to get back. They're on their own…'

Suddenly, she frowns. 'You shouldn't do that. Ever.' She lifts her hand and waves me away. 'They're far too young.'

'I know. I mean, I'd never normally but—' I bite my lip. I want to say how desperate a loss it seemed, how badly we need that money, now safe in my hand, inside my pocket, to get us through Christmas, through the whole month, but suddenly tears well up from nowhere and I have to swallow hard and choke them back. My jaw is hard and trembling. I don't trust myself to speak.

On impulse, I stride past her and gather up the bulky carrier bags. They're heavy with water and the handles slippery with slime. When I turn back, she's frowning and I hesitate, worried I'm doing the wrong thing. I take her arm and feel her yield, let herself be steered.

'You're soaking. Come back to mine and dry off, at least.'

*

Alex's face hangs at the sitting room window, peering down from the third floor, framed by the light inside. He lifts his hand to wave when he sees me and I sense his relief. Then he lets it fall. He's seen her at my side, wet and dirty, turning in at the gate with me and shuffling down the path.

The stairwell is deserted and I realise, as I hurry her up the stairs, that I'm glad. Grateful that the doors on each landing are closed. Worried that her sour, rancid smell will linger and get me into trouble.

By the time we enter the flat Alex has disappeared: he's fled into their room to hide.

I close the door and put my finger to my lips, whispering: 'They're both asleep.'

She says, a little pertly: 'I should think so.' She stands in the narrow hall, looking around in the dim light, taking it all in: the open door to the small corner sitting room, cluttered with furniture and the children's things; my room, next to it, with its crumpled duvet; the closed door of the children's room; and, to her right, the short distance to the bathroom and the open kitchen-diner at the far end, the heart of the flat.

I'm expecting her to be grateful – overwhelmed by my kindness in opening our home to her, even for a glimpse.

Instead, she wrinkles her nose and says: 'It's a bit small, isn't it?'

I take a deep breath. 'Cup of tea?'

She nods. When she takes a step forward, her wet feet leave splodges on the carpet.

'Is that the bathroom?'

I set down her dirty bags on the doormat and nod.

'Good.' She takes a few more steps and peers inside. 'What I'd really like is a hot bath. Would you mind?'

I fetch clean towels, picking out the old ones we used for swimming and holidays, and wonder what in God's name I've just started.

She disappears into the bathroom. I creep around, listening, trying to work out what she's doing. It's very quiet. Then the taps run. They go on so long, I start to worry the bath will overflow. We run shallow baths – the kids are well-trained – to keep bills down. Then silence. I pluck up the courage to tap on the door.

'Maddy. I'm putting a wash on. Do you want…?'

'If you wouldn't mind. Do it all on hot. Kills the germs.'

A pause, then the door opens a crack and puffs of fragrant steam billow out. She's clearly helped herself to bubble bath. A thin, bare arm pushes out a large heap of soiled clothing. A sodden mass on the carpet. The door closes again.

I try not to gag as I turn my face away and scoop it all up in a filthy bundle, carry it through to the kitchen and drop it on the floor in front of the washing machine. I'm not squeamish. I'm used to cleaning dirty underpants and bedding. Rosie still has accidents, once in a while. And she's prone to being sick in the night, poor love. A weak cry of: 'Mummy! Mummy!' and I drop whatever I'm doing and come running, usually finding her sitting up on the bottom bunk in the darkness, her hair straggly and face pale, struggling to say: 'I need the bowl!' before she starts vomiting. Alex, snoring in the top bunk, always sleeps through it.

This is different, though. This is not just an adult's filth but a stranger's. I don't know what she might have. Germs. Lice. I stand over the heap of clothes and gingerly break it open with my foot. There's a yellowing bra – sturdy, utilitarian style. Three or four crusty thermal vests. A thin black cardigan and a thicker red one. A fleece. The torn, padded jacket she wears on top. At least three thick socks, dark with mud. There must be underpants somewhere in there. I don't want to look any closer.

I fold the jacket into a ball and bundle it in like that, in case it bleeds any more stuffing. I can stitch that for her, if there's time after her bath. Then I shove everything else into the washing machine, add as much powder as the tray can take and put it on a long cycle, on extra hot. As it starts to churn and slosh, I go to the sink and scrub my hands.

The children's room is shadowy and silent when I ease open the door. Rosie lies sprawled on her back, her duvet kicked off, her arms splayed. I smile to myself, lean in and kiss her on the forehead and inhale her clean, fresh smell. I cover her up again and she sighs and stirs in her sleep.

Alex, in the top bunk, is hunched towards the wall, casting a low light as he plays something on his console. He's got his headphones on. He knows I'm here – I sense it from his stiffness and shallow breathing – but he's making a point of shutting me out. He's doing that a lot these days, since I left his dad.

I touch his shoulder. 'You OK, buddy?'

He doesn't move for a moment, deciding whether to acknowledge me. Finally, he turns a little, shrugs off his headphones and says: 'What's she doing here?'

I hesitate. 'I nearly lost our money. Our Christmas money. She looked after it.'

He doesn't answer.

'She won't stay long.' I stop, listening to the rain on the windowsill. 'It's pouring outside.'

He grunts. 'She smells.'

'That's not kind. Come on.'

I sigh. I don't want any more battles with him. We're holding down a fragile truce at the moment, my son and I. He puts up with sharing a bedroom with his little sister and keeps on top of his school work and, in return, I stop grumbling about his screen time. I look at him now, large-limbed, lounging sulkily across the top bunk. He used to be such a sweet boy, as big-hearted as Rosie.

I say, trying to appease him: "Anyway, she's in the bath, getting clean.'

He twists around to look at me, his eyes round with horror. 'In *our* bath?' He checks my face. 'Gross.'

I stroke the hair from his forehead and he pulls back, irritated. He worries too much. I know he already feels responsible for Rosie and me – he has since the spring, when I left Mark. Alex is the one who was closest to him, who misses him most. Mark makes the most of it, too. I've heard Mark telling Alex that he's 'the man of the house' now. Telling him to 'look after your mum and sister.' It's a cruel burden to place on the shoulders of a fourteen-year-old. And it's sexist, too, suggesting I'm somehow not a real adult because I'm a woman. Typical of Mark.

Now I say: 'Don't be like that. It's all right.'

He frowns. 'What if they find out at school?'

'They won't. I won't tell if you don't.' I kiss my fingertips and put the kiss on the tip of his nose. 'Now go to sleep.'

I potter around the kitchen in the quiet, making pasta and grating cheese and defrosting a tub of tomato and vegetable sauce and straining to listen for noises from the bathroom. The kitchen clock counts off the minutes. The washing machine stirs and spins.

My phone buzzes and I hesitate before I check it, worried it's Mark. I keep asking him to cut down on the endless texts, the calls, the unannounced visits at all hours. He always just hangs his head and says: 'I just miss you, is that so terrible?'

It's more than that. I know him. He can't accept I'm moving on.

But it isn't him this time. It's Sarah, downstairs.

Hi hun. Can R come to play Weds, after school? S x

I cross to stare at the calendar and check. No need to ask Rosie. She and Sarah's daughter, Ella, are inseparable. They have been since they started school last year.

I text back.

Perfect, thks. X

She answers at once.

How u?

I picture her on her own three floors down. Ella will be asleep, Sarah will be pacing around the flat, the TV flickering with the volume low, probably with a drink in hand.

I pause. Sarah's becoming a close friend now so why don't I want her to know about Maddy? She'll disapprove, I'm sure. And I'm embarrassed to admit what I've done. So I don't tell her. I just text back:

Fine. C u soon. x

The wind throws rain against the kitchen window. I try to imagine what it's like for Maddy, living without a home, and wonder where she can go at night. There must be places, surely? Hostels. Charities. They can't all be full.

'Might I borrow something? A gown?'

I go into the hall. She's peering out of the bathroom, the door almost closed so only her face and a hand are visible. Her hair falls in limp, wet strands. *A gown?*

'A dressing gown?' She looks at me again, impatient. 'You've got my clothes.'

'Hang on a minute.'

I rummage in my room and pull out an old gardening T-shirt and a sweater I keep meaning to take to the charity shop, socks and a pair of Lycra jogging trousers. I don't know if they'll fit but they're loose and stretchy and, anyway, I don't have much and I'm not handing over my best jeans.

I'm straining the pasta and bringing the sauce to the boil when she appears in the kitchen. She has one towel wound around her head and drops the other in front of the washing machine. I point to a kitchen chair and try not to stare at her as I set out the bowls and the dish of grated cheese and pour us both water.

She looks so different. Cleaner, of course, and sweet-smelling, which is a relief in itself. She must have given herself a really good scrub. The black lines which looked so deeply ingrained have gone and her skin's ruddy. She holds her shoulders very straight, perhaps to balance the weight of the towel turban, and it changes her whole bearing. She looks regal, with those piercing blue eyes and no-nonsense look. And so much younger than before. The sight of her now and the memory of how she was just an hour earlier strikes me as terribly sad.

She reads something in my expression. 'Behold,' she says, with a flourish and an impish grin. 'Behold, Venus is risen!'

It's odd, seeing her in my old clothes. We're similar heights but she looks scrawnier than me, the trousers hanging loose around bony hips.

I ladle sauce onto her pasta and gesture to her to help herself to cheese. I expect her to fall on the food – who knows when she last had a normal, home-cooked meal? – but she sits for a moment, contemplating the bowl in silence. I hesitate. For a moment, I wonder if she's saying grace but she doesn't look pious, just as if she's waiting for something.

'Black pepper?'

She says it politely but I feel rebuked and, flustered, jump up and rush to the food cupboard to see what we've got. I find a cheap plastic cylinder of peppercorns from the supermarket with an end that grinds. She looks at it quizzically, as if it isn't the standard she expects, and then showers her bowl. Another pause. Much longer and the food will be cold. I feel a surge of annoyance. I'm hungry, even if she isn't.

'I don't mean to be a bother,' she says carefully. 'But might I trouble you for a napkin?'

I tear off a piece of kitchen roll and push it across to her. 'That's what we use,' I say. 'It's all we can afford.'

She smiles and spreads it daintily across her lap as if it's fine cotton, then lifts her glass of water and raises it in a toast, treating my small, shabby kitchen as if it's a banquet hall.

'To my kind hostess,' she says. '*No act of kindness, however small, is ever wasted.* You know who said that?'

I shake my head, pick up my spoon and fork and start to eat.

'Aesop.' She frowns. 'You know, as in *Aesop's Fables*? I forget which one.' She looks troubled as she starts to eat. 'I used to read them in class. Don't suppose they do that any more, do they? Big, hardbacked book with delightful illustrations. It's about a lion… not the thorn in its paw, that's Androcles… What was it? I can see the picture in my mind – a lion with a big mane. My father used to say things like that – "I can see her face" – when he started to forget names. I didn't understand at the time. Too young. I do now.'

We sit in silence for a little while, eating. I feel very aware, sitting beside this woman, how little I know about her. I just wanted to be kind, inviting her to our home to dry off, giving her a hot meal. I didn't really think it through. Now, sensing the force of her personality, I wonder if even this is a mistake. If I've started something I'm going to regret.

Maybe Alex was right. I should have insisted she took the twenty pounds and walked away from her.

The washing machine spins and shakes as if it's trying to take off, then finally comes to a stop and beeps. I get up from my chair, still munching, and click it round to the drying cycle.

She asks: 'How old is Rosie?'

'Five.'

My mood has shifted. I'm tired now and grumpy about giving up the few hours of the day I have to myself and thinking of the extra work she's causing me. There are dishes to do and I'll have to clean the bathroom after we've eaten, too.

'And your son?'

'Fourteen.'

I feel rude but, suddenly, I don't want her to know too much about our family. I'm still wondering about her. Maybe she's on drugs or self-harms or carries some disease which might be a danger to the children? Why is she homeless when there's surely no need to be, nowadays? What's gone so wrong in her life that she's ended up in a doorway?

'How marvellous!' she says suddenly.

I look up. She has a wistful smile on her face and I turn to see what she's looking at. Nothing. Just the wall. The small window there, with a potted cactus on the sill. The cork notice board, cluttered with the children's drawings and school letters. What's caught her eye?

'How lucky you are,' she says, her tone rather self-pitying, 'to have a clock.'

I sigh and don't answer. Outside, the rain sounds harder than ever, bashing the window in sudden gusts. I can't help it, but I resent it. I resent her.

When she reaches the end of her pasta, she pats her lips with the kitchen towel and smiles. 'Ambrosia,' she says. 'Food of the gods. It's one of life's great blessings, a good meal in a real home.'

Suddenly I feel guilty that, despite everything, I have so much and she clearly has so little. She does seem eccentric – all those quotes and fastidious table manners – but I do have a roof over my head and food on the table and wonderful children, and what does she have? I stand up and clear away the dishes, clattering them into the dishwasher and put the kettle on.

'Tea or coffee?'

'I'm putting you to a lot of trouble.'

I make us both tea from the same tea-bag, splash in milk and set it in front of her in one of my chunky earthenware mugs, daring her with my eyes to ask for a china cup and saucer.

She smiles meekly as she thanks me. 'You're kind. Very kind. I can't tell you what it means.'

Her eyes well and I turn away, embarrassed. I feel suddenly conflicted – where will she go now if I turn her out?

'Isn't there a hostel you can go to, or something, for tonight?' It's important that she start thinking of where she'll go next. I'm just drying her out, not taking her in. 'Somewhere you can stay?'

She speaks very quietly, as if it's painful to explain: 'Not really. There are more people than spaces, you see.' She hesitates. 'And they're not places you'd want to go. Trust me.'

I shake my head. Trust her? How can I? I don't know her, or what she might do. But how can I turf her out when it's still raining? It isn't right.

'Do you want to… I suppose you could sleep in the sitting room…' I hear myself say.

Her eyes light up at once.

'But just for this one night. And that's it. OK?'

She nods, looking so relieved and so meek that I feel wretched. I wag my finger.

'And you stay in there, right? I'm a light sleeper. If I hear you—'

She holds up her hands at once, her face wide-eyed and innocent, surrendering to my rules.

I take my own mug of tea and stomp out of the kitchen to my room to dig out clean sheets, then go into the small sitting room and start trying to clear enough space to open out the sofa bed.

She trails after me and re-appears in the doorway, her cup warming her hands, awkward as she watches me fold and tuck the corners, force the spare pillow into a clean pillow-case. More washing.

'It's lovely and cosy in here.' She pauses. 'I'll be snug as a bug.'

I toss the pillow into place. I don't want to think about bugs just now.

'Look – I'm sorry, but I've got to ask.' I take a deep breath, steeling myself for the question that's been on my mind since she entered the flat. I stop straightening the covers and make myself look over at her. 'I've got kids. You're not on drugs, are you?'

The question hangs there for a moment. For a moment, she seems too indignant to speak and I burn with embarrassment. *I had to ask. I had to.*

Finally, she says, enunciating each word with theatrical care: 'I can assure you that I do not partake of illegal substances. Never have, never will. Nor do I have a criminal record.'

She crosses to the window, fiddles with the catch and then prises open the sash with a clatter. A cold draught snakes in at once. She considers, then lowers the window until it's just an inch from the sill. I wonder about telling her to shut it again, then take a deep breath and bite my lip. I've probably caused enough offence already.

Her eyes move to the bookcase. 'Do you read much?'

I try to swallow back my irritation. 'Don't have much time, sadly.'

'I used to teach English,' she says. 'I always loved books.'

'Why did you give it up then?' I manage to stop myself adding: *if you loved it so much*. It's a struggle to keep the sarcasm out of my voice. Her regal act is getting on my nerves.

She looks away and carries on without answering my question. 'That's what I miss most. My books.'

I'm barely listening. I'm already regretting all of this, and I just want to get through the night and say goodbye, then never set eyes on her again.

She rambles on: 'Not clean clothes or a hot bath or good food or even privacy. Although I miss all those things. But books. Just having them. Going across to a bookcase and running your eye down the spines, choosing one and lifting it out. Opening it and starting to read.'

I nearly say: *Can't you go into a bookshop or the library*, then realise that actually, maybe she can't. Not in the state she's usually in. She probably isn't welcome.

I look up and see how bright her eyes are, brimming tears again, and I should feel compassion, I suppose, I should feel moved but actually I think, as I bend back over the sofa bed, my head and arms and feet all aching and desperate for quiet, for bed: *Bloody hell, all her problems and she's going to cry about books. She really is bonkers.*

'I'm going to bed now.' I stand up, ease the knots out of my lower back and turn to face her. I sound as firm as I feel. I can't wait to get into my bedroom and close the door on her, to be alone. 'You can have breakfast here in the morning, if you like. Toast and cereal. I'll have your clothes dry by then. But you'll need to leave when we do. Just after eight.'

I take disinfectant into the bathroom and run a cloth round the bath and toilet, then finally have a quick shower and get ready for bed. I pause outside the sitting room, listening at the closed door. Not a sound. No sign of light. I think of Alex and Rosie, sleeping so close to her and wonder what I've done, whether she might be dangerous, whether to barricade her in.

I retreat to my own room and lie on my bed in the darkness, stare at the shadows on the ceiling, my stomach in knots. A few moments later, the sitting room door is eased open. I sit bolt upright and stare as the handle to my room twists and the door opens. I feel a surge of panic, imagining her wielding a kitchen knife, attacking me in my bed.

She doesn't even come in. She just pops her head around the door. Her teeth glisten in the low light as she smiles.

'Mouse. *The Lion and the Mouse*. That's the story.'

I just blink at her, clutching the sheet close.

'The lion catches the mouse and lets it go when it begs for mercy. Then later, the mouse repays the lion when it's trapped in a net. Gnaws through the rope. See?'

I don't move a muscle.

'*No act of kindness…*' She nods as if this settled something, as if it's proof that she hasn't lost it, not yet. 'Goodnight, sweet princess. Goodnight.'

And she's gone again, leaving me sitting there, clutching the sheet to my neck, wide-eyed in the dark.

SARAH

I see it as a game. A game of wits. It's a metaphor for life, isn't it? The big guys out there, the shop owners sitting on millions, with their yachts and mansions and who knows what, they're making big enough profits. They don't give a damn about the rest of us.

I should know. I work all day in a shop, not that I'd want the shoes we sell. All those hours on my feet and for what? It's barely enough to cover the bills.

So if I'm smart enough, if I use my wits, I don't see why I can't help myself to the things I need and can't afford. Just using the brain God gave me, same as the chain store millionaires. And it's seldom for me, not any more. When I go on the prowl, it's for Ella. She's everything to me. She deserves to look her best, just as much as the next kid. It's not her fault I'm a single mum, is it?

I figured it out years ago, when I was a teenager. The Parents never gave us much pocket money. It was part of their moral high-mindedness. *Commercialism is bad! Designer brands are wrong!* So I had to stomach watching the other girls at school brandishing their new phones and posh trainers and smart gear and know I'd never get that sort of stuff myself, however much I begged. I don't want Ella to feel like that, not ever.

It's not that hard, if you're clever. You do your homework and plan ahead. Never strike in the same place twice – not in the same month, anyway. There are plenty of shops out there.

I'm browsing now, flicking through the clothes. Kids' section. I like the look of the shoes down there. Ella would love the sparkly ones. But they're hard to get right. Can't take them back if they don't fit, see? And you want medium ticket items. Don't risk it for under a fiver. But more than a hundred and they'll be well protected.

I keep my eyes peeled as I move, trying to look casual and a little vague, as if I'm a poor tired mum. Security camera up there, top left-hand corner, blinking red light on the top. I need to be out of range of that one.

I move along to the kids' jumpers. Thick wool, bulky but warm. Ella's wearing a cotton cardigan to school and the weather's turned just this month. She needs a better one.

I finger the jumpers, take one off its hanger and make a performance of looking at the label, at the size. Actually, I'm checking out the security tag. Some amateur put that in. It's secured on the washing instructions. I can tear that out in a jiffy. Almost too easy. I take two, just for fun, one red and one blue, and head for the women's changing rooms – they have individual cubicles there. I slip the jumpers in my bag as I pick up a woman's coat, then go to try it on.

The assistant is harried and waves me through with the coat. Cutting the security tags out of the jumpers takes all of two seconds, invisible under the coat, and I'm out again, heading for the small exit at the back of the store – that's where the recce comes in – pushing the tags under a pile of men's sweaters on the way – and out onto the street. Bingo!

I walk away smartly and look natural. Never run. I blend right in, just another solitary woman, wrapped up against the cold, drifting down the endless stream of frazzled shoppers.

I wait until I reach the corner and turn into Regent's Street before I start laughing. Too damn easy, that's what. I think what the stuck-up parents at school would say, the clique of power mums who hang around together at school functions and look down their noses at single mums like me. Becca's not like that. We hit it off from day one, just like our girls did. But the other mums are even snooty about her, too, now she's left that bullying husband of hers and struck out on her own.

I smile to myself. They wouldn't have the guts, those yoga, coffee-shop mums, to go out there and take something for their children. But wouldn't they love the scandal if I got caught? I pop into a café on the way back and treat myself to a latte.

I'm no Robin Hood but I do try to look out for Becca. She needs a helping hand. I know what it's like, you see.

*

'Are you sure?'

She holds up the blue sweater, judging the size. She's thrilled but also embarrassed.

'You must let me pay you for it, Sarah.'

I wave that away. 'Come on. It was two for one,' I lie. 'Cheap as chips. You're happy with blue?'

I pull out the red again and hold it alongside. We both beam, excited, thinking how pleased the girls will be, how gorgeous they'll both look. They're lovely jumpers. Why is it that clothes always look better when you get them home?

'You're sure you won't take anything for it?' Becca spreads the blue jumper out on the kitchen table and runs her hand over the surface, stroking it. 'It's just her colour. Gorgeous.' She looks up. 'You are kind.'

I smile and bat that away, pleased but embarrassed. I'm not used to it. I'm always the oddball, the misfit, the chippy one who's quick to take offence. It's just hard to take offence round Becca, she's too kind.

'They're gonna love them.' I can just picture them both, side by side, here in Becca's kitchen in their matching woollies, heads bent together over some drawing or book.

Becca looks past me to the kitchen clock. 'You're sure you're OK to pick up Rosie today?'

I get up, taking the hint, and grab my jacket. 'Sure. I'll give them sausages and beans for dinner. All sorted.'

I don't get many days off during the week, only when I've got a Saturday shift coming up at the shop, and that's when I ask Becca to take Ella for me. I owe her. This isn't even close to payback.

I head down the stairs two at a time, still elated about the jumpers. About how pleased Rosie and Ella will be. How glad Becca looked. I head into the street and turn towards school. Maybe I could get some cute hats and gloves for the girls next week. They'd love that. A different store, of course. I'll add it to the list.

MADDY

'Ooh, look at you!' Mick, large and loud, as always. He comes striding towards me down the embankment, weighed down with bags and belongings.

I don't mix with the street crowd. Some women say you've got to hook up with a man on the street, just for protection. I can see that but there's an argument, too, for keeping away from the lot of them. I've never done other people very well, on the streets or off. They think I'm odd and I play along for the sake of a quiet life. Most of the time that suits me. Arm's length. Keep myself to myself. Hurl a few quotes from books like hand grenades at anyone who gets too close, or do my Lady Macbeth act. No one likes to stay around to be cursed. Just in case.

But it's different with Mick. Maybe I shouldn't, but I drop my guard. I can't help it. He's all heart, that man.

'Were you nicked? Surely not. Nice girl like you.'

He peers down at me, taking in the new trousers, thin, stretchy material but clean and no holes, then looks over the stitches in my old blue jacket which now hold the stuffing in.

I shrug, pleased that he's noticed the change but pretending not to care. 'Friends,' I said. 'The kindness of strangers. Anyway, I'm back now.'

I'm excited, not just because I'm clean and had a decent sleep in a safe bed. Truth is, I can't believe my luck. That woman and her kids, her kind-hearted little girl – Rosie. I don't yet know how but maybe they're what I've waited for, all these months. My way in.

'Oh, well, nothing wrong with a few nights in the cells.' Mick doesn't believe me, clearly. 'Hot grub. Hot shower. Regular mini-break.'

He turns, drops his bags on the pavement and sinks down beside me with a heavy sigh. His smell closes in at once. Stale beer. A rich bouquet of distilled sock and piss. *Piss pot* – that sounds like Falstaff. What did Falstaff say that used to make the boys snigger in class? Something about *peeing his tallow*. And the boar's head joke. They seemed to think I didn't get it, being a teacher and a female and old, in their eyes. Ancient. I was all of twenty-three when I started.

Mick rummages in his bag and pulls out a can of lager. Thick fingers, blackened with dirt, pull back the ring and it cracks, gives a low hiss. He takes a swig, wipes it off, hands it to me. I do the same, greedy for the taste after a night away from it, for the chance of a drink to soften the edges. Needs must. That's another reason why Mick and I get along. We both need drink more than food, more than shelter, more than anything. Not everyone gets that.

'Might be your lucky night. I'm looking for a good-looking girl to take out.'

It isn't late. Four or five o'clock, who knows exactly. But already the sunlight has almost vanished. The shadows reach, long and low, across the river. The wrought-iron lamps on the bridge, newly lit, cast dancing pools along the ripples. On the far bank, multi-coloured strands of Christmas lights trace the outlines of cafés and restaurants. A giant illuminated Father Christmas, vulgar to my taste, climbs one of the roofs on a ladder outlined in white bulbs. The colours bleed into the water and disperse there. Undulating. We learnt that word: *undulating*. From the Latin – *ululare*. I frown. No, that was something else. Something else completely. But what? No one to ask. That's the horror of forgetting now.

A duck swoops low across the water, lands with barely a splash and disappears under the bridge. The wind, blowing up from the water, carries ice from it, freezing my cheeks. A little while longer and it'll be time to force my numb legs back into life and seek out the safety of the park. The river is soul food, that's all. A nightly indulgence. The sight of the darkening flow of the mighty Thames, pouring itself from the dark capital city towards the sea.

'Word is, it's Christmas dinner at St Matthew's tonight.'

I consider. 'Bit early, isn't it?'

He shrugs. 'Don't knock it. Can't have too much Christmas pud.' He gives me a sideways look. 'Maybe a glass of wine. Seeing as it's Christmas.'

I swallow the bait but don't answer. I don't like being around other people but if there's drink involved… And I'm still elated, still full of hope. I feel like a celebration.

'Thing is, we need to get going,' he says. 'There'll be a crowd. First come, first served.'

I'm not sure I can move. Already the lager is cutting through and weighing me down. 'Bit of a walk…'

He cocks his head, drains the can, reaches into his bag for a second. He's always well stocked, some way or other. He has a knack for getting things. Best not to know how.

'What, you got a better offer?'

I never mind Mick. He's one of those men with nothing to prove, with an easy manner, impossible to offend. And he knows everyone. Maybe I'm grateful, too. He's one of the few who stop to pass the time, now and then, who speak to me, treat me like a normal person. That's worth a lot.

'Drink up.' He hands me the second can, still half full. That's another thing about Mick. Generous with drink. 'We should get going.'

He hauls himself to his feet and starts to gather up his bags again. If he let me keep the can, the rest of the beer might do me. I don't need food if I've got a drink. But he pokes me in the thigh and keeps hassling me until I finally stir and let him heave me upright again. I've lost feeling in my feet.

It's time, whatever time it is. The river has blackened to tar. We set off, ambling side by side, laden, bulked out by extra clothes and bags. I've forgotten what it feels like to walk normally. Briskly. To wear heels and clickety, clack. To hurry. Mick reaches for the can and shakes it, listening, then winks at me. He isn't a bad man. It isn't bad walking somewhere with him, to be taken along. I smile to myself. *The Odd Couple*. I saw that once, many moons ago. At The Grand in Leeds. In life before.

Mick starts to sing, loud and tuneless. He lifts a hand, clumped with bags, and waves it about, conducting. A young woman emerges from the side street up ahead, sees us and crosses quickly to the far pavement. Can't blame her. I'd have done the same, once.

I turn to Mick, grinning. 'You really know how to treat a girl. I'll say that. Roses all the way.'

He grins back, nods at me, and carries on with his serenade.

He drifted down to London from Manchester. He'd been a factory worker, had a wife and kids once. Then that went south – he never said why exactly – and so did he, washing up in Victoria Coach Station with the rest of the detritus. That was all he'd ever said. And all I need to know. He knows far less about me. He calls me Professor sometimes, as a joke. He knows I had an education and a proper job. That there was a man once, just one. That I like a drink or ten. He doesn't know what really happened. No one does. You hear some pretty grim stories on the street, but even Mick would be shocked by mine.

No one talks much about the past. What they'd once been. What they'd once dreamed of being. The past is a foreign country. *The Go-Between*. Huntly. Not Huntly… Hartley, you idiot. *The Go-Between* by L.P. Hartley. Every schoolboy knows that one.

Mick's past spills out sometimes in unexpected fragments. 'When the kids were young' or 'before the old girl left' or 'in my old place.' A flash of colour under a long, black cloak of nothingness. Best not to let too much show.

The dinner's all right. They've made an effort. Pathetic, really. Strings of paper chains and those paper snowflakes stuck on the windows that children cut out at primary school. All for a plate of stringy chicken, mashed potatoes, carrots and peas. No Christmas pudding, after all. No wine.

A woman from the church comes to talk to each of us as we eat. Earnest and rather pious. She enfolds people's hands in hers as if homelessness is infectious and she wants to follow the example of Our Lord and show she's not afraid. That's the price you pay for charity, being blessed.

When she gets to me, she shows me a leaflet about a nearby women's hostel and reads it to me very slowly as though she assumes I'm barely literate. It brings out the worst in me, I'm sorry, being patronised. I know the hostel by reputation. All drugs and self-harmers and cat fights. And there are never spaces anyway, even if you are desperate. I've tried them all.

She gets to the end and looks at me hopefully. She's probably much my age – mid-fifties – but cleaner, plumper.

I can't help myself. I say: 'Blessed are the poor for theirs is the Kingdom of Heaven.'

She looks at me, uncertain, wondering what's coming next. Her eyes are ringed with kohl and she wears lipstick. The invisible, stealthy kind, as if she's trying to come down to our level but couldn't help giving herself a little boost.

I say: 'I always wondered about that. Being so well and truly blessed with poverty, as I am.'

She manages to smile and moves straight past me, on to the next person, and Mick shoots me a look that says: 'What are you like?' But a fond look. Or so I choose to think.

They put us out at nine thirty, back into the cold. I hesitate, there on the cobbles outside the church, considering the graveyard and whether the bushes there might be decent places to sleep. There'd be a certain pleasing irony in sleeping amongst the dead in the shadow of the church. *Lest we forget. Memento mori.*

Mick appears at my side and gives me a nudge in the ribs.

'The night is young,' he says. 'And so are we.'

I raise my eyebrows and am about to make my excuses and bail out, back to my small park, when he opens one of his bags just enough to reveal the silver top of a bottle and winks and I think: *You know what, Mick's all right. I'm safe enough with him, no funny business and anyway, I think I'd risk it for a drink.*

We get away from the crowd and head back to the riverside to a deserted stretch of tow path, overhung on both sides by a tangle of trees and bushes. It's a rough track used during the day by runners and cyclists and families with young bicycling children but silent now, and unlit.

Mick crawls ahead of me under low-hanging branches and through a mess of undergrowth, dipping down towards the water. I push after him, catching fragments of dry bark and dead leaves in my hair, my nose filled with the wet, damp smells of winter earth and moss.

On the far side, hidden from the path, Mick is settling on a small patch of damp grass, laying out grubby plastic bags for us to sit on. There's barely room for two between the bushes and I sit close to him, feeling the warmth of his thigh against mine. His smell, stale but human, reaches for me and I wonder what he makes of mine.

He pull out the bottle with a 'Ta-dah!' It's cheap whisky, a supermarket brand, but who cares, it's the brown stuff. The sweet scent finds me the minute he unscrews the top and takes a deep draught, then passes it over. I glug as much as I can, taking deep mouthfuls. A thin line trickles from the corner of my mouth to my chin.

He says: 'Steady, girl!' and snatches it back again, puts it to his own lips.

It plays me like a violin, the drink, plucking my nerves, setting everything humming, every finger, every toe. Its warmth runs up and down my limbs and sets my organs on fire and oh, the bliss of it, thank God, blurring the edges of it all, past, present and future.

He drinks too fast and coughs and I see his arm slacken and seize my chance, grab the bottle back again, drink again, feeling its hot lava pour into me, completely under its spell now, floating, hot and dizzy with pleasure.

We're much the same, Mick and I. In thrall. No stopping until the bottle's dry. Riding the wave of euphoria right up the shore.

When the last drop is spent, we take turns running our tongues round the inside of the rim, in the metal cap, sucking the last traces. Finally, Mick lifts his arm and hurls the bottle out into the river. The glass glistens as it arcs, far above the water, then it hits the surface with barely a splash and disappears into the blackness. We're at once bereft, staring after it, still buzzing but melancholy.

'A hand should have caught it,' I say. My lips are numb with cold and whisky and it's a struggle to form letters. 'The Lady of the Lake.'

He gives me a bleary look. 'What?'

I raise my hand to demonstrate. 'The Lady of the Lake. King Arthur's sword. Excalibur.'

His face comes close to mine as he struggles to focus.

I say, teasing: 'Did you even go to school?'

He shrugs and looks away, towards the water. The streaks of silvery light rising from it catch the contours of his face. A kind face. Sagging skin. Straggly hair. A thick scar above one eye. I wonder what he looked like as a young man. What kind of person he was then, when he still had hope.

I say: 'King Arthur pulls the sword out of the stone, you must know that? Then later, when he's dying, he sends someone, I forget who, to throw it into the lake and a hand comes out and catches it. That's the story.'

He sighs and I'm not sure he's even heard but after a while he says: 'The stuff you know.'

I don't answer but I'm pleased.

Something beneath us in the darkness stirs and splashes in the water, sending out ripples. A frog, perhaps. The air blowing in from the river is icy but I'm still whisky warm and happily anaesthetised and I could stay here all night, feeling the heat of a friend beside me, looking out at the fast-flowing current, stealing in silence through the city, heading towards the sea. Escaping it all.

He stirs and I sense he's steadying himself to leave and wonder what I could do to hold him here, next to me, a moment longer. But he just shifts his weight and settles again, crinkling the plastic bag.

'She was right, that woman. You ought to get into a hostel, clean yourself up. You shouldn't be out here. You're not made for it.'

I try to understand this through the thick fug of alcohol. 'I manage.'

'You don't need to, though, you know? I mean, you're clever. What're you doing, wasting your life like this?'

That hurts. A dull pain right in my gut, as real as a punch. Is that what he thinks of me? Is this somewhere else I don't belong? I clench my jaw.

'Come on. Don't be like that.' He reaches a clumsy arm round my shoulders and pulls me to him in a hug. The knots of muscle along his arm are hard through his shabby coat. It feels good. It's a long time since I was hugged by anyone or even touched.

He says: 'I'm just looking out for you, Professor. You know? Gotta look out for each other out here.'

I say: 'What about you?'

He shrugs. 'I find my way all right. I'm used to it. I get what I need, see? Do what I need to do. But look at you. You're skin and bone.'

I don't answer.

'How long have you been on the streets, anyway? I never saw you before the summer. Five or six months?'

I shrug. He's right, it has been about that but I like to feel invisible. It's a shock that he's even noticed. And he wouldn't understand. I didn't just drift down here, like he did. I came on purpose. I came in search.

'So what happened? Someone throw you out?'

I close my eyes and there are racing threads of light there, behind my eyelids, green and yellow flashes. I don't know what to say. I don't know where to begin. All that's happened. Every time life knocks me down, it throws me back into the open arms of my old friend, drink, who draws me down into darkness, each time falling a little lower, each time a little harder to climb back out.

'It happens,' I say at last. 'It's not the first time. It's like we live inside a bubble, right? You float through life, holding it all together. Work, money, bills. Then something, someone, comes along and bursts it just like that. Gone. And then you need a drink.'

'A prick,' says Mick, and starts laughing. 'A prick comes along and bursts your frigging bubble.'

I laugh too and we rock there for a minute, clinging to each other, hiccupping and giggling like schoolgirls.

Finally, he catches his breath and quietens and says: 'So, who was the prick this time?'

I'm wondering how much more to tell him when suddenly there's a roar right there behind us and crashing bodies through the trees and dark weights hurling heavy on top of us, knocking us apart, kicking the wind out of us.

I pull away from Mick and curl in a ball on my side in the wet grass, buffered by the thick padded coat, my arms up round my head, warding off the blows. A crack to the side of my head, another on the back of the skull, white lights flaring and shooting stars in the blackness and my face burrowing into my sleeve as if it could tunnel underground and hide there. My hands are pressed against my ears, shutting *them* out. Their breath is hard and short and hot on the back of my neck when they bend low.

Close there, at my side, Mick cries out once, a high animal yelp of pain. Then there are just low gasps and wheezing, gurgling for air, and that's worse. They make the sounds then, whacks and cracks of blows hitting home and the sickening crunch of bone.

It ends as fast as it started. Boots beat the ground, scrambling through the branches, back to the path and away. My ears sing, a single, high-pitched note and even as I lie there, feeling the ground pitching and rocking underneath me and my stomach heaving, I have a sudden memory of school and the rising tone of the children's voices at Christmas. I manage to get my head up and turn to the side as my stomach pulsates and I let out a sour stream of whisky onto the earth.

Afterwards, as my body grows quiet again, my fingers trace their way over the foreign country of my skull, feeling new contours, new rivers, where the blows fell.

I get myself onto all fours and the trees sway and shudder as I try to bring them into focus. I grope towards Mick. He lies still and silent in the grass.

'Mick!' My voice is thin and high-pitched. 'You all right?'

His head's twisted to one side, one cheek to the ground. His eye is engorged, the lids pressed tightly together. A dark trail oozes from the side of his skull down the side of his stubbly face. His arm juts out to one side at an unholy angle. The sight of it makes me retch.

I reach out a hand and touch his hair, frightened. It's coarse and loosely matted. What just happened? I don't understand. Why did they attack us, those thugs? They seemed to know where we were, to know exactly what they were doing.

'I'll get help, Mick. Stay there.'

I don't know what I'm saying. My body shakes and I lurch to my feet and grab hold of a trailing branch, trying to steady myself. I focus all my efforts in lifting my left foot, swinging it forward, placing it deliberately on the ground, then inch forward and begin again with my right. My ears scream. What if they come back, those men? What if they finish me off? Suddenly, that's all I can think of – getting the hell out of there.

I don't remember much after that. Somehow I manage to stagger the short distance to my usual park, a little further along the riverbank. I don't know how I hauled myself onto the low wall by the bushes and somehow over the railings into the greenery on the other side. I don't know what animal instinct pushed me to crawl, on hands and knees, to the dark mass of rhododendron bushes and creep under their cover to collapse in the space within, on the damp, warm earth, my head spinning, my senses drowning in the heady smell of leaf mulch.

I spin in and out of consciousness. For a time, she's there, my girl, such a beauty with those deep brown eyes, John's eyes, and clouds of curly hair. She's still a toddler, still mine, running towards me across the grass on plump, shaky legs, and I'm crouching low, arms open, laughing, saying: *Come on, poppet. Come to Mummy! You can do it!* And she's smiling too now, giggling, her eyes on mine and the laughing knocks her suddenly off balance and she veers sideways and then she's gone and my arms are empty, always empty, reaching for a child who never comes.

Later, much later, I hear children's voices, screams of excitement, drifting across from the playground. My head aches. My eyes are crusty with sleep and when I lift my grubby hands to wipe them, flakes of black, of dried blood, coat my fingertips. Winter sunshine falls in shafts through the sieve of the branches and warms my cheek.

It comes rushing at me, the memory of the night before. Mick, my friend. He needs help. I need to save him, to raise the alarm.

But I can't move. The pain is overwhelming. When I close my eyes, I see his twisted arm and feel the blows from those men who fell on us with such fury. Who were they? Not just louts showing off, or drunks spotting a soft target. They were more sinister. Silent. Deliberate.

But when I try to move, when I open my mouth to scream for help, the slightest effort sets the branches spinning and the pain raging in my head and I close my eyes, trying to fall again into the past.

BECCA

It's December the eighteenth. School breaks up and they let the children out earlier than usual for the end of term and it's so busy in the wine bar – all the office Christmas lunches, the loud, boozy tables of workers happy to drink away the afternoon – that I have to run all the way to school to meet Rosie and Ella and by the time I get there, breathless and red in the face, most of the children have already gone and there they are, sitting on their own outside the school office, heads bowed, swinging their legs and clutching their school bags and stapled newspaper folders stuffed with paintings.

'I'm so sorry.' I bend down and kiss Rosie. She looks cross and hurt and embarrassed in front of her friend. I give Ella a hug too. Behind them, the school secretary watches over the top of her desk.

'It's sunny.' I gather up their bags and they jump down from their chairs and trail after me. 'Let's go to the park on the way home.'

It's a crisp winter's day, cold and damp underfoot but the sun, finding my face through the trees, is warm. We make our way along the tow path, watching the ducks feeding close to the bank and counting the boats out on the river. The girls have revived, jostling each other and playing Chase, excited to be free from school and together.

'You're It.'

'Not fair! I'm always It.'

'No, you're not.'

Ella gives in, as she always seems to. She stands, rigid with concentration, and gives Rosie a head start, then sets off after her, arms pumping at her sides. Rosie taunts her and weaves, twists, giggling. Then they're off again, Ella setting the pace this time, tearing along the path.

'Look where you're going!' My voice disperses, too slow to catch them both.

They zigzag, spill this way and that across the mud. A young woman, jogging towards us, headphones on, has to bounce on the spot for a moment until she can get past them. When she reaches me, I mouth: 'Sorry' but she doesn't seem to notice.

At the park gates, the girls pull free and race, arms out to block each other, hair bouncing, across the grass and over to the playground. It's almost deserted. A weary mum holds a coffee in one hand and pushes a toddler on the swing with her other. Another woman, a nanny perhaps, huddles on a park bench and stares at her phone as the children play.

I set the children's bags down at the bottom of the slide and go to watch as they climb and swing and slide down metal poles. Rosie takes the lead. She's a natural gymnast, lithe and strong. Ella is less confident, eager to copy but more likely to fall. I stay close to them, just in case.

My mind drifts elsewhere. Alex announced that morning that he's going to the mall with friends after school. I didn't make a fuss about it. I gave him the money he wanted so he could buy himself something to eat there – I couldn't let him be the only one who couldn't afford a burger – but he seems to be out more and more lately. Since I left Mark. Perhaps it's inevitable. Alex is a teenager. Growing away from me. But I feel it keenly. I hardly seem to see him nowadays.

'Can we play Hide and Seek?' Rosie tugs at my trousers. 'Can we, Mummy?'

I nod. 'Just for five minutes and then it really is time to go.'

She beams. 'You count. We'll hide.'

I peer out at her through the web of my fingers as I count, making sure I never lose sight of them. She runs straight out of the playground and heads off towards the trees at the far end of the park, followed by Ella. I slow the pace of my theatrical counting to give them both time to reach cover, then pick up the bags and head slowly after them.

'Where did they go? I can't see them anywhere. They've vanished. Hmmm.'

I keep up a loud monologue for their benefit as I approach. They're wearing their new jumpers, one blue and the other bright red. Not hard to spot in the thinning winter landscape. Most of the trees are bare.

'Behind this tree? No! Well, where are they? They must be invisible. Hmm.'

I pretend not to notice as Rosie scoots from one trunk to another, running at full pelt, giggling. A moment later, Ella dashes after her. I don't mind. We're going in broadly the right direction, towards the gate and the road home. I herd them that way as I pretend to search.

When the line of trees ends, Rosie dives under the big rhododendron bushes, her feet scrambling through dead leaves. Ella hesitates, anxious about leaving the safety of the last tree. She takes these games too seriously, liable to burst into tears if I'm not careful.

I leave Ella where she is for the time being, crouch low and creep forward after Rosie. She's so deep inside that I don't think she can see me and I circle round to the next bush and bend double, peering into the gloom, ready to shout 'Boo!' when she reaches me. It stinks under there. Foxes perhaps. Dogs. I lift a branch, trying to let in a bit more air, willing Rosie to hurry up. She'll be filthy by the time she comes out but at least she won't need her school—

I drop to my hands and knees and crane further forward, pushing myself deeper into the umbrella canopy of the bush. The sole of a boot, toe dug into the ground, heel sticking up to the sky. I stare, my eyes adjusting to the deep shade after the sunlight. A second foot nearby, the legs splayed, higher, disappearing into the bushes, the dull shape of a body, face down, encased in a padded blue jacket.

To one side, leaves rustle and shake. Rosie comes scrabbling through the undergrowth. Fragments of twigs stuck in her hair.

I push further in and put out my arm to her. I want to pull her out of there as soon as possible, to stop her going any further and seeing the body.

'Come here. Quick. Let's move.'

Her face folds. 'No, Mummy. You looked!'

'Please, Rosie. I'm not playing any more.' I reach my arm under the branches. 'Now.'

She purses her lips and shouts. 'No! It's not fair. You've ruined it.'

'Rosie!'

The thick leg shivers. The boot creaks.

Rosie stops suddenly, notices the body.

'Mummy!'

'It's all right, Rosie. Look at me. Come OUT of there.'

My voice rises to a shout. Her eyes are fixed on the prone figure. She begins suddenly to shake.

'Is it real?'

'Come out NOW.'

She shrieks. 'It's Maddy! Mummy, it's Maddy!'

She seems about to move further in to investigate and I launch myself at her, a web of dry branches scratching tracks down my cheeks. I grab Rosie's arm and heave her towards me, out of the bushes and onto damp, cold grass. She falls on top of me and we struggle there for a moment, licked by mud, trying to regain our balance. Ella runs out and stares anxiously down at us both.

Rosie's voice comes as a worried whisper: 'Is she dead?'

I pull out my phone and dial for an ambulance.

I don't mean to get sucked in – it really isn't our business and, besides, we've got a lot to do. I've promised Rosie we'll all make mince pies later, and I need to go to the shop on the way home as well, to stock up before the supermarket gets any crazier before Christmas.

I think we'll just wait there until the ambulance turns up and then, as soon as we know she's in safe hands, we'll make a discreet exit. But Rosie has other ideas. Once the paramedic has established that it was me who called the ambulance, he asks me to stick around while they check Maddy over. I don't see why. She's got nothing to do with us.

Ella hangs back, staying close to me. Rosie bounces on the balls of her feet as she watches, enthralled. The blue lights of the ambulance, parked up there on the side of the road at the park gates, strobe the grass. A man and woman have climbed down, carrying a folding stretcher, their uniforms bristling with interesting equipment. The whole drama of a rescue.

'Can I see?' Rosie pushes her nose in as they snap on plastic gloves and crawl into the bushes. I have to grab her by the shoulders and hold her off, the way you might an over-eager puppy.

'You all right, love?' The man checks for a pulse at Maddy's neck with the impersonal cheeriness of medics. 'Took a turn, did you?'

Rosie turns to me with shining eyes. 'What's a turn?'

The sun is losing its power, falling low through the winter sky. The shadows across the park are long and cold. I wrap my arms around the girls and hug them to me. *A few more minutes*, I think, *and we'll go*. The nanny passes by on her way back to the gate, pushing a small boy in a buggy along the path, staring across to see what is going on. At the gate, she pauses, turns back, lifts her phone and takes a picture.

They draw her out, strap her onto the stretcher. I take a step back and try to turn the girls away, to hold them against me, even as they struggle to see.

The fetid smell comes out with her. Her skin is waxy and thinly stretched over the bone as if it's shrunk in the wet. Her eyes are closed and puffy. Her cheeks are streaked with mud and bits of dead leaf. On one side, from her hair down to cheekbone, there's a dried stream of blood. I think of the twitching leg and wonder if she really is still alive.

'Will she be OK?'

The woman paramedic talks into the walkie-talkie stuck on her uniform, just below her shoulder. Some coded description. I don't understand.

'You know her?' The man nods to us as they lift her past and turn, ready to set off to the waiting ambulance.

I shake my head but at the same time, Rosie pipes up, excitedly: 'It's Maddy. She's my friend. She stayed at our house.'

Ella gapes, impressed.

He looks at me quizzically, then back to Rosie. 'You can ride in with her, if you like?'

Rosie pulls free and twists to look at me. 'Can I?'

I say: 'She's all right, though? I mean, it's getting late. We should really—'

He shrugs. 'Suit yourself.'

I let Rosie and Ella go with them as far as back of the ambulance and we watch while they stow Maddy inside. The interior is fitted out with gadgets and tubes and plastic boxes.

The female paramedic climbs inside after her and the man slams the doors shut and makes to walk round to the front.

'Which hospital is she going to?'

'St Winifred's.'

I follow him as he climbs into the driver's seat and reaches for his seatbelt. I feel guilty. I don't want to get involved but Rosie will worry, I know she will, and I don't mean to be hard-hearted if there's something small we can do to help.

'What's wrong with her? Is it serious?'

He shrugs and starts the ignition. 'Hard to be sure. Hyperthermia. Malnutrition. Pneumonia, maybe. And then there's the fact she's been coshed on the head. Anyway, merry Christmas.'

Rosie stays angry at me all the way home.

'It's not fair!' she keeps saying, her mouth in a tight pout. 'I wanted to go.'

Our landlord, David, distracts her, in the end. He lives in the next block and he's out on the street, outside the flats, washing his car. He's got a posh sports car – not a boy racer, but something a bit more stylish, in silver. A Merc, I think. I don't know much about cars. He's already let Rosie sit in the driving seat once or twice. I've got a photo on my phone. Her hands reaching up high to clasp the steering wheel, her face lit with pride.

Now, he beckons the girls over and gives them each a sponge, shows them how to clean off the panel he's working on. Steam rises from the bucket, the sponge, as they work, side by side, splashing water everywhere.

'Not too much water, Rosie.' I can't help myself. 'Don't fill your shoes.'

'So…' He takes a step back to stand beside me. 'All ready for Christmas?'

'Hardly.' We both speak without looking at each other, with our eyes on the girls, a safe neutral focal point. 'I've got as far as ordering the turkey. And making lists. You?'

'Lists are good.' I sense him nod. 'Are you going away?'

'Not this year.' I wonder how much more to say. 'You?'

'I'm keeping the door locked and bingeing on Netflix, cooking some good food and opening a decent bottle of champagne. Or two.'

'Sounds great.' I wonder what he'll watch. How he defines good food. I try to look at him out of the corner of my eye, without making it obvious. He always looks right, somehow. Monied. His jeans and that sweater, pushed up to the elbows, strike me as expensive. His forearms are pale and coated with downy black hair. Hairy chest, then.

Rosie sploshes her sponge in the bucket and makes circles with it. Water slops over the edges and forms a dark ring. Ella still crouches low, her face intent and serious as she works.

'Leave that now, Rosie. Let's go, girls.' I add, to David: 'Sorry.'

'That's OK.' He turns to me, his eyes amused. 'I'll soon have them trained.'

Rosie stands in front of him and looks up, eyes imploring: 'Can I have a go at driving?'

I cut her off: 'Not today, Rosie. He needs to finish washing it. It's cold.'

'But after—'

'Not today.'

David stoops to her height. His hair is short and spiky and stands up at the back of his neck. 'Maybe another day, OK? When we've got more time.'

His phone rings and he shifts into another gear at once, looking away from us, across the street, his tone suddenly adult and business-like.

'Come on, you two.' I hold out my hand to Rosie and Ella and they allow themselves to be led away. When I look back, at the door to the block, he's still talking, his head nodding and free hand gesticulating. Whatever deals he's striking or clients he's helping, it seems high-powered. I smile to myself and carry on thinking about him as we head past Ella and Sarah's front door and take the stairs to our flat. Rosie and Ella scramble, shoving each other as they race.

We've only just started these chats, David and I. Half-conversations.

Enough to know each other's first names, to know he owns half-a-dozen flats altogether, including the one here on the ground floor that Sarah and Ella rent, and ours on the third floor. He lives alone. No kids.

Enough for him to know I'm newly separated and work part-time. Enough to sense he might be interested and to wonder if I might be, too. I'll take my time. It's too early to think about all that. But there's a gentleness about him that I like. A shyness. So unlike Mark.

After dinner, I let Rosie and Ella help with the mince pies and we turn some into jam tarts, for them. I give them the scrag ends of pastry to mould into shapes and nibble when they think I'm not looking.

By the time Sarah swings by to collect Ella, tired after a hectic day in the shoe shop where she works, the girls seem to have forgotten about Maddy and the drama in the park. I don't mention it, either; there seems no need.

Rosie is naughty in the bath, soaking the bathroom floor and she ends up losing her bedtime story because she messes about so much getting into her pyjamas. I tuck her in and leave the door ajar to give her some light. As I clear up from the mince pies, my movements are trailed by her high voice, drifting along to the kitchen from her room, tunelessly singing, again and again: '*When Santa got stuck in the chimney…*'

I make myself something to eat and sit at the kitchen table, grateful for the chance to think, making lists. All my stress is focused on the fact Mark and his mother are joining us for Christmas lunch. I'd much rather it be just Rosie, Alex and me. I'm cross with myself for giving in to him.

I add the ingredients for bread sauce and fresh stuffing to the list. I shouldn't feel under pressure to impress Mark's mother – it's absurd – but I have some pride.

Every now and then, I check the clock and then my phone. Alex should have been home by now. I frown, trying to remember exactly what he said. A friend's mum would bring him home, that's what he promised, but at what time? Wasn't it by eight? Or was it half past? I start to message him: *Everything ok?* I think how embarrassed he'll be, reading a text from his mother when he's with his friends, hesitate, then delete it again.

I cross to the kitchen window and put my nose close to the glass, trying to see past my own reflection and out into the night. The strip of communal garden below gives way to a fence and a patchwork of small gardens backing onto Victorian terraces. Several are in darkness. Some show thin lines of light around closed curtains or blinds. In one or two, the curtains are open and wall-mounted televisions strobe coloured light, competing with the fairy lights decorating mirrors and windows, Christmas trees and mantelpieces.

Someone coshed her, the ambulance man said. I think of her pale skin, of her body lying face down on the earth. Wonder how long she'd been lying there and how much longer she might have stayed there, unseen, if it hadn't been for Rosie's game of Hide and Seek. *Maddy*. I look round the kitchen at the coffee machine, the neatly stacked dishes, the cooling rack of mince pies and jam tarts. Rosie's Christmas angel, brought home from school today, a lop-sided and rather squashed decoration made out of a cardboard cone and a slice of paper plate, hangs from the corner of a cupboard door. It has googly eyes and a broad, wobbly smile. *She's my friend*, she'd said without hesitation. *Maddy*.

It takes me a while to find the phone number for the hospital and then get the switchboard to put me through to the right ward. I don't have a lot to go on. Maddy. Middle-aged. Homeless. Hit on the head. We found her under a bush. Accident and Emergency finally transfers me to a women's ward which confirms she's been admitted.

'How is she?'

Far below, a man opens up the back door of one of the houses and steps out into the garden. A minute red glow. Smoking, then.

'Are you a relative?'

'No. We found her, that's all. I called the ambulance.'

The woman sighs. She sounds tired. 'I can't give information over the phone. Not unless you're related.'

I blow out my cheeks. The dark figure in the garden walks up and down along the back of the house and peers in through the window, as if he's trying to keep following the TV programme.

'Can you just tell me if she's OK? I mean, is she badly hurt?'

'I'm sorry.' The woman tuts. 'You can always come in, if you really want to know. Two till four. Eight till nine thirty.' And she's gone.

I pace around the kitchen, trying to imagine her in hospital. She's being cared for. Fed. Kept safe. It's very sad but she really isn't my problem. I have other priorities.

I look at the clock. Check my phone. Still no sign of Alex. Another ten minutes and I'll text him. Embarrassing or not, it's getting late.

MADDY

My head hurts. They stitched it up, I don't remember much about that. I'm used to a pounding head, a thick skull, any time the booze wears off. But this is a different sort of ache and I'm stuffed up with painkillers. I lie here, legs straight, pinned to the mattress by starched sheets, hands by my side. Washed and laid out, like a corpse.

But I can't be dead. A tube feeds liquid into my arm from a drip which whirs and clicks. And I'm shaking. The tremors are bad this time. The shudders run up and down my skeleton as if I'm a puppet being shaken by a giant hand. Beneath me, the mattress sways and bounces. I'm wet with sweat.

When I open my eyes, a young nurse is standing right there beside me, fiddling with the bag of liquid on its pole.

I try to whisper but no sound comes. My throat and mouth are dry as dust. I strain. Croak.

She turns and bends low over the bed to hear. 'What's that, Madeleine?'

'Mick.' I mouth the word, uncertain if she can make it out. 'You find Mick?'

She frowns. A moment later, she comes back and pushes a pill into my mouth, impossibly large, then presses a paper cone of water to my lips, one hand raising my head.

'Swallow this, darling. Go on.'

Waters dribbles at the corners of my mouth and she wipes me off with a practised hand, lowers my head back to the pillow. How did my poor neck ever support such a weight?

'Get some rest now.' She pats my hand and bustles away.

My eyes fall on the drip, the plump bag of liquid emptying itself steadily into my veins. Whisky. No, too light. Gin, maybe. Or vodka. I tremble, imagining alcohol pumping through my body, soothing the shakes, bringing me peace. I struggle to keep my eyes open. Mick, still and crooked under the branches, his eyes closed. I need to tell them. He needs help. But I'm sliding backwards, warm and heavy, back into darkness.

Time passes. Sometimes, the ward is bright with electric light. Heels squeak as the nurses hurry to and fro. They wear plastic aprons and gloves and they strip me off, heave me this way and that, a dead weight of woman, disinfect me with their wet cloths.

My brain has swollen to three or four times its normal size and chafes constantly against the inside of my skull but when I try to tell them, they look at each other across the bed and smile.

'Come on, Madeleine. Up we come.'

They treat me like a child. I'm as helpless as one.

I manage to tell the young nurse, the lass with the song of Ireland in her voice, that I need a drink. Just one. Just a wee dram. Just to ease the pain in my head. It's all I can think about. Couldn't she just…? No one need know. An act of kindness…

She says: 'That's the last thing you need, darling. The very last thing.'

I don't know how many days I lose in all. Slowly, the sweats ease and the shaking too and I lie there, weak as a kitten, wondering what the hell happened to me. And I realise I've survived. I've come through the fire, yet again. I'm in a bed. Warm and safe and clean and fed. I'm being looked after. That's a wonderful thing. I can't tell you how long it's been. I'm being cared for by other human beings, even if it is their job. I'm still here, still alive, still in the game, after all.

But is Mick?

A police officer comes to talk to me. The nurses pull the curtain around my bed and set a chair inside the tent with me, close to my head, and a young woman thickened out by her uniform and bulging pockets strides in and sits beside me, draws out a notebook and takes notes. Her hair is scraped back into a bun with kirby grips and an old-fashioned hair-net and I can't take my eyes off it. It reminds me again of Cyprus and crouching with Daphne in the scrub, peering in through the open window of the recreation hall in the afternoon, watching the older girls do ballet, all in a line, hands on the barre, backs straight, heads up, as Mrs Crouch hammered out a tune on the old piano and that teacher – what was her name, it begins with L – tapped the wooden floor with her cane, marking time. *One, two, three. One, two, three.* The memory smells of floor polish and the clean sweat of the straining girls and, under-pinning it all, always, the salt of the sea.

'Madeleine. Madeleine Crosby?'

For a moment, it seems that it's the ballet teacher talking, reaching out across all those years to catch me watching at the window. I blink and refocus.

The police woman is bending forward, her face too close, talking a little too loudly as if she thinks I'm deaf. Or just plain stupid.

'What happened, Madeleine? Can you remember?'

I turn my head to her, cross. 'Of course I can.' She's barely more than a child. What does she know about anything? About the blackness, the struggle, the viciousness of life? 'We were just sitting there. That's all. Sitting by the water having a drink. No law against that, is there? And they jumped us from behind. Unprovoked.' I point at her notebook. 'Write that down. *Unprovoked assault.* Can you spell that?'

Her look hardens.

I say: 'Did you find Mick? How is he?'

Her face tightens. 'Mick?'

I sigh. 'You're the police, aren't you? Mick. Stocky fella. He was with me, by the river, where it happened.' I see him again, lying there, head twisted, eye battered, arm smashed. 'I got off lightly, compared to him.'

She looks suddenly worried, gets to her feet and is gone. The curtain swishes closed behind her. A radio squawks, her voice, then a burst of static, fading as her footsteps carry her away. I let my eyes fall closed.

What if they didn't find him? What if he's still there? I swallow. He was a good man. What if he's dead?

Later, another woman comes. Not a uniform, this time. Gentler. One of those do-good types. She lifts my hand from the bedding and holds it for a moment, looking into my eyes. Her fingers are plump and warm, embedded with too many rings. She's asked me something or other but she lets the silence stretch for so long, her face so earnest, that in the end, I forget what it is she wants to know and, by the look of her calm but vacant expression, perhaps she has too.

Then she asks tougher questions, not about that night but about earlier.

'What happened, Madeleine? May I call you Madeleine?'

I pull a face. 'You might as well. Everyone else here seems to.' I pause. I know she's only trying to help, really. 'My friends call me Maddy.'

'So, Maddy' – her smile is cloying and already I regret my moment's thaw towards her – 'let's have a chat about arrangements, shall we? When you're ready to be discharged from hospital, where will you go? Do you have anywhere to live?'

I look past her to the curtain. The woman in the next bed has a lot of visitors and they push their chairs out too far, beyond the boundary, into my space. The square bulge in the curtain shows they're doing it now. I keep telling the nurses.

She starts again: 'Tell me a bit about yourself, Maddy. Have you got any family?'

I don't answer.

She tries again: 'Where's the last place you lived? Let's start there, shall we? Can you remember?' Her face shows a neutral, I'm-not-judging-you look and she waits and time opens up and swallows us both as we wait to see who will crack first and end the silence. Not me.

After a while, she looks at the file in her lap, all disappointment.

I lean towards her and lower my voice. 'I need to know what happened to Mick.'

She nods and her eyes narrow a fraction as they watch me and I see at once that she knows, that she's holding that knowledge like a weapon.

'There was a man admitted to St Winifred's about the same time as you, Maddy. Found down by the river. The victim of an assault. Michael Reeves.'

I frown. It's him, of course, I just never heard his full name before. It sounds so strange. He was always just Mick. 'And?'

'He's doing well. Early days, but he'll be OK.'

Some tightness that I've held inside me, ever since I found myself in hospital, seems to slacken. I nod, exhale.

Her eyes are on my face. 'Strange thing is,' she goes on, 'he says he was alone at the time of the assault. Denies all knowledge of you.'

I frown. 'Why would he say that?'

Her eyebrows raise a fraction. 'I don't know, Maddy. The police don't, either. It is odd, isn't it? Almost as if he's trying to protect you. Trying to hide something.'

I look away, stung. I misjudged her. She's not as stupid as she looks. I wonder how much she knows about me. They've got my name. There can't be many Madeleine Crosbys in England. Maybe just one. I close my eyes and my body starts to shake, not with DTs this time, but with fear. What if they've got records? What if they know what really drew me down to London? What if they've found out what I did?

*

Where do you start? Once you pull a thread and your life starts to unravel, where does it end? Where will it ever end? I've been through worse. I tell myself that on the bad days. Been through worse and come out again. But I'm older now. It's harder, all harder. What does Macbeth say about Lady Macbeth? *She should have died hereafter.*

Perhaps that's the place to start. The death of my sister-in-law, Christina. John's twin. We always called her Christy.

I was working at the caravan park then, dried out, getting back on my feet, keeping my head down. The park owners were lucky to have me. They knew and I knew that in any other life, I'd be doing more than ordering fresh stocks of bread and biscuits for the site shop and checking in caravans and posting off booking forms and all the other menial tasks that were demanded of me.

I didn't need more. It was impossible to go back to teaching, after all that had happened. I was just doing my time, hiding away from the world, counting down the years until I could go in search of her, until I could introduce myself and beg her for a fair hearing and explain. And ask forgiveness – I planned to do that, too.

Christy had my address at the caravan park. She could have got in touch. I posted a Christmas card to them every year with my address written in neat capitals, correct punctuation, on the outside of the envelope and repeated inside the card. Just in case. She never replied but she knew where I was. She could have told me what had happened and given me the chance to make up with her, to put it right at the end, but she didn't. I think that was the hardest part, afterwards, when I thought about it.

I'd been at the caravan park for eleven years. Caravans and trailers and a batch of mobile homes; they called them that but they weren't very mobile – most of them had gardens and outside toilets. There was a field down near the stream which the farmer let out to campers in July and August, if there was demand. Families sometimes came for a week or two in the long summer holidays – you know, not much cash to spare but doing the best they could to give their children a treat.

If someone asked me, I'd say I liked it there. Not happy, exactly, after all that had happened, all I'd lost, but a sort of creeping contentment that helped the years to pass. I knew by then the value of having a dry, warm place to sleep. Of a door you could lock to keep your possessions safe, and know, within the bounds of reasonable doubt, they'd still be there when you went back at night. Of having enough money in my pocket to buy food. To cook. And yes, even books. Not as many and not the ones I'd choose. Not the bookcases filled with classics that I'd once loved and thought to have forever. But books, just the same, discarded by campers and caravaners and holidaymakers, enough to be proud.

And then the letter came. Badly written. From my nephew. Not Andrew, the older one – I remember Andrew when he was little. Even at that age, I didn't much like him. The sort who pinched other children and took their toys and looked you right in the eyes to say, *No, I didn't, it wasn't me*, when you took him to task. No, the letter came from her second boy, Jeremy. My favourite and hers too. He was a sweet boy.

He would barely remember me. He was too young when I last saw him. But he was big-hearted. He wrote to me once before, when he was getting married, to say he'd have invited me to the wedding if he had his way but, things being as they were, he wanted at least to tell me and know he'd thought of me.

It meant a lot to me, that first letter of his. I toasted him and his bride with orange juice at the back of the trailer, the summer evening they were married, and tried to imagine Christy in a ridiculous hat – she never had much style – and that stuck-up husband of hers, Tom, with his little moustache, all quiet self-importance. I blame him for what happened. He was the sort of man who rarely said much but made mischief later, behind the scenes. Poured poison into his wife's ear, as deadly as Claudius.

And then this second letter from Jeremy. An epistolary hand-grenade.

'My mother didn't want you to know,' he wrote. 'She made us promise not to tell you she was ill. But now that she's gone, I feel you should be told. You're her sister-in-law, after all. I know you were all close once.'

Breast cancer. Of course it was. She was so like her mother. The same loud laugh that made people in cafés look round. The same way of standing in judgement, all black and white and no grey. And the same genes, it seems. I'd have told her, if she'd stayed in touch, to have regular checks. *No matter how busy you are. Pay for them, if you have to.* I'd have told her so many things, all those long, missed years.

I phoned their local undertakers and got the details of the funeral, then told the site owners that there was a family emergency and I needed to go away for a few days. They weren't pleased – it was April, one of busiest seasons, not just the Easter clients but the rush of interest in summer bookings as well. But they let me go, to give them their due. I'd hardly taken holiday for eleven years. It would have been churlish to refuse me this.

It wasn't easy, going back there. I sat alone on the train, the tiny three-carriage train that took us out from the city to the town. The houses falling away and the rest of the world too and the fields stretching, green and lush and the first few lambs, new-born with spindly legs, nudging between their mothers' hind legs for milk.

There are moments when time folds and comes together and this was one such moment, the unchanged countryside so familiar and the memories of my childhood so clear, once we came home from Dad's tour in Cyprus. The million times I took the train back and forth with my mother, when she was still alive and then, after her death, when I was only a teenager, with Christy. She was more than just a friend to me, she was family too. Christy and her handsome, cool, crazy twin brother, John. My John, in the end.

I arrived at the church early. The weather was all wrong for a funeral: all new life and green leaves and clusters of flowers. I followed the path towards the back of the church and it was only then, when I smelt the dry earth and saw the gaping hole where the grave was freshly dug, ready for Christy to be lowered into the ground, that it hit me. That I realised she really was gone forever and all those things I planned one day to say to her, the calm explanations on good days and the angry shouts on bad ones, the conversations I rehearsed in my head so often as I swabbed out a caravan or lugged welcome packs down the field or just sat quietly in the trailer in the evening, wrapped in blankets, listening to the drum beat of rain on the roof and wondering what happened to put me here, those things really would never be said. *It's never too late.* But it was. *Never, never, never, never, never.*

By the time the service started, I was a wreck. It was only a small church but she filled it. Trust Christy, she always did know how to draw a crowd. I kept my head bowed as the muffled footsteps started to sound down the aisle. Low voices. Awkward.

I shuffled to the far end of the pew, close to a pillar and kept my head bowed, just snatching glances as the mourners gathered, middle-aged couples in sombre browns and greys. I barely recognised a soul. It struck me that I might be the only one present who remembered Christy as a girl, before she ever met Tom.

The church smelt of must and dust and wax and it took me back decades, to Mum's funeral and then Dad's and then Christy and Tom's wedding when I was a bridesmaid, dizzy with love for John which was still secret then, so new it was just for the two of us. I remember shaking as I stood there in my frilly pink bridesmaid's dress, feeling his eyes on me, knowing how sexy he'd look in his rented suit, wondering if we'd dance together at the reception, in front of them all, or if I'd have to watch him out of the corner of my eye all evening. *Lord, what fools these mortals be.*

Tom and the boys carried in the coffin. That's what finally broke me. The sight of the wooden box, all polished as if Christy herself had got out the Pledge and duster and given it a good going over. Tom looked old, too old. Bald, now, so the little moustache was all he had left to treasure. Vain little man. And Andrew beside him, his self-righteous firstborn. And then Jeremy, the kindness clear now in his face, tall and handsome at the back. Broad-shouldered, too. She must have been proud. He was a man now of… around thirty – I couldn't focus enough to work out his age. But I still saw the little boy in him. The toddler, just learning to walk, stumbling to keep up with his big brother.

They set down the coffin and the vicar started and I couldn't take my eyes off the wood; I couldn't stop myself from imagining the body lying cold and stiff inside, and think of the girl whose skin smelt like toasted marshmallows in the sunshine and who first taught me how to apply eyeshadow – blue, always blue – and who once ate flour and raw cocoa with me to see which made us sick, and who showed me how to braid my hair in a hundred tiny plaits and hugged me when I cried about my mum.

Now, remembering her and all that happened to drive us apart, I broke down and sobbed. I couldn't help it. The people in the pew in front of me straightened their backs and sat a little forward as if they feared I'd slobber on their necks. It wasn't just the funeral. Or her death. Or what had happened between us. It was the whole sorry mess of my life and the part she'd played in it.

I sat in my corner for a long time after the service. I couldn't join them at the grave for the burial. I couldn't see Christy lowered into clay and covered. The church emptied around me with a creaking and sighing as if everyone there was heaving themselves with effort away from eternity and back into the sunlit world.

By the time I emerged, blinking and shaking, almost everyone had disappeared. I hesitated at the entrance. The spring flowers in the churchyard were such vivid purples and reds and the sap leaking from the trees and bushes all around smelt of life. I felt an imposter amongst it all.

A stout woman stepped across to me. I didn't recognise her.

'You coming for a drink?' Her voice was gentle and I wondered who she was and if she'd seen me crying in the church. 'We're off to the The King's Arms. You know it? Just up the road.'

She hesitated and I looked away, back towards the gate. We went to The King's Arms after Mum's funeral. Pork pies and sausages and shandies in the pub garden. The memory was blistering. Dad sat in a corner, crying and getting quietly drunk, while Christy and I handed around plates of meat-paste sandwiches. I wondered what Christy would think if she'd known we'd see her off the same way.

The powdery-cheeked woman threaded her arm through mine and led me down the path towards the road. I found myself leaning on her.

'Let's walk. It's not far.' She propelled me along, past the knots of people, still chatting in the sunshine, out through the wrought-iron gates and onto the street.

She said, to fill the silence: 'Beautiful day.'

I clung to her. I felt sick, thinking about our lives and the fact my own must stretch on alone now, without her, without the hope of seeing her.

'Here we are. They said they'd be in the garden.'

Here we were indeed. They'd remodelled the car park and the entrance but the rest of the pub looked depressingly the same. I almost stumbled on the step and the woman caught me, steadied me, helped me inside, into the cool, wood-panelled shadows.

The familiar smell reached for me at once, as soon as I crossed the threshold. It grabbed me by the throat and made me gag. The cloying thickness of beer, cut through with whisky. Musty wool and floor polish. Chip fat.

I found my way to the bar, swaying as if I were already drunk, and leaned heavily against it. The brass taps shone as the staff pulled pints. Shards of light bounced off a row of mirrored tiles. I managed to lift my eyes and check the faces. The staff at least were new. No one here would remember me. I bought myself an orange juice, no ice, and headed out into the garden.

Tom was there, at the centre of a small knot of stooping women. Andrew stood close at his side, beer in hand, gesticulating. And Jeremy, all grown up and looking so smart in his dark suit and tie. He was the one who saw me. His small frown, as he tried to place me, turned hastily to an attempt to smile. I wondered if Tom and Andrew knew he'd written to me, if it had occurred to Jeremy that I might find out about the funeral and come. I suspected not. I started to turn away.

He reached my side as I re-entered the pub.

'Aunt Maddy?' A gentle voice. His warm hand cupped my elbow. I looked at it, trying to focus. A man's hand with broad, strong knuckles and a gold wedding ring. 'Thank you for coming. I didn't mean…' He broke off, embarrassed. We both knew what he meant. 'I didn't expect to see you.'

I steadied myself, took a deep breath, tried to reconcile this man with the child I knew. 'Hello, Jeremy. You did well to recognise me. The stranger at the feast.' I tried to smile. 'You got married, didn't you? Is she here?'

He drew me further into the pub, past the bar and through to the small hallway where it was quieter. 'She couldn't come. She's not very well just now.'

'Nothing serious?'

He shook his head but didn't say more. I tried to peer more closely at his face, to read him. His cheeks had fleshed out and his nose was broad, like his father's. But he still had Christy's brown eyes. John's, too.

I said: 'You were her favourite, when you were tiny. You know that, don't you? Did she tell you?'

He flushed. *Ah, the tales within a family that are never told.*

'I'm sorry. I won't stay.' I paused, wondering how to redeem myself. 'I meant well.'

'Of course.' He hesitated. He looked anxious. His fault, I suppose, that I was there at all, that I even knew about his mother's death. It would all come out in a family inquest if I caused trouble. 'Could you just wait a minute? I've got something for you. I was going to put it in the post later but now you're here…'

I stood there on the bristly hall mat, with the framed hunting pictures and rows of coats, and drank down my orange juice, wondering. A memento, clearly. Some photograph of us all together, perhaps. In happier times, as they say in the newspapers.

He looked tense as he came back. Afraid of being seen with me, perhaps. He had a long, thin envelope in his hands. It was addressed to me in his neat handwriting and already stamped. All ready to send. He really hadn't expected to see me today then.

I thought of my father and the care he took to float off unfranked stamps and dry them along the top of the radiators until they were stiff and curled, then use them again. I swallowed. I hadn't thought of that for forty years.

I expected Jeremy to hand me the envelope straight away but he didn't. It seemed hard for him to pass it across and I wondered why.

'Look, I never understood…' He faltered. 'I mean, I was too young, I didn't…' He raked his free hand through his hair and I wanted to say something, to make it easier for him, but I didn't know what. 'Anyway, I'm sorry for what happened. That we never saw you.'

Silence. Finally, I managed to say: 'It's not your fault, Jeremy. Any of it. You were just a child.'

He looked down at the envelope and went on: 'I found this in Mum's papers. I don't know…' He broke off again, looking past me to the hunting scenes on the walls, his face rigid with tension. 'I don't know why she didn't send it on to you at the time. She never mentioned it.' He hesitated. 'Don't be too hard on her, please? I know you'll be angry. You have every right to be. But she wasn't all bad. She was hurt, too, you know. And I think she felt guilty, towards the end, about the way she treated you. I mean, the fact she kept this from you… Maybe that's why she hung on to it. Maybe she knew it would find its way to you in the end.'

I didn't say a word. I just watched his face, his struggle, and waited.

'Anyway.' He nodded as if he'd reached a decision. 'I hope I'm doing the right thing, giving it to you now. Just between us, yes? Dad and Andrew don't know.'

He pushed the envelope into my hands and patted them. A goodbye pat.

He gave a tight smile. 'Goodbye, Aunt Maddy.'

And he was gone.

I read the letter on the train back.

I hadn't had a drink for eleven years. Eleven long, sober years. When I reached the main station, I walked straight into the pub there and headed for the bar. A triple Scotch. Down the hatch. The whisky opened its arms to me and welcomed me home, burning a path down my throat, through my empty stomach. My old friend. It made my heart tremble and my fingers tingle, all the way to the tips. I stuck my tongue into the rim of the empty glass and licked off the last drops.

The barman looked amused as he poured me another. He seemed sterner when he served up the third but I was past caring by then. No such thing as half-measures for me. All or nothing. Finally, the sharp, hard edges of life began again to blur.

I bought a bottle of whisky to drink on the train home. The carriage was quiet and I had a window seat. The countryside blurred into green streaks. It wasn't a hot day but my hands were slick with sweat. And that was it.

It was ten days, apparently. I don't remember. *Stop the clocks.* They're strange things, binges. It's like stepping out of your life for a holiday and putting yourself down for a rest. Numbness. Flying. Sweet oblivion. Blackness. But like all blow-outs, you pay the price eventually – when you crawl back into your skin shell some time later, battered and bruised, vomit-stained, mouth dry, head exploding. Then, the final phase – the detective work. Figure out what happened. That drunk person who took over your life – what the hell did they do? Piece together the evidence. The bank statement that shows a throat-slit account, steadily bleeding away each day, from cash machines, bottle bills at shops and supermarkets, taxis home.

I don't remember getting back to the caravan park. God knows how I managed the journey. I remember waking up underneath the trailer. Something dripped on my head. Bang. Bang. Bang. The drops hit my skull like hammer blows. Only water, it turned out. It had rained that night. I had just been too drunk to turn the key and drag myself inside.

One of the mobile home owners found me the next morning. A holier-than-thou scoutmaster type. Socks and sandals and shorts in the rain. I stank, apparently. There's no stench like stale alcohol. And plenty of other evidence, anyway. Empty bottle still clutched in my fist. Lying in a pool of vomit. If I'd been him, I'd have shaken me awake, brought me a bottle of water and a strong coffee and left me to sleep it off. It would be clear to anyone that the hangover was punishment enough.

Not my scoutmaster. He took photos as evidence. He filed a formal complaint. He made sure I was well and truly finished.

They gave me twenty-four hours to pack and leave. After eleven years. Not even a bit of extra cash to see me on my way.

I never even had the chance to confront the scoutmaster. Anyway, what could I say? *Have a happy bloody holiday.*

And there I was, out on my ear, back in the gutter once more. Leaving behind the books and the pots and dishes in the trailer. Clutching what I could carry in plastic bags. Drawing out the money I still had and spending it on booze, that old familiar friend. Turned out it had always been there, all this time, waiting for me, just out of sight, half-hidden in the shadows, waiting with its arms open and its soft, whispering voice, until I came again to find it. Promising oblivion.

I bought a ticket for a long-distance coach and drank my way down to London slumped in the corner of the backseat, carried on the stream of all desperate things, down to the streets of our glorious capital. I didn't know what I'd do there but I knew where I was heading. I had the letter in my pocket, the letter Christy had kept from me, the letter Jeremy handed to me, with an address at the top. Was it stupid, pitching up like that, homeless and penniless and numb with drink? Probably. I had no choice. I had to go.

I've thought a lot about it since. Lord knows, I've had time.

On good days, when my head's clear and the sun shines, I think: *Maybe it could have been different.* If only someone kind had found me that morning and helped me out. If only the boss had showed some mercy and given me a second chance. Maybe I could have climbed back onto the wagon, hard as that is. I've done it before. And then? I could have written my own letter and responded properly, thoughtfully, with dignity. We could have made a plan to meet, like two normal people. Who knows what might have been?

But on bad days, when the mist comes down and the need to drink, to dull the edges, to escape myself, has me in its grip, I look back and all I can see is a sickening predictability. I was set on the road to destruction from the start. There was no escaping it. Once I entered that pub at the station and knocked back that first whisky, I was lost.

I had the address. Yes, I would go and look. Watch from afar. Find out what I could. But then?

Don't be a drunken fool. Look at your wretched, blathering self. Why would anyone want to know that? How could anyone ever love it?

BECCA

We get through the weekend without too much drama.

Alex skulks in his room and disappears into the strange world of computer games and, for now at least, I leave him alone.

Rosie and I do the shopping and then have a short play in the park both mornings. On Saturday afternoon, Ella and Sarah come up and the girls watch a Disney movie together with microwaved popcorn, while Sarah and I drink tea and chat in the kitchen.

Nothing from Mark. No crazy begging letters. No surprise visits. No late night calls. Not even a text. When I go to bed on Sunday night, I feel stronger than I've felt for a long time. I lie very still in my rented bed and look at the patterns of light across the ceiling and think, for the first time in years: *I can do this. This being happy. Maybe I really can.*

On Monday, Alex sleeps in late, sits grouchily over breakfast, barely speaking, then disappears into his room. When he finally emerges and appears in the kitchen doorway, he's wearing an old hoodie and jacket.

'I'm off out.'

'You mean you're "going out",' I correct. 'Where to?'

He shrugs as if it isn't my business. 'Dunno. Off to meet mates. The mall, I suppose.'

'The mall? Now?'

He rolls his eyes. 'What?'

'Haven't you got homework?'

He groans. 'Mum, it's Christmas, right? Holidays?'

'Don't talk to me like that.' I turn away, annoyed with him and annoyed with myself for letting him get to me. I take a deep breath and focus on loading the dishwasher. Finally, I straighten up and start to turn. 'It's just that—'

Too late. Down the hall, the door opens and then slams, and he's already gone.

At lunchtime, Rosie comes to work with me and tucks herself away at the back of the long, steamy kitchen of the wine bar, getting on with some secret colouring. Every time I try to dash across to her, she bends forward and covers it up with her arms, her face cross.

'Don't look, Mummy! Go away!'

I'm happy to leave her to it. I give her a packed lunch and she sits there, legs swinging, munching her sandwiches and crisps and watching us as the bar opens and quickly fills and the young waitresses, schoolgirls most of them, run to and fro. Dennis commands the kitchen and the two of us struggle to keep up with the orders.

It's busy all lunchtime. Not three-course lunches but small orders – bowls of soup and hot sandwiches and dishes of chilli and rice. Fast turnovers between one cover and the next which doesn't leave us time to catch our breath.

'Christmas shoppers,' Jane says, when she comes rushing through from the front to see if we're managing. 'Cold out.'

As the tables start to clear, finally, she runs through to me again, beckons me out to the back door.

'Quick word?'

It's the nearest thing to a private place, where Jane has her awkward conversations with suppliers, and staff are confronted and fired. My stomach twists.

'Everything OK?' Already, my mind races ahead. *What have I done? What if she fires me? I can barely cover the bills as it is.*

Jane is flushed. The warmth of the wine bar, the constant running back and forth, overseeing the two teenage waitresses. But is there more than that?

'I've been thinking,' she says. She looks off to one side, gazing somewhere near the door handle. 'About your hours.'

I take a deep breath. 'I know. I know you always let me out promptly, to get Rosie. I really appreciate it. But if it's not working, maybe—'

She tuts. 'Natasha's leaving.'

I pause, wrong-footed.

'From January, I'll have four nights a week going. Are you interested?'

I blink and my heart flips with excitement, with nerves. 'You serious?'

She carries on as if I haven't spoken. 'Second chef. Same as you do now. But you'll have the chance to learn a lot more in the evenings. You'd be in from six, prepping with Dennis. Then cooking to order. Getting the food out. It's usually busy. You'd have more responsibility. But you can do it, you're ready for it.' Her eyes are on my face now, reading me. 'I could let you get away by ten, if that helps.'

I hesitate. For a moment I'm exhilarated, imagining myself rushing round the kitchen, getting proper meals out instead of just soups and salads. I'd learn a lot, I can see that. They offer a gourmet menu once a month. Maybe I could help on that, after a while? Even suggest some dishes of my own, once I'm established.

'It's good money,' she goes on. 'More tips. You'd do better than you do at the moment. And you could keep your lunch shifts as well, if you like. Up to you.'

I chew the inside of my lip. It's such an opportunity, I can't quite believe it. I want to say yes at once, to make sure she knows I'm keen and before she gives it to someone else. And proper money, too. It might even give me the chance to put money aside, to protect myself from the risk of Mark pulling the plug, as he keeps threatening.

I hesitate and my stomach contracts. How can I? I'm not a free agent – what about Alex and Rosie? I can't afford the cost of a sitter. Not for that many hours. Sarah might take them for the odd evening, but not four nights a week.

I can't bring myself to say no. Not straightaway. Maybe there is a way. Maybe I just can't see it yet.

'Can I think about it?'

She nods, brisk again. 'Think it over.' And she's gone, back into the main body of the wine bar to supervise, leaving me dazed in the kitchen, wondering how I could possibly make it work.

They're fully booked for that evening. The usual story: if it weren't for Rosie, I'd offer to stay on and help. Jane and Dennis will be hard-pressed to replenish the fridges by the time the bar opens again at seven.

As it is, it's after two by the time I drop my apron into the basket and reach for my coat. I go over to Rosie, sitting there at the back counter. Bored, now.

'What a good girl.' I put my arms around her and kiss the tip of her nose. 'Can I see it now?'

I point to the picture she's coloured.

She puts her head on one side, considering, then lifts away her arms. A unicorn, one of her favourite animals, standing by a Christmas tree. Blue sky above and a strip of bright green grass below, studded with flowers.

'Well done, Rosie. That's so neat.'

She beams. 'Is it the best picture you ever saw?'

I make a show of looking more closely. 'Do you know, I think it probably is. You've worked so hard on it. Well done.'

I help her down from the stool and hold her coat, button it up.

'Shall we put it on the fridge when we get home?'

She shakes her head. 'It's not for keeping. It's a present.'

'For me?'

'For Maddy.'

I hesitate. I thought she'd forgotten about Maddy.

'That's a bit tricky.' I wave goodbye through the bar to Jane and steer Rosie towards the back door. 'Because we might not see Maddy again.'

She stops and turns to face me, her face set. 'Yes, we will. She's in hospital. We can take the bus.'

I stall. 'Maybe after Christmas. We're busy now.'

She stamps her foot. 'No, Mummy!'

'Rosie.' My warning voice.

Her face reddens. 'But you said. You said if I was really, really good, I could have a treat.'

I frown. 'You can have a treat. At home.' I was thinking a small chocolate bar, maybe.

'But it's KIND. She's all alone. In the hospital.'

I take a deep breath. 'Well, maybe we could post it—'

'Noooo! I want to see her.' She tosses her head. Her arms flail at her sides with frustration. She isn't often so set on something but when she is, she's hard to talk round.

'Calm down. Now. I'm not talking to you at all if you're cross. OK?'

Her body is rigid with tension as she struggles to control herself and her rising anger. She breathes heavily. Finally, she says in a quieter tone: 'Please, Mummy. Please. Just to give her my picture.'

I think of the traffic and how long it would take. But I think too that maybe I should be proud of her, that she's right, she is trying to be kind. It is Christmas, after all. And perhaps, if we go quickly, hand in the picture and come away, it needn't take too long.

I sigh. 'What do you say?'

'PLEEEEEAAAASE.' She grabs a fistful of my coat, her face beseeching. 'I'll be good all day. Promise.'

I take a deep breath, open the wine bar door and usher her out into the cold air, still trying to persuade myself that it's no big deal. She sat quietly and coloured that card for hours while I worked. She's a good kid. It's my job to encourage the children to be compassionate, to be grateful for what they have and to give to others.

But even as we get the bus and I look across at Rosie's beaming face, I have a sense of foreboding. A sense that we're being dragged inexorably into a dark, downwards spiral from which we might never emerge.

I've always hated hospitals. They frighten me. The sickly chemical smell of them. The bland colours and long corridors and slapping plastic doors. The sense of imprisonment. The memories of visiting elderly relatives when I was a child, shrinking behind my mother, frightened. The false brightness in people's faces – the nurses and the visitors – which even then, as a girl, I knew was a lie.

I adopt the same fake cheeriness now with Rosie as she skips past the card shop and cafés and flower stall on the ground floor, all dolled up with Christmas greetings and special offers, shiny foil angels and silver snowflakes on ropes and glitter balls. She bounces on the spot and watches as I buy a box of chocolates from the newsagents.

The air is close and humid and carries the scent of tropical plants as well as detergent. It doesn't feel much like a hospital. More like a shopping centre with its massive atrium and giant fish tank and six-foot Christmas tree, decorated with baubles and tinsel. And everywhere, letting in the grey winter light, endless sheets of glass.

Here and there, a patient in a dressing gown is pushed in a wheelchair or hobbles on a relative's arm and they're a surprise, as if we've caught them semi-naked in the street.

We take the same lift as a patient on a mobile hospital bed, an elderly man with silver stubble on a bony chin. He has a mask pressed over his face and a drip attached to his arm and it's hard to tell if he's conscious. A member of staff, in green scrubs, pushes and pulls the wheeled bed into position as if he's parking a car, pressing us into the corner. I look away.

Rosie pulls on my hand. She seems relaxed, unafraid of the strange and the sick, and excited about delivering her picture.

I bring her to a halt at the reception desk on the women's ward.

'Is there a woman called Madeleine here, please? She came in at the end of last week. She collapsed in the park.'

The nurse hesitates. 'Are you a relative?'

'No. We just wanted to—'

Rosie cuts in. 'She's our friend. We found her under a bush. Is she better?'

The nurse smiles at her. 'Almost. Do you want to come and see her?'

I say: 'Is it a bad time? We could just leave this—'

But Rosie's already skipping down the corridor after the brisk nurse, the soles of their shoes squeaking out a rhythm together on the polished floor.

I follow them as they veer left into a bay with six beds. A large expanse of picture windows at the far end is shielded with blinds. Curtains are drawn around most of the beds. The square angles of beds, lockers and portable trolleys distort the lines. Behind one, the moving bulges of a person – the bottom or back of a nurse or visitor – bang shapes in one curtain as we pass and then swing and settle again.

'She's here!'

Rosie breaks into a run as she nears the end of the bay. She waves her picture like a flag, excited, and Maddy, sitting in a chair beside her bed, facing out towards the windows and the outside world, turns and opens her arms and smiles.

I hurry after her as Rosie climbs onto the arm of Maddy's chair. Their heads bend together over the picture.

'What fabulous use of colour,' Maddy says, pointing a finger here and then there across the paper as she praises it in an even, adult tone. Rosie twists back to me, eyes shining, then turns again to listen.

'Hello!' My lying hospital voice. The one my mother taught me. 'We've come to see you.'

Neither of them looks up. They're whispering together, conspiring, lost in the multi-coloured world of the unicorn and the flowers and the psychedelic grass. The nurse has already left and I find myself standing there, suddenly excluded, looking Maddy over.

She's wearing a thin, green dressing gown, fastened loosely at her waist with a cord. It falls open at the chest, revealing a flannelette nightie with a sagging neckline and mottled skin beneath. Her feet are in over-sized slippers. Nothing fits her or sits right on her. *Borrowed*, I think. *Charity. The poor box.*

One side of her head looks shaved and is dressed with a medical pad and bandage. It makes her look exotic but lopsided. Her skin, which on her face is stretched tight across her cheekbones and nose, is sallow, but it's clean and younger-looking than I remembered.

A plaster on the soft inner flesh below one elbow holds a tube in place and a drip above, hanging from a stand, slowly feeds her. Maddy sees Rosie looking and jiggles the plastic tube.

'It's giving me medicine,' she says. 'It's all right. It doesn't hurt.'

I look away. A trolley sits to one side of her bed with the remains of lunch. A bowl with streaks of custard stacked on top of a plate of half-eaten food. A lid tilts to one side. The cloying smell hangs thickly in the over-heated air. Stewed meat or gravy and mashed potato.

The smells stir memories. My mother sitting in a hospital bed like this, thin and gaunt, and trying to smile. Her hair was wrong, when we visited. Someone had washed and combed it who didn't know her, who didn't know the way she was supposed to look. I hated that. Her hands became translucent, towards the end, a map of raised veins threading their way over bone. I blink. She must have been a similar age to Maddy. I find a tissue in my pocket, blow my nose.

Maddy and Rosie are whispering again, complicit. I shake my head. What is it about this woman that fascinates Rosie? I think of the way her legs stuck out from under the bush. Felled, like the witch in *The Wizard of Oz*. And now what, now she's survived? Now what happens to her?

A nurse bustles in and hands Maddy a paper cup containing tablets and a cone of water and waits while she swallows them down, making a performance of it to amuse Rosie.

'That one tastes of melted rainbows,' she says. 'But what about that one?'

'Chocolate ice-cream,' says Rosie. Her favourite.

Maddy swallows it, considers. 'By golly, you're right!'

They smile.

As the nurse leaves, she says: 'Your gran's doing really well, lovey. Might be home for Christmas, eh, Madeleine?'

My stomach clenches. Maddy doesn't react at all but I feel it on her behalf. We barely know her. She has no home. I think how awful to be stuck here, with nowhere else to go. To end up in hospital for Christmas in a borrowed nightie that doesn't fit.

A moment later, another, harder voice in my head is already interrupting and saying: *Stop it! She's not your problem. Ten minutes is plenty and then we go, honour is satisfied. Rosie's been kind, this has gone far enough.*

I set the box of chocolates on the end of the bed and they both look round, as if they're surprised I'm still here.

Rosie cups her hand to Maddy's ear and whispers, her eyes on mine, her expression mischievous. When she breaks off, Maddy fastens me with her blue eyes.

'Well, that's very kind. What can I say? Thank you.'

It's only chocolates. I glance at the lines of tinsel and shiny twists festooning the windows, embarrassed. It's hard to make a hospital look cheerful, even at Christmas.

'You're really sure?' Her hand is round Rosie's shoulders. The fingers are long and artistic. 'I don't want to impose.'

I look at Rosie who's twisted around to see me, her face beaming. I feel slightly sick. 'What do you mean?'

Maddy falters and the light in her eyes dims. She says to Rosie: 'Are you quite sure that's true, Rosie? Do you think you might have made a muddle?'

'I haven't!' Rosie's fists clench. 'It is true, isn't it, Mummy?'

'What?'

'About Christmas.'

My cheeks flush.

Maddy, watching me, says at once: 'She's got it wrong, hasn't she? Of course. A misunderstanding. Happens all the time.'

Rosie looks from one of us to the other, horrified.

'But, Mummy! She must come! Just for Christmas.'

'Rosie!' I shake my head at her. My mind's racing to catch up, to find a way out of the embarrassment. 'You've given Maddy her card. Now we need to get going.'

Rosie, refusing to be distracted, says: 'She can't be on her own. That's horrible. She might go into a hotel. The doctors said. Because she hasn't got a house.'

Maddy says: 'Not a hotel, Rosie. It's a hostel. But I expect it's just as comfy.'

I don't want to know any more about Maddy's hostel. It isn't our problem. At least she'll have a roof over her head, thanks to social services, presumably.

I say with as much conviction as I can: 'I'm sure she'll be fine. They probably have Christmas all together there. Isn't that right, Maddy?'

Maddy, red in the face now, turns to Rosie with false cheeriness. 'I'm sure they do. And Father Christmas always brings extra special presents to people in hostels. I wouldn't want to miss that.'

Rosie frowns and her lips pucker.

Maddy doesn't meet my eye. 'It's all right, Rosie. Your mummy can't add another person at the last minute. There won't be enough food.'

Rosie's voice rises in protest: 'But there is!'

Maddy puts her hands squarely on Rosie's shoulders, pulls her forward and plants a kiss on her forehead.

'Rosie,' she says. 'You are the kindest little girl in the whole world and I hope Father Christmas still has a few presents left for you, after he's brought me all mine. Will you draw me a picture of them?'

Rosie twists away, buries her head in my stomach and starts to cry.

I give her a hug, turn her around and start to steer her away, still sobbing, towards the entrance to the ward.

'Bye, Maddy.' I call back over my shoulder. 'Good luck.'

The double doors slap closed behind us as we emerge into the main hallway.

'Now, sweetheart, calm down.' I duck down to Rosie's level and try to get her to look at me. Her face is blotchy and streaked with mucus and tears. 'How about we go and have a hot chocolate?' A quick one.

'Don't want to.' Rosie, still crying, starts to hiccup. 'Why, Mummy? Why can't she come for Christmas?'

I shake my head. 'We haven't got room. It's going to be a squeeze as it is. Daddy's coming, remember? And Grandma?'

'They won't mind.' She pulls at my sleeve. 'Please, Mummy. Just for Christmas dinner and we can give her a present and she won't be so sad.' Her face is desperate with pleading. She takes a deep breath and trembles. 'I won't have any presents,' she says. 'Not one. Just this one tiny thing. OK? Deal?'

I hug her to me. 'Oh, Rosie. I wish there were more people like you. I really do. But it's not that simple.'

'It is!'

'What would Alex say?'

She starts to smile, sensing that I'm wavering. 'Alex doesn't matter. He won't notice. He'll play computer games all day anyway.'

I think of Mark and his mother and how shocked they'd be. *They might even think twice about forcing themselves on us next year…*

I blow out my cheeks. 'I can't believe I'm even talking about this.'

She sees something soften in my expression and reads it as victory. She throws her arms around my neck and kisses me. 'Thank you, Mummy. It'll be the best Christmas ever. I promise.' She wipes off her face with her hands and jumps up and down. 'Can I go back and tell Maddy now? She'll be so happy.' She beams. 'She can cuddle Bunny if she likes.' She considers. 'Just for a borrow.'

I follow her back into the ward, wondering quite what I've just done. I'm buoyed by Rosie's elation that we're going to make a homeless person happy at Christmas but, at the same time, wondering what Christmas lunch will be like with Maddy at the table, what Mark and his mother will have to say about it, and if we'll ever escape from the clutches of this strange, homeless woman.

SARAH

I say: 'You've having her for Christmas? That tramp who sleeps in a doorway?'

Becca hasn't told me. Rosie let it out. She never can keep a secret. Becca sits quietly, her eyes on the kitchen table, looking embarrassed.

Rosie says: 'She sleeps under a bush, actually. But she was coshed on the head. That means hit. We found her, didn't we, Ella?' She considers. 'Well, I found her. She's my friend. You were just there.'

Ella gazes at her with admiration. I purse my lips. I wish she'd stop idolising Rosie and be more confident, be her own person.

I say, trying not to show Ella that I'm cross that she hasn't told me about all this: 'What an adventure. You were there too, Ella? You never mentioned it.'

Becca steps in. 'Her name's Maddy. She just had an accident, that's all, and she doesn't have any family. So Rosie was keen to ask her round. Just for Christmas lunch.'

Rosie says: 'She stayed the night, the other day. She's like an extra grandma.'

I raise my eyebrows, trying to catch Becca's eye. 'Did she?' Sounds as if there's a lot I haven't been told.

Becca says: 'She did me a good turn and it was so wet out, she slept on the sofa bed one night. No big deal.' She turns to Rosie: 'Don't exaggerate, Rosie. We've talked about this. She can come for Christmas Day and that's it. Right?'

Rosie pouts and lowers her head over the Play-Doh. We're sitting at Becca's kitchen table, rolling out brightly coloured sausages to coil into baskets. Becca, her own basket progressing well, smooths out the sides with the pad of her thumb. Her hair falls forward over her face and she tosses her head to flick it away, as she does a hundred times a day.

I say: 'How much do you actually know about her?'

Becca doesn't answer.

Rosie, always literal, says: 'She's got a bandage that goes all the way from here to here.' She illustrates by touching her own head. Ella's eyes widen. 'We went to hospital to see her. She was wearing a nightie and slippers and she had a plastic thing stuck right in here.' She shows Ella the inside of her elbow.

Ella whines. 'Why couldn't I come? I never go to hospital.'

I sigh.

Later, the girls disappear into Rosie's room to play and I help Becca tidy up.

I like this flat. The stairs are a pain – there's a lot to be said for living on the ground floor, especially when Ella was still in the buggy – but Becca gets more privacy and more light up here. I look out now at the row of backyards down below, the sloping roofs and gutters, black with leaf mulch, at the scribble of bare branches and the birds wheeling over the trees. It already looks so familiar. It's only eight months since Becca and the kids moved in upstairs and already it seems like forever. We knew each other pretty well before, first chatting at the school gates and then, as the girls became inseparable, hosting play dates.

I was glad to help when Becca said she was thinking about leaving Mark. I encouraged her. As soon as one of David's flats came up, he did her a good deal on the rent. I knew he would if I asked. Now the girls are in and out of each other's homes all the time, we're practically neighbours. Even Alex hangs out at my place, once in a while, to have a break from this little flat and check out my stash of computer games.

'Where's Alex tonight?'

Becca rolls her eyes. 'Out.' She doesn't need to say more. I get the picture. I remember being a teenager and the trouble I caused. Alex has been through a lot this year and he's a funny kid – a bit of a misfit, I can sense it.

'Don't worry.' I shrug, trying to be reassuring. 'He'll be OK.'

It's after five. I tug open the fridge and take out the bottle of white wine I brought round. 'Quick drink?'

She shakes her head – Becca's not much of a drinker – but I unscrew the top and pour myself a large glass anyway and sip it as we talk. It's one of the things I like most about the fact Becca's so close now – these informal drop-in visits here and there for a cup of tea or a glass of wine. Easy company.

Becca takes a seat opposite me. She pulls at the loose skin around her nails. 'Do you think I'm being stupid? Letting a homeless woman come?'

I shrug. 'Probably.' She's too kind, that's Becca's problem. Hates to hurt anyone's feelings. That's why it took her so long to leave Mark. Why she's still struggling to sever the ties. 'Why'd you say yes?'

She sighs. Pick, pick at her nails. 'It was so awkward. Rosie's really taken a shine to her. She sort of invited her and then, well, it was just awful. She's got nowhere to go. I couldn't say no…' She trails off.

I nearly say: 'Well, you could have, actually. It's not that hard to say no, if you've got a backbone,' but I manage to bite it back. Becca looks forlorn enough already. Instead, I say: 'Is this because Mark's coming? Getting your own back, somehow?'

She looks up at me and says a little too quickly: 'Of course not.'

I take a sip of wine. I wouldn't blame her. I'd like to see Mark's reaction when he turns up and finds a bag lady at the table. Serves him right.

It's no secret that I'm not a fan of his. I had a bad feeling about him from the start, when Becca and I first became friends, at the school gates. I never liked like the way he treats Becca. All the emotional blackmail, all the bullying. Even now, even though she's moved out, he's still making a nuisance of himself. Texting. Phoning. She doesn't need to tell me, I can see. I know his type.

'And his mother's coming too, isn't she? What's she going to say?'

She pulls a face. 'Stop it.'

We sit for a moment.

Finally, I say: 'What's her name again?'

'Maddy.'

I consider this. 'Probably the best name for her – she's stark raving mad. And Becca, she's a fully grown adult. You mustn't feel sorry for her.'

Becca frowns at her fingers. She hates it when I lecture but sometimes she needs to hear it. I feel I've got a duty to look out for her. She hasn't lived on her own before. She doesn't know what it's like out there, how many people are on the hustle.

I carry on: 'If she lives on the street, it's because she chooses to do that. You know that, don't you? She doesn't have to.'

Becca stares at the table and doesn't answer.

I shrug. 'I know. It's complicated. I'm just saying, she could get help if she wanted.' I pause, thinking. 'What do you know about her, anyway? Is she on drugs?'

Becca looks uncomfortable. 'I don't think so. She said not.'

'Just be careful. I know you've got a big heart, Becca. I love that about you. But, you know, watch your back.'

I take another glug of wine.

Becca closes me down by changing the subject. Typical Becca. Always avoids confrontation.

'The invitation still stands, if you and Ella want to come round for Christmas, too. We'd find room.'

I shake my head at once. Much as I'm tempted to see Mark forced to pull a cracker with a bag lady, I could do without the drama. We've got enough of our own. 'That's kind but we're OK. It's always just the two of us at Christmas. It's what we're used to. We like it that way.'

Ella comes flying out of the bedroom and runs down the passage to join us, Rosie not far behind.

Ella says, panting: 'She's not sharing, Mummy.'

'Rosie!' Becca gets to her feet.

Rosie, indignant, shouts: 'She's telling a lie! I *am* sharing. She hit me.'

'That's enough, you two.' I knock back the rest of the wine and get to my feet, put the empty glass on the draining board. 'Anyway, it's time we were going. Say thank you to Rosie and her mummy for having you.'

I gather together Ella's things and go through to the coat-rack to unhook our jackets.

Behind me, Rosie says: 'Thank you for coming, smelly pants.'

Ella, giggling now, says: 'Bye bye, poo poo.'

Becca screws the top back onto the bottle of white wine and hands it to me at the door. She knows me too well.

'Anyway,' she says in a low voice, 'if you change your mind about Christmas, you know you're welcome.' Then, as she pulls back from kissing me on the cheek, she says loudly: 'See you soon, smelly pants,' and the girls collapse with laughter.

Later, when Ella is settled in bed, I pour another glass of white wine, alone in the sitting room, curtains open, looking out at the darkness. The Parents never drank. A sherry at Christmas, maybe. A glass of champagne to toast a wedding. But 'drinking to excess', as my mother rather primly describes getting drunk, was one of the many things they never understood about me.

I don't understand it myself. Tonight I'm melancholy and I want to keep drinking to black out the sadness, but it isn't working. It never does. It's making me worse. So why don't I learn that?

I get up, restless, and pace through to Ella's room. I hesitate at the half-open door and listen, peer through the crack. I'd like her to still be awake. I'd like to have a cuddle with her and stroke her hair and tell her how much I love her, this beautiful, thoughtful girl of mine. This miracle.

But she's lying very still, breathing deeply. I creep into her room and stand over her, marvelling. She's sleeping on her back, one arm thrown up, palm cupped as if she were reaching to catch a ball. Her other arm is wrapped around her teddy, holding it close. I stoop and kiss her on the forehead and she stirs and twitches.

I stay for a moment and watch her sleep. She's growing so quickly. There's so much I need to tell her and keep putting off and she's asking more and more difficult questions. About why she doesn't have a daddy. Why we never see her grandparents. Christmas rakes it all up again. Even Rosie, grappling with the idea of living apart from her father, gets to sit down to Christmas dinner with a mum, dad and grandma.

I go back into the sitting room, refresh my glass and spread myself out on the settee. I'd just like it over, Christmas. I hate it. All the fake jollity and the rubbish in the shops and everyone pretending to play happy families. It brings back too many sour memories: The Parents dressing me up as an angel, a circle of tinsel on my head, and dragging me along to the church nativity play every Christmas Eve. Their sanctimonious presents on Christmas Day. Books and wooden toys that were made by some charity in the developing world and smelt strange, and sensible clothes I never liked.

I reach for my glass and drink. They meant well. That's the best I can say of them. They were kind-hearted and generous, just like Becca. And maybe a little naïve, too. But I was never like them. I always knew that. I never fit in. Worse than that, I was always a disappointment.

I close my eyes and the darkness spangles and swims. I think about my special book, the one I kept hidden. My mother found it, in the end, when I was a teenager and she went poking in my room to clean. She had no right.

She said she hadn't read it but I never believed her. I wrote my innermost thoughts in that book. I copied my best stories into it and the scraps of sentimental poetry I wrote now and then, just for myself. She had no right to pry.

I lift the glass and tip more wine down my throat. My limbs slacken and relax. There's a low buzzing in my ears and I listen, wondering what it is.

I burnt the book, after she found it, secretly on the garden bonfire. It was late in the afternoon and the fire had died down. She'd gone inside to start cooking dinner. I pushed it into the centre with a stick and poked the pages and watched them curl and brown and finally burst into flames, one clump at a time. It hurt, seeing it burn. It hurt a lot, but I couldn't stop myself.

Something twists now, inside me, and hardens. I think again about Ella and Rosie and this homeless woman, Maddy. They found her, beaten up, in the park and they didn't tell me? Becca must have told them to keep it a secret. That was wrong of her. Irresponsible. Why would she keep something like that from me? Why?

I'm grateful that she takes Ella so often when I'm at work. I'm always saying how grateful I am. Always giving her presents. But that doesn't give her the right to keep secrets from me. What if that woman is on drugs? What then? She could have been a danger to the girls.

I try to think what this homeless woman looks like. There is one I've seen around here. Slumped in a shop doorway across the road, some evenings. Or huddled on the high street. I wonder if that's the same one. There are so many, nowadays. There's that man with a ponytail and a bedraggled dog who sits behind a cardboard sign by the station. *I'm hungry. Please give money for food.* There's that plump woman, quite a young face actually, who plays the accordion near the shopping centre. And others. I've lost count.

And what did Rosie say? Becca let her stay the night once? I tut to myself.

I get up to switch on the television, more from habit than anything, and my head swims. I sway, stick out a hand and lean heavily on the edge of the table to steady myself. It tips up and I slide down the polished surface, crash, onto the floor. The wine bottle goes, too, and rolls with a clatter across the wood.

I lie on my side for a moment, longer than I need to. Dazed. I blink slowly, surveying the ski slope of the toppled table, the dusty chair legs, the balls of fluff along the skirting.

I take my time, clumsy, getting up again and sitting back on the settee. I lift my hands to my face and rub them slowly, steadily, down the sweaty, slightly numb skin there, tracing the bones as I go, the cheeks, nose, chin. Making sure I can still feel myself. Making sure I'm still real.

BECCA

On Christmas Eve, late afternoon, just as I'm drawing the curtains and wondering how to calm Rosie down before bedtime, the doorbell rings.

Rosie jumps down and gets there first. I hear her high voice, over-excited. 'My friend's coming tomorrow. It's Christmas. She got whacked on the head.'

A rich, male voice, amused, says: 'I'm sorry to hear that. Being whacked on the head is never good.'

'Don't worry. She'll be fine. I've made her a Christmas card. Do you want to see?'

Rosie turns to run past me to the kitchen as I reach the door.

'Hello.' David, my landlord.

'Do you want to come in?' I'm suddenly nervous, wondering if something's wrong, what state the sitting room's in. He looks so poised, standing there in a cashmere coat, a woollen scarf loose round his neck.

'Don't worry.' He smiles. 'I just wanted to drop this by.'

He lifts his hand to offer a carrier bag, a plain red one. I try to peer in, confused, as I take it. A bottle, clearly, and something heavy and solid. For a second, I think he's taken in a delivery for me.

'Happy Christmas!'

From him? 'Oh! But you shouldn't have – I mean…' I peer more closely into the bag.

'It's a fruit cake. It'll keep. I bought one for myself and I just thought, well, I thought if you've got a full house, you can't have enough cake.'

'Look!' Rosie's back, pushing a homemade card into his hands, showing off the picture. 'It's a tree. See? A Christmas tree. Mummy wouldn't let me use glitter. Those are balls.'

'Baubles,' I say.

'Stunning.' David studies it with care. 'I can honestly say that is one of the best Christmas cards I have ever seen.'

Rosie looks delighted.

'That's so kind.' I'm still digesting the existence of the cake and bottle. 'You shouldn't have.'

Rosie says: 'What?'

'David's bought us a lovely cake, look, and a grown-up drink for Mummy.'

'But why did you say he shouldn't have?'

David laughs. 'Quite right. No reason at all. Anyway, I should head off. Have a wonderful Christmas.'

'You, too. Thank you. That's so kind.'

Rosie starts jumping up and down, bouncing out onto the landing as he heads back down the stairs.

'I hope Father Christmas comes!' she calls over the banisters. 'Have you been good?'

He turns to look back at her from the bottom of the first set of stairs.

'Terribly good. I'm keeping my fingers crossed.'

'Me, too!'

And he's gone.

In the kitchen, I examine the presents. Champagne. Expensive. The cake, too. At the bottom, a card.

Wishing you all a very merry Christmas. Best wishes, David.

I study his handwriting. Neat and even. For a moment, as I watch Rosie put the final touches to her homemade card, I feel elated. Then it hits me: I'm being ridiculous. He must take presents to all his tenants. It's what landlords do.

Still, instead of putting the card on display in the sitting room, I tuck it away in my bedside table. It's personal, part of my new life, and instinctively I want to hide it away from Mark. He'd only cause trouble.

I put the champagne in the fridge and find a tin for the cake and focus on this evening, on cooking fish pie and trying to calm Rosie enough that I might have a chance of getting her to bed at a sensible hour.

So much has changed since last Christmas. However hard it's been this year, I've come through it and I'm not going back.

*

I'm up early on Christmas Day and sit, bleary-eyed, nursing a coffee, as Rosie and Alex tear through their stockings on the sitting room floor. They haven't got a lot. I couldn't afford it. But Rosie is crazy with excitement and even Alex cracks an occasional smile. Afterwards, we have *pain au chocolat* for breakfast. A big treat.

When I begin work in the kitchen – clearing up the breakfast dishes and then starting to peel sprouts, carrots, parsnips, potatoes – I put the radio on. It's a Christmas morning service and the music, the voices of choir and congregation, washes over the room. I look out at the cold, grey sky and the flats with their curtained bedrooms and listen to the hymn and, despite all the tears and bitterness of the past year, I'm glad to be here, glad to be alone.

Last Christmas, just a few months before I told Mark I was leaving, I was constantly anxious. I didn't see it at the time, but I felt trapped and unhappy and didn't know how to end it. I felt as if I were losing myself completely, after all those years with Mark. I was always exhausted and resented caring for two children, being chronically sleep-deprived, shopping and cooking myself into oblivion when all Mark seemed to do was to turn up, grin over everyone and somehow take the credit. If I tried to ask for help, he simply made fun of me or ignored me.

'Oh, look, guys, Mummy's grumpy again! What can we do to make her laugh?'

Mummy had been close to breaking point.

Now, everything's different. I can hardly believe how much my life has changed. I'm still chronically sleep-deprived and exhausted and worn down by worries about money, about Alex, about everything. But I'm living my own life. I'm starting to find myself again, to piece together some self-esteem. I have a job and I love it and I'm good at it. However hard it is, I'm managing on my own.

I cut crosses into the bottom of the sprouts and pile them in a bowl. This Christmas, I'm determined to put on a good show; to demonstrate to Mark that there are no cracks beneath the surface, as he likes to imagine. There are no hidden signs that I secretly want him back because, however hard it might be at times, I am doing absolutely fine without him.

Mark and his mother, Elizabeth, arrive soon after ten, earlier than I hoped. Rosie has only just got dressed and Alex is still languidly picking up the shreds of old wrapping paper that I asked him to tidy away about three hours ago. The intercom sounds from the front door.

'They're here!'

'Daddy!'

There they are on the doorstep. The intercom image is wobbly but it's them all right. Mark, lunging with confidence at the camera, the fish-eye lens making his nose loom large and, in the background, poking her head around him as if to make sure she isn't overlooked, is Elizabeth.

Rosie runs screaming to the door and jumps up and down on my toes: 'Daddy! Granny! Yay!'

Alex rolls his eyes, but I can tell he's pleased, too.

I open the front door. 'Go down and meet them, would you, Alex?'

He sighs dramatically and sets off down the stairs to the ground floor towards them. Rosie, in her socks, bounds after him.

I dash around the sitting room, trying to hide as much mess as I can. By the time I take up position again at the flat's front door, they're nearing the top. Elizabeth's voice drifts up the stairwell.

'Well, you find me the hairbrush, dear, and I'll do it. What about a nice plait? You can't go around looking like a ragamuffin on Christmas Day.'

I take a deep breath and steady myself as they come into view. Rosie is holding her grandma's hand, making a show of helping her up the stairs. Mark and Alex climb behind, carrying bags of presents. I'm feeling on edge already, just seeing Mark's beaming smile. He always spends too much money on the children. They don't need it. It's embarrassing.

'Well, look at you, Mummy!' He calls up the stairs, his voice reaching for me.

I try not to bristle as I greet them. 'Hi, Elizabeth. Mark. Happy Christmas.'

'Merry Christmas, dear.' A peck on the cheek and she's already in the hall, looking round, no doubt seeking out something to criticise. I never liked her much, even in the good old days. She's a born matriarch. And it was clear she was appalled when I walked away from her beloved only child. How could I explain? She never saw that side of him. The put-downs. The subtle way he undermined me. His need to control everything.

She says: 'I don't know how you manage. So high up. With shopping and everything.' She turns to Rosie. 'Now, princess. Let's sort out that hair.'

I try not to roll my eyes. Mark pushes a bag into my arms. The hard, curved weight of bottles and boxes that will no doubt be chocolates and shop-bought mince pies. He always insists on buying mince pies, even though he knows I'm proud of my own. As if mine are somehow not good enough.

He gives me a quick kiss on the lips before I can pull away.

'Happy Christmas, Mummy.'

That's something else I hate. When he calls me Mummy, as if he's my third child.

I turn without answering and head for the kitchen. Their voices drift through, already dominating the small space: hers, faintly disapproving, taking charge; his, jolly and childlike, joshing with Alex as if they were buddies instead of father and son. I take out David's bottle of champagne from the fridge and put it on the tray with glasses and crisps, then try to find room in the over-crowded space for the newly-arrived bottles of white wine. I slam the fridge door hard, setting jars inside rattling, then stand quietly for a moment, looking at my mottled reflection in the cooker hood and trying to compose myself, before carrying the tray through.

We're just finishing with presents when the buzzer sounds. Eleven-thirty. Right on time. Mark and his mother look up in surprise.

'I've invited an old friend of the family to join us for lunch,' I lie. 'I hope you don't mind. She'd be on her own, otherwise.'

I give Alex a warning look as I head for the door. Rosie smiles. I've given them both a stern talk about keeping their mouths shut and not causing trouble but I'm not sure which of them is worse at keeping secrets.

Maddy's footsteps come heavily up the stairs. I feel a surge of relief when she appears at the top. She looks formidable, stronger than before, and as if she's done her best to make herself presentable. Her hair is cut into a short, spiky style which makes its unevenness less obvious. Where her skull was shaved, the skin has a coating of fresh, downy growth, partly concealing a jagged pink scar.

'Happy Christmas.' I hesitate. 'Are you OK?'

She nods, briskly. She's avoided telling me the name of the hostel so I have no idea how far away it is. When I offered money for a taxi, she batted me away, saying she'd walk.

She hands me a plastic bag. For a moment, I hesitate to take it, remembering the filthy carrier bags she deposited, dripping, on the mat last time she came. Dirty washing, perhaps, or some sort of rubbish salvaged from the street?

She reads my face and says tartly: 'It's quite safe.'

I look inside. A cheap colouring book. A plastic Batman keyring. A cheap box of chocolates.

'I didn't have time to wrap them.' She looks embarrassed. 'Sorry.'

She looks so forlorn, standing there, that I surprise myself by reaching forward and kissing her on the cheek. Her skin is smooth and smells of lemon soap.

Behind me, the sitting room has fallen silent. Waiting.

I whisper: 'My ex is here. Mark. And his mother, Elizabeth. I've told them you're a family friend.'

She visibly brightens and whispers back: 'Quite right. Indeed I am. Just a recently acquired one.' She straightens her shoulders and seems to steady herself. 'Nothing to drink,' she says.

I'm not sure if that's a reprimand, a way of pointing out that I've already failed in my duties as hostess by not offering her anything. I bristle. *She's hardly come through the door…*

'Well, do come and meet everyone and perhaps then you can have—'

'No.' Her face is stern and she looks me directly in the eye. 'Nothing to drink. No alcohol. Please.'

I manage to nod. She sheds her coat, revealing dark trousers and a long-sleeved, brushed cotton blouse. Clean and neatly pressed. *You've really tried*, I think.

She seems to gather herself together as she faces the open sitting room door.

'*Once more unto the breach, dear friends*,' she says softly. '*Once more*.'

I move along to the rack to hang up her coat – it has a stranger's name inked across the inside label – and turn back in time to see her sailing through the door into the sitting room, her arms slightly raised, as if she were an actress moving from the wings to the stage.

'A merry Christmas to us all. God bless us every one!' Her voice rings out, clear and confident. 'Elizabeth? What a pleasure to meet you.'

I hesitate in the hall, suddenly awkward as I wait and listen. I've been worrying about this moment since Rosie strong-armed me into inviting Maddy in the first place. I feel as if I've just thrown a firework into an already fraught room.

'And you must be Mark. Of course you are. Alex is so like you. You must be so proud of him. What a delightful young man.'

I brace myself and follow her to see what's going on.

Rosie already has her arms round Maddy's waist, hugging her. She's wearing the knitted hat and gloves set she just opened from Sarah and Ella, thrilled because they're posh ones, decorated with a row of dancing unicorns. I'll have a job getting her to take them off to eat. Sarah's very generous. I don't know where she finds the money. All I gave them was a box of chocolates and a colouring set.

Alex is sitting in a corner of the settee with his head down, still exploring his new phone. Ridiculously extravagant present for a fourteen-year-old but that's Mark all over.

Mark is on his feet, drink in hand, smiling as if he were the head of this small, dysfunctional household.

But it's Elizabeth who makes me stop and stare. She's standing close to Maddy, her hand on Maddy's arm, her face unusually warm with approval.

'I'm so glad you could join us,' she says. 'How lovely to meet you. Alex is *so* like his father, isn't he? I saw it as soon as he was born. The eyes. The shape of his face.'

Elizabeth seems to have taken charge of Maddy. She steers her to a chair beside her own.

'And are they alike in other ways? I mean, in personality?' asks Maddy.

And Elizabeth is off, rattling on about what a marvellous person Mark is and how much he adores his children. I stand there for a moment, watching, taking her comments as some sort of veiled attack on me for leaving him and still stupefied by the way they're apparently getting on. The two of them are acting as if they've been pals for years.

I know Elizabeth. She prides herself on good manners. There's part of her, I suspect, that's putting on a show, making sure I see how a polite hostess should behave. And yet it's more than that. As the two women talk and Rosie balances forward over the arm of Maddy's chair and bounces on the balls of her feet, I have the sense that I'm the outsider. Standing there, in my own sitting room, my sense of exclusion, of failing to belong, makes me feel both indignant and deeply sad.

I find myself wondering whether Maddy, for all her problems, all her madness, might fit into my family better than I do.

Elizabeth is saying now: 'And tell me. Maddy. Is that short for Madeleine?'

'Exactly.' Maddy pauses for dramatic effect. 'I never quite forgave my parents. For naming me after a cake.'

And Elizabeth instead of looking baffled, as I did, lets out a short, hard laugh as if she understands completely and at once.

'I love Proust,' she says. 'Do you know, I was a headmistress for thirty years and I don't think I employed a single teacher, not even the literature staff, who'd actually read him.'

Maddy leans forward. 'I was a teacher myself. English literature. My passion.'

Elizabeth claps her hands. 'Who said this: "There's no better basis for a friendship than a shared love of books"?'

Maddy inclines her head playfully. 'Fitzgerald?'

'P.G. Wodehouse!'

They both laugh as Mark, bemused but pleased, looks on. He clearly has no idea what they're on about and neither have I. No one seems to notice when I withdraw to put the carrots and sprouts on.

The kitchen is filled with the smell of turkey. I think of all the kitchens across London, across England, which, at this precise time, smell the same, and all the women who are frantically cooking while their guests chat over a drink. I can't imagine many of them are talking about bloody Proust.

I move the pots about and chop up the carrots I peeled the night before. A headache is building behind my eyes and I move carefully, aware that if I turn my head suddenly the kitchen swims in and out of focus.

I bring the sprouts to the boil and wonder how Sarah and Ella are getting on downstairs. Whether Sarah bothers with cooking a turkey and preparing carrots and sprouts and roast potatoes when it's just the two of them. Whether she heats a traditional Christmas pudding afterwards, when Ella's probably too young to want it. However strange our Christmas is this year, theirs strikes me as sadder.

I shake my head, guilty. They should have joined us. I should have insisted. Ella and Rosie would have had fun together.

I think of all the help Sarah's given me this year, swinging into action and organising the flat for me as soon as I told her, at the start of the year, that I was fed up with Mark. That I was thinking of leaving him and getting my own place. I owe her such a lot.

Sarah's so evasive sometimes. Rosie says Ella never had a dad. It sounds as if Ella's father, whoever he was, doesn't even know she exists. When I ask Sarah about her parents, about her own childhood, she makes it clear she doesn't want to talk about it, even though she knows so much about mine.

I stand at the cooker, stirring the bread sauce mix with a wooden spoon as it slowly heats and thickens. The steam wets my cheeks as it rises.

I should be happy. This is what I wanted, isn't it? To have my own space, my own kitchen. Not to walk in after dinner and see Mark's plate and cutlery, his glass, left there on the draining board for me to wash up. Not to settle down, finally, in bed only to have Mark stride in, switch the light back on and start telling me about his day, answering the questions I'd asked, only out of courtesy, hours earlier when he was first home.

This is what I wanted. So, tonight, why do I feel so sad?

*

I was only twenty when I met Mark. It was my first week at the company. I went in with my red strappy heels and a neat little skirt suit I'd bought to give me confidence in the new job, and a cup of coffee I'd picked up from the deli on the corner. The butterflies in my stomach were excitement as much as nerves.

I had a one-day induction course with the other newbies. It didn't feel like real work, all corporate videos and presentations from HR about the transformation of the telecoms industry. It was relevant, I see that now, but at the time I just wanted to get it over with, get my sales targets and hit the phones to show the team manager what I could do. My life was never all about work, even then. Work to live, that's my motto. As long as it's not too dull and I'm not doing anyone any harm, it's a pay packet, isn't it, not a career, when all's said and done? A means to an end. The end was a lot of fun in those days. A flat-share with two crazy girls from New Zealand who seemed to know everyone and loved to party. Clubs, restaurants, picnics and barbeques if the weather was good enough. It was the freedom I'd always wanted.

And then Mark walked into the presentation room. Handsome. Easy, charming manner. A suit, but a cool one, and a hint of stubble on his chin. He wasn't much older than me, but it felt like a big difference. He was a junior manager in those days.

I fancied him right away, but he didn't show any sign of interest – his lopsided grin was the same for everyone. At coffee, one of the other new joiners hung around him, definitely flirting. I watched from the far seats. He didn't fight her off, but he didn't encourage her, either. Strictly professional. I liked him for it. Then I started properly on the phones and began to get to know everyone else on the sales floor. He worked out of sight in the adjacent building with the marketing team and that was that.

Until the New Zealanders dragged me off to a party – a massive pop-up picnic in Hyde Park with about fifty people sprawled on blankets and endless bottles of fizz – and there he was. Hanging out with a group on a picnic blanket. Black T-shirt showing his muscles. Jeans. A wicker hamper and plastic plates and glasses.

I didn't dare to go up to him at first. He lolled on his elbow, drink in hand, listening to a stylish woman with long, dark hair. She was well toned and sitting cross-legged, her hair hanging like a curtain down her back. She had kicked off her sandals and her toenails, poking out from under her folded knees, were painted green.

I sat with the New Zealanders and their friends, a rowdy crowd, and tried not to watch him. His hair was dark and cut very short and his shoulders were broad. I thought about him at work, how effortlessly cool he seemed, how at home there. The young woman leaned in close to him as she talked, waving her hands theatrically. He gave a low, steady laugh and the corners of his eyes crinkled. He glanced over suddenly and caught me looking and I turned my head away, pretending to be fascinated by the young man clowning about near me and forcing a laugh in the hope it showed my dimples and white teeth.

It would be perfectly natural to go over to him, wouldn't it? I kept my eyes on the young man who was telling some story about his wild night out. I could just say hi. We worked together. He was probably trying to place me. It was always the same – you remembered the people above you in the chain, but it was harder to remember those junior to you. I reached for another sausage roll and thought about my over-sized T-shirt and floppy shorts and the toned stomach of his long-haired companion.

The clown plonked down beside me on the grass and started talking to me and I made the most of it and flirted a bit. I didn't fancy him, but I was grateful for the chance to show a few moves.

Mark didn't come across to me for ages. Not until the music was turned up and everyone kicked off their shoes and started dancing, there on the grass, drawing curious looks from the dog-walkers and parents with small children on bikes and scooters. I'd had quite a few drinks by then.

'Becca, isn't it?' He didn't ask me to dance, just sat next to me, drink in hand, and we started chatting. It wasn't fireworks and rockets – it was easy, comfortable. And it turned out that the long-haired girl was his friend's girlfriend after all, and he had noticed me at work – that was clear from the questions he asked about how I was settling in, by the fact he remembered my name, the fact he knew the name of my team leader. He'd done his homework.

He took me from the picnic to dinner. Nothing fancy, just pizzas and a bottle of wine, and we shared a piece of cheesecake. And it felt so easy, so natural, so much as if we'd been a couple forever.

He had his own place and his own car and he was nearly thirty. When he invited me back for coffee, he actually lifted me up, carrying me upstairs like some old-fashioned film star – a bit tricky round the bend in the stairs but that just made me giggle – and he dropped me down in the middle of his king-sized bed. The wardrobe down the side of the bedroom had mirrored doors and then we were kissing, and then his T-shirt was off and his chest was as broad and muscular as I'd imagined and I thought of it in his fashionable suit, in meetings, giving presentations to newbies like me and then my T-shirt was off too, and my shorts, and the more excited I acted, playing it up a bit to be sexy and because I was a bit drunk too and it had been a long time, if I'm honest, since there'd been anyone peeling off my clothes and stroking my breasts, anyone at all, the calmer and gentler he became, until I was crazy for him and, all the time, we both kept half an eye on the thrashing, coupling couple next to us in the mirrors and it seemed the sexiest thing, even as I wondered how many other women had been reflected there.

The next day, he brought me tea and toast in bed. We stayed there all morning. It was that sweet start-of-a-relationship time of revelation. *I saw you at the coffee machine and I wanted to come and talk to you, but I didn't dare.* When? Really? *And then in the canteen, but you were with the sales crowd and I was too shy.* You? Shy? *I fancied you the first time I saw you.* You didn't. You didn't even notice me. *I damn well did. You were wearing a red top with white lace at the top and a blue jacket and skirt.* And you wore that fancy suit with big pockets. *My 'top executive' suit.* Oh, please. *Seriously, why do you think I returned for the feedback session at the end of the day? I don't usually.*

And so on. And so on.

And more sex, and more mugs of tea and then a takeaway and a lazy afternoon sprawled together across the settee, my bare legs draped over his knees, his hand straying often to my breasts under my T-shirt, watching a corny old black and white film, and that was it, the start of it. Easy. No drama. As comfy as an old pair of slippers.

I thought it was a good thing at the time. He kept telling me it was.

So, after a few months, I started keeping a few things at his place, just in case I stayed all weekend and needed to go straight to work on Monday. He gave me some space in the wardrobe and my own shelf in the bathroom. Then I started staying for days at a time. It was getting colder, and his house was always warm, an adult's house, not like our draughty old rented flat where the boiler kept breaking down.

Finally, it seemed stupid to keep paying all that rent when I was hardly ever there and he persuaded me to move in with him. Easiest thing in the world. And it was fun, commuting to and from work together, having a final kiss in the shop doorway around the corner from the office and then walking to our separate buildings, trying not to look as sexed up as we were. Furtive fondling in a nearby pub at lunchtime. Keeping it secret from everyone, our clandestine love affair, for as long as we could. And when, after all that, after just over a year together, the little blue line told us both that Alex was on the way, he couldn't have been more thrilled.

I left work after Alex was born. They didn't offer much maternity leave and I thought at the time that it was only temporary and I'd find another job once Alex was a toddler. But that never happened. Every time I raised the idea of looking for work and trying to get my career back on track, Mark had a fit. I'd never seen him act like that before.

How could you be so selfish? A child needs its mother. Don't you want what's best for him?

Later, when I tried a different tack and pointed out that we could use a second income, he was just as angry.

What are you trying to say? Aren't I earning enough for you? Don't you think I can provide for my own family?

He wore me down in the end, just as he always did. He made me feel wrong for trying to carve out some space for myself, for wanting my own identity again, even for just a few days a week.

Other people didn't see what went on between us. I never complained. It felt too disloyal. They probably thought I wanted to be a full-time mother. And, when it suited him, Mark certainly acted the perfect father. He made a show of doing all the traditional things dads do with sons – football and cricket and cars and bikes and lots of treats. Short of taking him fishing, they were a greeting card manufacturer's dream. Alex adored him. I was the unhappy one. Constantly exhausted and unfulfilled and guilty about wanting more for myself.

Mark just didn't care. He made fun of me.

Look out, Alex. Here comes Mrs Crosspatch. See that frown! Watch out – we're in trouble again! What have we done now? Oh dear, what is she LIKE?

Sometimes I could hardly stand to be in the same room as him. At night, I could hardly bear to share the same bed. I was just getting through, one day at a time, in bed and out of it. If my lack of passion bothered him, he never spoke about it. Maybe he didn't notice. Much of the time, if I managed to get to bed first, I just pretended to be asleep.

Once Alex turned eight and was getting more independent – old enough to enjoy after-school clubs and to go back to friends' houses for play dates without me – I started to send off my CV to recruitment companies. I told myself there was no need to tell Mark. It might not come to anything, after all. No point having an argument for no reason.

I wasn't the most attractive job candidate. I'd been out of the workforce for eight years and I'd only had a few years' experience before that, but eventually, I was shortlisted for a post. It was a starting position with a small management company, but I was excited. I dug out my old suit and heels and took care with my make-up and went to meet them in their offices. A dynamic, friendly team. I remember the train journey home after the interview, my head buzzing, face glowing. They'd practically offered me the job. And I wanted it. I could do it. I imagined the commute, taking this journey each day, buying lunch around the corner at the deli where I'd picked up a coffee. It might lead somewhere, if I worked hard. It really might.

Mark was waiting for me when I walked in.

'Where the hell have you been?' He looked me up and down. The make-up. The jewellery. The heels. 'You look ridiculous, you do know that?'

He crushed me. I was deluded to think I could survive in that job, he said. I'd done nothing for eight years. The world had moved on. And who did I think was going to look after Alex? Had I even thought about that? The demands of a full-time job? The hours they'd expect from me?

I tried to defend myself. I tried to argue back. Of course I'd thought about childcare. We could figure it out. Other people did. But he was relentless. In the end, I burst into tears and sobbed upstairs in the bathroom until it was time for me to wash and change, and then collect Alex from school, plastering a smile on my face as if nothing had happened.

Mark was there when the agency called, glowering behind me, listening to the conversation. What could I do? I told myself there'd be other jobs. Maybe, over time, I could talk him round.

Then, a few months later, the little blue line appeared again. It was more shock than surprise this time. I still don't know how it happened. After all, we hardly slept together any more.

But it was too late. Rosie was on the way. The door had closed.

Mark was thrilled.

That'll give you plenty to do, all right.

I tried to stick it out. I did. For the children's sake. In many ways, Mark was a good father. He was very patient. He was the one they went to if they wanted a tangled knot sorting out or a new toy constructing or someone to kick a ball outside. I was the irritable one, the one who was always tired. And then I began to realise how often he checked up on me with a phone call or text. How many jokes he made about me to his friends, to the children. That it was all right for him to be out a few nights a week but never for me to meet new people.

I began to realise how tense I felt when I heard his key in the door, his too-cheery voice singing out, in mock irony, every time: *Honey, I'm home!*

It was exhausting, holding in my feelings, day after day.

I told him one evening. I'd been practising on my own, for weeks.

'It's not you, it's me.' A variation on a theme.

He laughed it off at first. 'You don't mean it.'

'I do.'

'Come on, you're just tired. We'll talk about it when you're feeling more yourself.'

'Yes. I do. I really mean it. I'm leaving you.'

'You can't.' And then: 'Where will you go? What about the kids?'

'You'll still see them. You're their father.'

'You don't know what you're saying.'

'I do, Mark. Listen.'

He shook his head with a frown and put the TV on and I had to wait until the following day to start all over again. We did it every day for a week. It hurt like hell, but I couldn't give up. I kept thinking: *If I don't get away now, I never will.*

I found this small flat and moved out with the children. He agreed to pay me maintenance, just enough to cover the rent. I didn't like accepting his money – I feared it was his way of staying involved, of keeping control. But I wasn't in a position to say no, not yet.

At first, he joked about it. 'Don't worry – it won't be for long. You'll soon be back.' On other days, when he was angry, he threatened to stop the payments, to put me on the street, see how I liked that. If it hadn't been for the children, *his children*, perhaps he might have.

So as soon as Rosie went to school in September, I started working. Making up salads and short orders for Jane's wine bar first and then, slowly, learning her style of cooking, under Dennis. It doesn't pay much but I've got by, so far. And maybe I can extend my hours soon, take up Jane's offer and get serious about cooking. If I can, I'll start saving, just in case Mark ever does stop the rent.

They say you never really know someone until you live with them. Now I wonder if you ever really know them until you leave them. When I first met Mark, he seemed so calm and easy-going, then suddenly he was behaving in ways I never thought possible. He seemed possessed by demons, fuelled by a determination not to let me go, by a rage I'd never seen in him before.

In the first weeks in the flat, I never knew what to expect. Sometimes he turned up late at night at the front door, clutching a bouquet of roses or expensive presents I didn't want, with a pathetic, begging expression, asking if he could just come in: *Please, that's all I want, let's just have a chat, can't we?* On other days, I came home to find those crude, vicious letters on the mat, calling me all sorts of names and making vague threats about how sorry I'd be, that it was no use to go crawling back to him, and warning me what he'd do to me if he ever caught me with anyone else.

And once, just once, he used that old chilling line: *If I can't have you, nobody will.*

SARAH

Ella's in a funny mood. Restless. Dissatisfied. Maybe it's me. Maybe it's catching.

The sitting room floor is littered with torn paper and presents. She had quite a haul this year. All the things I wanted at her age and never got. A mini dolls' house and tiny furniture to go inside. Brightly-coloured plastic animals on springs. Glitter pens and sparkly keyrings and sticker books. A plush hat and scarf set, decorated with dancing dogs. Chocolate coins. Small things. Fun things. Easy to palm.

I thought she'd be thrilled. But she isn't. She's subdued, perhaps even sad.

I fix us toasted sandwiches for lunch and set it out on the coffee table in the sitting room and let her graze there. A treat. There are crisps too, and caramel bites, and a big gingerbread biscuit, iced, in the shape of a Christmas tree. I've tried but it looks meagre. A poor offering. I wonder what Ella makes of it.

Upstairs, Becca's family will be sitting down now to their feast, a proper Christmas dinner with all the trimmings. Becca's been talking about it for weeks. Rosie has a real family. A brother and father and grandma, too. My stomach contracts with guilt. Maybe I should have said yes. Maybe we should be there too, pulling crackers and acting like normal people.

Then I remember their other guest and I harden. That down and out. Probably a druggie. Probably alive with lice. God knows what she's doing there – Becca doesn't even know her. I shake my head. I was right to say no, after what Ella saw that day in the park.

Ella crouches by the table and munches steadily, her large eyes on her food.

I say for the tenth time: 'You OK? Having fun?'

She nods but there's something forced, something joyless about this Christmas together and it strikes me that now, at five, she's already old enough to judge me and wonder why we're always alone.

I open a bottle of red wine – it's Christmas after all – and stand at the windows, looking out, as she eats. It's eerily quiet on the street. A lot of people are away. A lot of windows are dark. The road, usually overcrowded with cars, is deserted. There's even a space where David's car should be. I try to imagine him having Christmas lunch, see him there at the table, absurd in a paper hat but charming, no doubt. I blink away the thought.

When I turn back to Ella, I catch her watching me for a moment until she swings away her eyes and stares again at the table. She's such a solemn child.

'You can have the cookie, if you like. You don't have to finish your sandwich.'

She considers. 'Let me tell you,' she says, and her forehead creases into a thoughtful frown. 'Some people have a mummy and a daddy. And some people just have a mummy, like me.'

I cross the room and kiss the top of her head.

'Your mummy loves you so much, it's enough for a mummy and daddy and a grandma and a grandpa and everyone else. You do know that? I love you so much, little Ella, I can't even tell you.'

She reaches for the cookie and says, matter of factly: 'I know, Mummy. You said.'

BECCA

I finally dish up Christmas dinner. I'm flushed with the heat of the oven and my head's pounding and the smell of the food makes me feel sick. Maddy and Elizabeth appear next to me to help, processing through from kitchen to sitting room with dishes of vegetables and the roasties and gravy as if we're feeding a thousand. I wondered what Maddy makes of all this indulgence, if she's judging us.

I set down the turkey on its platter – the same glazed plate we've always used at Christmas, a wedding present from Mark's cousin. The meat looks dry. It used to be a regular Mark joke that I overcook the turkey, but he doesn't dare this year. He takes up the carving set like some Victorian patriarch and comes out with other stupid old lines, his other Christmas jokes.

'So, Alex – are you a breast man or a leg man, or do you like somewhere between?'

'Dad!' Alex, already annoyed about Maddy being with us, shakes his head in despair and his cheeks redden. I try to imagine the day he'll bring a girlfriend home for Christmas – it won't be too many more years now – and wonder if he could be any more embarrassed by his parents than he already is.

Rosie and Maddy pull a cracker and a plastic puzzle flies out and plops into the gravy. Elizabeth goes around the table doling out roast potatoes and I trail after her, light-headed, with the carrots and sprouts, which no one actually likes but that's another Christmas joke, and suddenly Mark's finished his carving and is passing around the plate of turkey and sausages and Rosie and Alex are squabbling about whether he must wear a paper hat, really, and it's starting to look a lot like Christmas, despite everything. Despite the fact we're in a cramped, rented flat because I smashed our family into two this year and despite the fact Mark, Alex and Elizabeth might never forgive me for it and despite the fact we seem unable to escape from the attentions of an eccentric and possibly crazy homeless person, it's still Christmas.

Mark fills my glass with red wine without asking if I actually want it, then taps his own with his fork and says: 'A toast!'

The noise dies down for a moment and faces turn to him.

'To the lovely Becca. Thank you for being such a wonderful cook – and mummy.'

Elizabeth says: 'To Becca!'

An awkward silence. Then Maddy pipes up, in a high-pitched, mock-child's voice: 'God bless us every one!' and Elizabeth smiles and now Maddy is rattling on in her real voice, effortlessly taking the lead, even though she's supposed to be the outsider here: 'Well, tuck in, everyone, don't just stare at it. Do it justice. Now, Rosie Rabbit, let's start with you. May I read your joke?'

Rosie says: 'I'm not a rabbit.'

Maddy shrugs and scrabbles amongst the bits of broken cracker for the slip of paper with the joke. 'What did the tomato say to the fries? You go ahead and I'll ketch-up! Do you get it, Rosie? Ketchup but it's also like "catch up", you see.'

Alex looks strained. Mark turns to him with some of their same-old boys' chat about football and, after a while, he brightens up.

I let the chatter wash over me as I eat, my eyes on my food. Mark's at the far end of the table, lording over it. I can't bring myself to look at him. It's as if I've never moved out, never been through all the heartache of the last year, as if he's right back again with his feet under the table. I have a sudden sense of panic that it might be the same next year and the Christmas after, that I think I've left him but maybe, after all this, I'm just on a slightly longer leash. This has to be the last time. Next year, we'll figure out a way of taking turns. He and Elizabeth can cook Christmas dinner for the kids, if they want that. I'm done.

Afterwards, once the whole Christmas lunch is over, I dismiss all the offers of help, manage to stack the dishes on the kitchen table and retreat there, nursing my thudding headache, leaving Alex hunched over his new computer game and the others setting up one of Rosie's new board games.

I've got as far as covering leftovers and finding room for them in the fridge when Mark appears, carrying the final bits and pieces. His cheeks are ruddy. I see the tremble in his hands as he sets down the gravy boat and the cranberry sauce with too much of a clatter.

'Brilliant, Becca.' He hovers, smiling. Too close. He smells of stale wine fumes and, faintly, of sweat from the damp patches under his arms.

'Thanks.' I turn my back to him. When I bend down, ready to start stacking the dishwasher, the floor sways and dances, speckled with white lights. I steady myself against the counter.

'You OK?'

'Fine.' I close my eyes and wish he'd leave me alone. 'Do you want to put some coffee on?'

'No rush.' He doesn't move.

I reach slowly for the dishes and he catches my wrist.

'Hey, you.' He lowers his voice. 'You're looking lovely, you know. Better than ever.'

'Don't, Mark.' I try to pull free. 'Come on.'

He lets go of my arm and spreads his fingers in the air in a 'no big deal' gesture.

'I've got something for you, that's all.'

Oh God. 'You shouldn't, Mark. Really.'

'It's Christmas.' He dips his hand in his pocket, his eyes on my face, and brings out a small, square present, wrapped in gold paper. 'Happy Christmas.'

He thrusts it towards me. I hesitate, standing there, looking at it, unable to look him in the eye.

'I don't know, Mark. I mean—'

He laughs. 'Just open it. You don't know what it is yet.'

I sigh, wipe my hands on the kitchen towel and take it. My palms are clammy. I tear off the paper and find a jeweller's box inside. An expensive, hinged box with a pouched velvet lid. For a moment, I think it might be a ring – *Heaven help me* – and my fingers tremble. *No*, I think. *Too big a box.*

'Well, go on. It's not going to explode.'

That isn't even funny. The lid springs open with a thud. There's a thin gold bracelet inside, intricate and set with pearls. I lift it out. It's exquisite and expensive, too delicate in my large, hot hands. The chain glistens and glows where it catches the low winter sunshine.

He inches closer. 'It's eighteen-carat gold. And look, I had them engrave your initials on the clasp. You see? RW. So don't go thinking you can take it back!'

'Mark. It's very kind, really, but you know, I can't—'

He reaches a hand to my neck and strokes the soft skin there with his fingertips. 'Don't think so much, Becca. It's OK. Don't overanalyse. It's a Christmas present. That's all.'

He's suddenly closer, his chest almost touching mine. I try to take a step away and back into the hard edge of the kitchen worktop. I lift my hands to fend him off, the bracelet in one and the box in the other. His breath is warm on my face, his hand lightly stroking my hair.

His eyes glisten as he moves in to kiss me, his arms tightening around me.

'No, Mark! Stop it.' I twist away, struggling to escape. His lips land on my cheek, then touch my ear as I fight to get free. 'What're you doing?'

'Oh, I do beg your pardon! Am I intruding?'

Mark swings around at once. Maddy stands there in the doorway, her face calm but determined, wearing a polite smile. I wonder how much she saw. As soon as Mark, distracted, loosens his grip, I push myself out of his arms and retreat to the other side of the kitchen table. I dump the box and the bracelet on the side and make a show of clearing up. My hands are shaking.

She doesn't say anything. She doesn't need to. She just steps past us both, reaches for the kettle, fills it and switches it on, then nods to us both as if to tell us to behave ourselves and sweeps out again.

It only takes moments but the atmosphere in the kitchen is transformed. It reminds me of something and it takes me a moment to place it. Of my father, that was it, all those years ago, bursting into the sitting room and switching on all the lights if I had a boyfriend round for the evening. Just to make a point, to make sure we weren't up to anything.

Mark turns to me as soon as she leaves. 'And what's that all about?' He stabs a finger towards the door. 'Old family friend? Come on.'

'Rosie asked her, if you really want to know.' I dump pots in the sink, angry too now and determined not to let him close again. 'She'd have been all alone at Christmas. OK?'

'Since when was the five-year-old in charge?'

'I didn't say—'

'So? Who is she?' His eyes are hard.

I falter. 'I told you. A friend.'

'Don't lie to me.' His tone is suddenly cold. 'You think I don't know what goes on around here? She's a bag lady. A tramp. Isn't she?'

I don't answer. *Alex, of course*. Why couldn't he keep his mouth shut, just for once?

'What do you actually know about her? Is she on anything? She couldn't keep her eyes off the wine. Did you see?'

'I saw she didn't drink any.'

'I'm really starting to wonder about you, Becca. All that nonsense about us. And now this. Inviting a tramp home. I mean, do you not care about Alex and Rosie? Don't you want them safe?'

'Of course I do.'

He's beside me again now, physically powerful, his hands on my shoulders, forcing me to turn to face him. His eyes, so angry a moment ago, soften as he looks at me.

'I just want to look after you, Becca. That's all. Look after all of you, you know?'

A movement in the doorway. Rosie, a small slight figure, stands on the threshold, watching with large eyes.

'Mummy?'

I pull free from Mark and stride across to her, brush my hand over her newly plaited hair.

'Is the game ready? We're just coming, sweetheart.'

I take her hand, turn my back on the kitchen, walk her briskly through to join Elizabeth and Maddy, and start to play.

MADDY

I thought at first that Becca was just stressed about having him around, that clingy ex of hers. I've seen him before, you see. He wouldn't know. He only thinks about himself, I can smell it on him. Not one to stop and say hello to a heap of homelessness like my good self. A damp huddle in a doorway. Not like Rosie. She takes after her mum.

I've seen him hanging about near their flat, in the evening, looking up at the windows, a pathetic look on his face. I didn't know who he was then but I knew her and their little girl and I put two and two together. So I added him to the list. I kept watch. You'd be surprised who's watching you when you don't know it. Check the windows, next time. Check the doorways. There are eyes everywhere in a city like ours. Silent eyes.

None of them knew what it cost me to get through that lunch. I tried so hard to put on an act. Jolly, mad Maddy. But however fragrant the food was, all I could smell was the red wine, its vapours curling out of the glasses and tormenting me. I was so greedy for the taste that my tongue ached, craving it. No one pressed it on me, thank the Lord. But my hands shook as I ate, knowing how close I was, teetering on the edge of the abyss.

Becca didn't look right either during Christmas lunch. It's hard work, that's part of it. I understand that. I cooked Christmas lunch once upon a time, a long, long time ago, in a land faraway. The land time forgot. For my husband and daughter. I remember.

But it was more than that. Her face was pale and her upper lip was damp as if she were clammy, and when I saw the two of them in the kitchen together, her hands were shaking. Emotion, but not only that. She isn't well.

So when Elizabeth and Mark finally push off at four in the afternoon and Alex disappears into his room, I ignore her hints about booking a taxi – as if I'd pay for one anyway when I can walk on my own two legs – and hang around, even when she settles Rosie down in front of *Lady and the Tramp*, just to keep an eye on her.

When the film reaches 'He's a Tramp' and there's no sign of her, I head down the corridor to the kitchen. She's slumped on a chair, staring out at the winter darkness, her hot face reflected back at her in the glass.

'You're not well.' Not a question, a statement.

'I'm just tired.' We both know she's just pretending that's all it is. She looks too worried about herself.

'Bad head?'

She nods, miserably.

'Sick?'

'And dizzy.' She looks about to burst into tears. 'I didn't drink much. It's not that.'

'I know.'

I take a deep breath. 'Right. This is what's going to happen. No argument.'

She looks up at me, bright-eyed with fever and startled.

'You've struggled through today. Well done. But you're not well. Flu, maybe. Some nasty virus. You need to rest.'

She sits in silence, depleted, letting me take charge.

'So, here's what we do. You are going to take whatever you usually take – aspirin, ibuprofen, choose your tipple – and go to bed. I'll sort out the kitchen and then Alex is going to help me put Rosie to bed.'

She blinks, frowning. 'I don't know. That's very kind but—'

'I'm not asking, I'm telling. You look shocking, frankly. You need to rest. We'll manage. All hands to the pump.'

She needs two attempts to get to her feet. I take her arm and she leans on me as we inch our way down the corridor. She sinks, fully clothed, onto the bed and closes her eyes.

I rap on Alex's door. He's lying on the top bunk, headphones on, playing some game. At least he doesn't need entertaining. I lift the headphones from his ears and he grabs at them, shouts: 'Hey, leave them alone!'

'Your mum's ill.' I set it out plain and simple. 'I'm staying the night. You're fourteen, aren't you?'

He glowers.

'That's older than Juliet was when she met Romeo. You know, *Romeo and Juliet*?' I sigh, try to search my mind for a better analogy. 'It's not much younger than David when he killed Goliath. Yes? Anyway, you're more than old enough to get yourself to bed.'

He doesn't answer.

'And no telling tales to your father, either. Your mother needs to rest.' I consider. 'There's leftovers in the fridge. Just help yourself if you're hungry.'

I go through to the sitting room to watch the end of the film with Rosie – she needs someone to hide behind when Old Trusty is hit by the carriage – then play games with her until supper and put her to bed. Alex lies on his back above her, focussed on his screen, sending a low glow up to paint streaks on the ceiling.

I stand at Becca's closed door for a while and listen. No sound.

I make up my old friend, the sofa bed, and open the window a crack, as I always do. The air blowing in from outside is freezing.

I think of all the people out there, invisible in the darkness, in the shadows. Huddled in grimy blankets or sleeping bags. Drinking away the misery with bottles or cans. I wonder where

Mick is. If he's angry with me for abandoning him. *I didn't mean to, my friend. I really didn't.*

I'm getting maudlin. I give myself a shake. At least the fact I'm here means someone else will get a bed for the night, taking my space once the hostel puts me down as a no-show. They'll store my bags for a week or two. I don't much care. The only possession I really value is the letter, still tucked inside Jeremy's envelope, right here in my pocket. I never leave that behind. Not even for an hour or two.

I take a book from the shelf. A modern novel, not my cup of tea, but the idea of lying in a warm bed, safe and enclosed, and reading, is too much to resist. I open the book and the words dance. It's calling me, the thought of all that booze, right there in the kitchen. Tugging at me. Tempting me.

Finally, I set the book aside, pad through to the kitchen and start to search, fast and methodical, turning out cupboards like a professional thief.

A half-finished bottle of sherry. Middling quality. I've been sick on worse. I watch it swirl, brown and muddy, down the plughole. The smell is sweet and rich. I wash out the bottle quickly before I can stop to lick the neck, fearful of getting the taste and what it will do to me. A shark scenting blood. I find the main stash in a top cupboard – out of Alex's reach, perhaps. Not much. A bottle of gin. Half a bottle of vodka. Two bottles of supermarket wine. I find an old carrier bag in a drawer, bundle them inside and brace myself to take them down the stairs to the communal bins outside. I get as far as the front door, then stop, my hand on the latch. My heart is pounding and my stomach is cold. I know myself. I know what will happen. I'll leave them and then lie on that sofa bed, shaking, hearing them call me, imagining the taste and, more than that, the wooziness, then the oblivion. I won't be safe from them. Sooner or later, I'll creep down for one, promising myself I'll only have a little. Then I'll go again for a second. A third.

I close my eyes and let the bag ease to the floor at my feet. The bottles clink. I think of the sweats and chills in hospital, the tremors that seized me at night, the misery and the medicine they gave to help me through. I think of the letter in my pocket, the one I carry everywhere, and of the chance I have now to get back on my feet. Perhaps my last chance.

'Right, my girl. Onwards and upwards.' I force myself back into the kitchen and, in a flurry of activity, before I can stop to think, to breathe in too deeply the rising alcohol fumes, I start unscrewing the bottle tops and upending them in the sink, one after another, red wine mixing with gin and vodka, a bloody stream pouring itself down the drain. I rinse out the bottles, put them back in the bag and hide them at the back of the cupboard. By the end, my mouth is dust dry. I pour myself a glass of water and go to lie down on the sofa bed, trembling, feeling the breath of outside air reaching to me through the darkness.

I hear her in the night. It's too dark to see the time. I know that sound too well, even as I struggle from sleep. It's been so often my own.

She's in the bathroom, poor thing. Crouching over the toilet and retching. Whatever food was inside her has already gone. That was the easy part.

I stroke back her hair and hold it clear for her as she vomits. She's thin and her head is hot, but she shivers. She's only wearing a big cotton T-shirt. What happened to nightdresses and proper pyjamas? When she finally stops, I wipe off her mouth and flush it all away.

She says, 'Thank you' but weakly, and when she lies on the bathmat, she turns her head away from me, embarrassed. I shrug. The smell of vomit doesn't bother me any more. Not after all these years. Blood. Piss. Bile. What of it? We're all made of the same stuff. Nature, that's all it is. Binding us all. *The body of a weak and feeble woman*. And the stomach isn't doing too well, either.

I get her back to bed, eventually, and leave her with a glass of water at her side and the washing-up bowl for emergencies. She closes her eyes. Her pale skin glistens in the half-light, bleeding in through the thin curtains from the street lights outside. Her hair is straggly, stuck to her cheek. I can't see her being well by the morning.

I sit at the open sitting room window for a while, thinking in a sudden rush.

This is it, I think. Now is the hour. This is my opportunity.

I think of Becca and the way she's struggling here. Maybe I could help. I think of Rosie and the bond we seem to share. I could love that little girl, I can feel it. I frown. It's a dangerous thing, love. I mustn't hurt her, mustn't let her down.

But I will. I know it. How can I stay sober, even for her?

I think about the Christmas tree she drew me. The unicorn picture she brought me in hospital. Maybe she needs me, too. Maybe I can help her in some way, plug some gap in her life. I sense it without understanding it. But can I do that? Can I find the strength?

Voices drift up from below. Loud, cheerful voices spilling out into the street, saying thank you, calling goodnight. A car door slams and an engine starts, revs, fades as the car pulls away.

I'm shaking now, just thinking about it. Because I really could do it, if I could stay sober, and what then? Could I take a step further and do what I long to do, to meet her again? Meet her with dignity, sober and clean?

Even if I could, do I dare?

I turn away from the window and crawl between clean sheets, curl into a ball and hide under the duvet. It smells fresh, of clean laundry.

A voice in my head says: *You can do this, Madeleine. You can. But for heaven's sake, don't screw it up.*

SARAH

He comes around late and waits on the door step, outside the communal front door, until I let him in. He needn't – he's got a key to the block – but he's polite like that. Careful not to crowd me out.

He stands there in his smart coat and gives me a mock sad face.

'Happy Christmas.' He holds up a bottle of wine, expensive stuff of course, and a brown paper bag. It's from the posh deli around the corner. Cheeses in waxed paper and stuffed olives and maybe a *panettone*. He brought much the same last year.

'Ho bloody ho.' I stand aside as he walks in from the cold, then we go together through the open door of the flat. He heads for the kitchen and sets the food on the counter. He peers round, taking it all in. The empty wine bottles on the draining board – I've no one else to blame – and Ella, asleep on the settee in her pyjamas, her hair splayed across the cushions. The mess of paper and plastic on the floor that I can't be bothered to tidy.

When he opens his arms, I walk into them at once and sink my face into his shoulder. My head's heavy and starting to ache.

'How was it?'

'Well, you know.' He shrugs. 'Same as usual.'

'You hungry?' I open up the bag he's brought and set out the food in its papers and little plastic pots. I pick at the olives and realise how empty I am, how little we've eaten.

'You go ahead. I'm stuffed.' He shrugs off his coat and goes to Ella. He strokes her hair for a moment, then reaches under her and lifts her up, carries her off to bed. She stirs in her sleep and cuddles against him. I try to remember what that feels like, if The Parents ever did the same with me, when I was her age.

When he comes back, he unbuttons his cuffs, rolls back his sleeves and helps himself to a glass of wine.

'You been OK?'

I don't answer, just cut into the cheese and pile a plate with food.

He clears his throat and I know he's going to say something difficult and I wish he wouldn't, I really wish he'd shut up and leave it be.

'I know it's hard for you,' he says, his eyes on the floor. 'Christmas.'

I sit next to him and start to eat, mentally blocking my ears.

'But it's not just about you now, is it? It's about Ella, too.'

La, la, la. Not listening.

He carries on anyway: 'You'll have to tell her sooner or later. How can she understand what's going on if she doesn't know?'

MADDY

The next morning, Boxing Day, I wake up early, warm and safe, and find myself thinking about Mick.

I try to imagine him in hospital, poked and prodded by nurses, told to be a good boy and take his medicine, to behave himself and keep his voice down. No booze, of course.

He'd have to be very ill to put up with all that.

The flat is silent. I shut the window in the sitting room as quietly as I can and fasten the latch, then go through to the kitchen and put together some turkey sandwiches and other bits and pieces before I creep out of the front door.

I don't like to be shut in. I'm out of practice at it. That's another problem with hostels – all those locks and keys. They say it's for your own protection, locking you in, locking the world out, but too many people in there have had a taste of prison.

It has frozen overnight. A weak winter sun is trying to rise and colour the clouds but there's a cutting chill in the air which pierces my bones and dries out my mouth and nose. Puddles crunch with a thin coating of ice as I walk. That's the danger. You soften up quickly, once you get the chance. A warm bed. A hot shower. Good food. Your body lets its guard down. That's not always for the best when you're back out here again.

I walk steadily down the high street, past the familiar doorways. There are fewer shapes this morning. One I don't recognise. A drunk, maybe, who just couldn't get home. I see Billy, hunched in a sleeping bag, hugging that mangy dog of his. Trigger or Tigger or something. He swears it keeps him alive, brings in the cash when they sit together. More people worry about the dog being homeless, he says, than they do about him. He gets dog biscuits and offers to take him all the time.

The river opens up ahead of me and I take a right turn and walk along it towards the edge of the park. The tide is high and the icy wind whistles right down the water and freezes my face, my hands. The café isn't open yet but I see a dark figure there, huddled around the back, waiting in the shadows. *Mick*. He lifts his head as I approach, nods.

'Professor.'

I smile and open my arms wide, a theatrical gesture. I don't quite know what to do when I reach him so put an arm around his shoulders and pat him awkwardly on the back. One of his arms is encased in a plaster cast from elbow to wrist but he still has the same familiar smell of stale sweat and booze. He's still Mick.

He pulls back and looks me over, a bemused look on his face. I'm not usually one for a hug. As he looks, I'm conscious of my short, spiky hair and the jagged wound still healing on my skull.

He doesn't seem to mind, he just says: 'Look at you, lovely. All spruced up.'

I shrug, embarrassed. 'Cleaned up, anyway. Won't last, I shouldn't think.'

He considers. 'Back in bricks, are you?'

I look at my boots. The park around us is silent and thick with shadows. 'Not really. I was in hospital too, you know, for a bit. Then a hostel. Grim place. Then someone gave me a bed last night. Nothing permanent.'

He shrugs. 'Well, that's good. Don't knock it.'

I hesitate. 'You all right? I've been worried. Heard you were in hospital, too.'

He looks away. 'Not for long. Discharged myself, soon as. Hate hospitals.'

I nod, considering, but don't say any more, not yet, just pull the parcel of food out of my pocket. 'Hoped I'd find you down here. Brought you breakfast.'

'You Christmas angel of mercy.' He rummages at the silver foil at once, wolfish. 'I'd give you a drop of cheer but I'm all out.' I know that without being told. Maybe it's because I'm stone cold myself, but the stink of booze is even stronger than usual and his good hand shakes.

'Here. I can help.'

I put the parcel in his lap and help him open it up. He stirs the food with his fingertips, checking what's inside: a mound of turkey sandwiches and some cold sausages, a few mince pies. He lifts a sandwich to his lips, offers me a bite, then tucks in. He's swallowing without really chewing, without tasting, still drunk. I'm hoping the food may sober him up a bit, but I'm frightened it could make him sick.

I look him over in the half-light. One eye is little more than a slit, puffy with bruising and a palette of colours. Yellow, mostly. His scalp is shaved above his temple and there's a dirty dressing stuck there. Flakes of blood cling to the skin below. But his arm means trouble. Hard to fend for yourself on the streets with only one working arm. His cheeks are hollow, more haggard than I've seen before, and dark with stubble.

I gesture to his arm. 'Does it hurt?'

He shrugs. 'Nothing a drink can't deal with.'

'Didn't they sort a hostel for you?'

'Nah. You know me. Can't cage a lion.'

We sit in silence for a bit, close together, sharing each other's warmth. It's freezing but strangely peaceful, close to the water. *Time's ever-flowing stream.*

Finally, I say: 'Mick, who were they? Those men.'

He shifts his weight, keeps eating a mince pie a while longer, as if he hadn't heard me. Then he speaks. 'I'm sorry I dragged you into that. It wasn't you they were after. It was me. Got on the wrong side of some bad lads. End of.'

I shake my head. 'But why? What've you done?'

Mick raises his eyes. 'Best you don't ask. Keep your distance, Professor. I doubt they're done with me yet.'

I blink. 'But why? Can't I do anything to help?'

He shakes his head. 'I mean it. Best you don't know.'

A light goes on inside the café. They're awake then and opening up downstairs. Footsteps sound on the ground floor. A few more minutes and they'll unbolt the back door and see who's there, let Mick slip in to charge his phone, offer him a coffee.

Mick scrunches up the foil and shoves the parcel into a bag, then heaves himself clumsily to his feet. His plaster-cast hangs awkward and heavy at his side.

'If you've got a chance to get off the street, take it.' He lifts his hand in a mock salute. 'Goodbye, Professor. Good luck.'

He turns his eyes to the doorway and I feel dismissed. When I pause at the end of the path and look back, he's barely visible in the shadow, a lean silhouette, waiting it out on the back step like a stray dog.

I slip back into the block of flats when a man comes out, dressed for a walk. They let you in without a murmur when you're clean. Upstairs, their front door's still on the latch. The hall is silent. No one's even noticed I've been out.

I potter in the kitchen and marvel at the joy of it. The shiny kettle that boils the water for my tea. The cupboard of clean mugs and plates. The fridge, stuffed with food inside and decorated on the outside with pictures, school timetables marked up with lurid green and yellow highlighter pens, photographs, all stuck on in clumps by magnets.

I find a bread roll and butter it, then draw up a chair and sit with my tea, looking at Rosie's drawings on the fridge, trying to imbibe them. The building bricks that make up a normal life. All that love, all that purpose, all that connection with the world. People have no idea how extraordinary normal really is. Until they lose it.

I think about Mick. The hunted look that passed over his face when he talked about the men who hurt him, who might yet track him down again. I always knew he had a dark side. That he was into some dodgy deals. That's how he gets the cash for booze. I frown. I'm afraid for him. I want to look out for him, the way he's always looked out for me.

The children's bedroom door opens. A moment later, Rosie appears at the kitchen door. Her hair's tousled, eyes cloudy with sleep. She's wearing a long shirt with a sparkly unicorn on the front, bare legs sticking out below. When she sees me, she grins, suddenly awake, then rushes over to jump onto my lap.

'You're still here!'

Her hair is soft and springy under my chin and she smells sweet, of soap and shampoo and youth. She puts an arm around my neck and I slip mine around her waist and hold her there. Her warm, compact body, clean and innocent. The sheer weight of her, the bodily contact with a caring, vibrant human being, is overwhelming. It brings back in a heartbeat so many memories of the past, of my own little girl, when she was almost the same age. Of everything I've lost.

I can barely remember the last time someone really embraced me. It's one of the things I miss most, the lack of touch. The most dehumanising thing. Mick and I once or twice threw a comradely arm around each other's shoulders, mostly when we were both half-cut. Do-gooders might squeeze a hand or shoulder in a brief, awkward gesture, to pretend they're not repulsed when they clearly are.

Someone else is there. I see the reflection first in the kitchen window, the darkness at the door, then turn. Alex. He's already dressed in jeans and a football shirt. He scowls at the sight of Rosie in my arms and I twist around, set her down on the floor, suddenly embarrassed.

'Breakfast?'

He shakes his head and mumbles something, goes across to a cupboard and pulls out a chocolate bar and a packet of biscuits, then leaves.

'Don't you want more than that?' I follow him down the short hall to the door, where he's pulling on his coat and stuffing his pockets. There's a holdall at his feet. 'Where are you off to?'

'Football.' He barely acknowledges me as he opens the door. He lifts a woolly hat off a coat peg and pulls it low over his ears. 'With Dad. I'm back tomorrow.' He nods towards his mother's closed bedroom door. 'She knows.'

The door slams. I turn back and see Rosie, looking like a little waif in her bare feet, watching.

'It's all right.' She smiles, cheering me up. 'They do that. Go to football and stuff. It's a boy thing.' She too considers her mother's closed door, then looks back at me. 'Are you looking after me today?' And adds, when I nod cautiously: 'Cool!'

We're in the kitchen, tossing pancakes and rolling them with ice-cream and chocolate sauce, when the doorbell rings.

I give Rosie a quizzical look. Who would turn up on Boxing Day morning? Some relatives Becca hadn't thought to mention? I frown. However ill she is, she'd be fretting about it, if she was expecting people.

Mark, maybe? I think of Alex, dashing out with his pockets full of biscuits, heading to meet him. Maybe Alex has spilled the beans, told his father what's going on and they've come round to turf me out. Mark's the type. He'd jump at the chance to take charge while Becca's unable to defend herself.

So my features, when I open the door, are set and defensive. Ready to shut the door in his face, if he looks bullying and ready to cause trouble. I'm the gatekeeper. Just for today. Like it or not, I know where my loyalties lie.

It isn't him. A young woman stands at the door, a little girl at her side. The woman would be attractive if she didn't look so impatient, as if she's already late and it's somehow my fault. Her hair is cut in a neat bob, hinting at underlying curls. Her coat is good quality. Her make-up is cleverly applied. *Well groomed*, Christy would say, as if all women were horses. Or my father: *well heeled*.

The little girl stands very still and looks up at me, with solemn brown eyes. Beautiful eyes.

I stand there, looking at them. For a moment, I can't speak.

Rosie pulls at my arm. 'It's Ella,' she whispers. 'She's my friend. She was with me when I found you in the park.'

I hesitate, mortified, imagining it.

Rosie, misreading my silence, whispers: 'You'll like her.'

'Is Becca there?' The young woman is trying to see past me, into the hall. I don't answer. I don't know what to say. My hand, on the door, shakes and I wonder if she notices. All I need is a stiff drink. Just one.

'I'm sorry.' She doesn't sound sorry. She focuses on me and her gaze is full of disdain. My cheeks burn. 'I don't think we've met.'

I hear myself say: 'I'm a friend of the family. She's not well. Becca.'

'Not well?' Her eyes are sharp with suspicion. 'What do you mean?'

Rosie helps me out: 'She's got a sore head and a poorly tummy. She's in bed.' She reaches a hand to Ella and pulls, trying to drag her inside. 'Come on, we're making pancakes.'

Ella hesitates, uncertain, still staring at me. She tears her eyes away eventually and looks back at her mother, reading the tension. She's sensitive, I see that at once.

The young woman looks cross. 'The thing is,' she says, 'I'd arranged with Becca to have Ella today. I'm working.'

I say, trying to sound normal: 'That's OK. I don't mind looking after her here.'

She narrows her eyes and looks at me, weighing this up. She moves a hand to Ella's head and touches her dark hair, as if she's shielding the child from me. The nails are neat and painted coral. No ring.

'Can I see Becca?'

I stand aside. 'If you like. I think she's asleep, though.'

She crosses the passage, eases open the bedroom door and steps inside. The air that leaches out is stale with sickness. I hear the murmur of voices and, a moment later, she comes out again, her lips pursed.

Rosie has persuaded Ella to come in and the sound of their chattering drifts down from the kitchen.

The young woman says: 'Are you here all day?'

I don't like her tone. I straighten my shoulders. 'Look, it's up to you. If you'd like to leave her, I'll look after her for you. I'm here with Rosie, anyway. If you'd prefer not, I quite understand.'

She tuts, pulls out her mobile phone and checks the time. She's out of options and we both know it. She calls down to Ella: 'See you later, then. All right? Becca's right there in her room if you need her. She's just a bit poorly.'

Ella doesn't answer, probably didn't even hear. I sense that the remark about Becca was less for her benefit than for mine, a warning that I'm under scrutiny.

The young woman turns reluctantly to me. 'I'll be back just after five. What's your number? I'll give you a call when I'm on my way back.'

I don't answer.

She raises her eyes as it dawns on her that I'm not like normal people – I don't have a phone. She shakes her head. 'Ella knows where I work. Jason's. The shoe shop? It's just round the corner, on the high street.'

She steps briskly through to the kitchen to whisper goodbye to her daughter, then heads for the door. At the top of the stairs, she pauses and turns back.

'Thank you,' she says. I sense that it's something she finds hard to say.

'You're welcome.'

Her feet pound as she hurries down the stairs and I stay there at the door, listening, until the heavy front door to the block finally slams closed, far below.

BECCA

I hear the doorbell ring once, then again. I can't move. My head's exploding and I feel so sick.

For some reason, I think it's David. He's heard I'm ill and come round to see how I am. I think of his Christmas card, still tucked away in the bedside table. I lie still.

I try to listen to the murmur of voices through the fug. Not David. A woman. Sarah, of course. It's Boxing Day. She's working. It's the start of the sales. It comes back to me in a flood. I said I'd have Ella, as I do a couple of Saturdays each month now, when Sarah has to work at the shoe shop. I owe her such a lot, I'm happy to help where I can.

The bedroom door opens.

'Becca?'

I can barely croak. Sarah looms over me, her hair curling forward round her cheek. Her eyes glisten in the half-light.

'What's going on?'

I try to roll onto my side. A glass of water, large and bulbous, too close. I reach for it but I can't judge the distance and my hand falls limply. Sarah steps in, brisk, puts her hand under my head and begins to lift me. At once, the room tilts and spins and my stomach heaves. I groan and protest and she eases me back to the pillow.

'Is that her? The homeless woman? Why's she still here?'

I struggle to think. *Maddy. Of course. In the night, she looked after me.* In the hall, outside my door, low voices. Ella's giggle, then scampering feet as the girls run down to the kitchen together.

I say: 'Rosie? Is she OK?'

She pulls a face. 'I don't know. I guess so. They're making pancakes.' She pauses. 'Where's Alex?'

I fight through the pain. 'With Mark.'

She tuts. She's angry. She doesn't like Maddy, doesn't approve. But then Sarah rarely likes people, especially not at first. I've learned that about her. She thinks the whole world's out to hurt her. And hurt Ella, too.

I try to nod but my eyes are falling closed again. The spinning slows a little and I try to sink into the throbbing in my head, to let it out.

Distantly, Sarah says: 'I've got to go. It's the sale. I can't call in sick.'

I manage to say: 'It's fine. Tell the girls I'm here if they need me.'

A pause. She says: 'Are they safe with her?'

What does she want me to say? I'm worried, too. I just can't do much about it, not right now. Not until I'm well.

A floorboard creaks as she shifts her weight. 'Look, I must go. You know what a fuss they make if I'm late. They've already threatened to fire me.' She adds from the door: 'Maybe they're safer together. The girls. They'll look out for each other.'

I don't move. I just want to be left alone to sleep, to die. A moment later, the door shuts. Quiet. I fall back into the blackness.

Later, the door creaks open. I peer out through barely open eyes. Maddy, standing there in the doorway, my apron tied around her waist. The blue striped one that Mark's mother gave me two Christmases ago. Odd, seeing it on her. She stands, listening, and her breathing is thick in the silence.

She whispers: 'Are you awake? Can she just see you? She's worried.'

Giggling. Rosie creeps in and comes close to my face. A small cool hand touches my cheek and strokes me. 'Poor Mummy.'

I manage to look. Rosie's face hangs there, right against mine, more cheerful than sad, as if she's enjoying the drama.

'Hi.' My lips crack as I try to smile. 'You OK?'

She nods, happy. 'We're playing Chase. It's fun.'

The effort is already more than I can bear and I let my eyes close and wait until they withdraw, closing the door softly behind them. Then: 'Sssssh!' in the hall as the girls run shrieking past her. Clomping feet. *It's OK. Rosie's OK. I can sleep a while longer, thank God.*

Later, I surface again. The water is still there, large in my vision when I try to look out. Beside it, a cup of tea. I stretch out a hand, cautiously. Warm. Maddy must have been in again. Maybe that's what woke me.

I need the toilet. I inch my legs out of bed, my head still on the pillow, then slowly, little by little, get myself to sitting. The room sways, then slowly settles like falling dust.

I walk myself down the wall towards the bathroom. The girls are in the kitchen, laughing and loud. I catch glimpses of them. Rosie, a colander on her head for a helmet, brandishing a wooden spoon. The tea towels, my good, clean tea towels, are rectangles under her feet and she's skating on them, polishing the floor as she glides. Beyond her, Ella is licking out a mixing bowl. Her face is daubed with brown – chocolate by the looks of it – even the tip of her nose, and she smears her finger, then licks, smears, then licks. Chaos but happy chaos, I see that at once.

Maddy is there in the midst of it all, the apron crooked at her waist, moving around the kitchen as if it were her own.

My panic shifts and eases at the sight of them. The girls look happy. They seem safe. This woman, Maddy, is caring for them. I realise how little I know about her. Was she a mother once? Did she run a home? Why has she ended up dirty and unkempt, living on the streets?

I'm too weak, too ill to think about it now. All that matters is that the girls seem fine. I stagger on. I don't want Rosie to see me in this state. Somehow, I make it to the bathroom and back to bed, my head finding the cool pillow as if it were home. *Please God, if I can just sleep. If I can just get strong again.*

Time passes. Maddy stands at the end of the bed. *How long has she been there, watching? Did she wake me? Did she speak?* My head aches but the pain is less intense.

'How are you?'

I close my eyes, shutting her out. It's too much effort to speak.

She persists: 'Can I get you anything? A little toast?'

I shake my head. 'Are they all right?'

'The girls? Absolutely. We've had a ball. We haven't been too noisy, have we?'

'I'm sorry.' My tongue is large and dry in my mouth. 'I'm really sorry.'

'Don't be absurd. You can't help being ill.' She's tugging at the duvet now, straightening the bedclothes, smoothing me out. 'Glad to help. We baked a cake for lunch.'

'Cake?' Then I remember the mixing bowl, the chocolate face.

'I found fish fingers in the freezer. For dinner.'

I don't answer. I can't think about food, not yet.

'Thank you. I don't know what—'

'You'd have managed. People do. Especially mothers.' I sense something jagged in her voice and wonder what it means. She straightens up and moves towards the door. 'We made a den with the sofa cushions. We'll have dinner in there.' She pauses, her hand now on the handle. 'Don't worry. I'll stay another night. You're not well.'

I don't know what to say. I should get up and take back control, look after the children myself. There'll be baths later and teeth to clean and settling Rosie in bed. But the truth is, I can barely get my head off the pillow without the room spinning. I'm grateful just to lie here, to set it all down, like some heavy sack that's been crippling me. I'm grateful to have someone kind here to look after Rosie. To look after me.

I open my mouth to say so but the door clicks and she's already gone.

MADDY

Ella and Rosie. Sweethearts, both of them, in their different ways.

'Poo poo smelly pants!' Rosie, eating her fish finger sandwich in the sofa-cushion den, dissolves into giggles.

'Poo on your head.' Ella can barely speak for laughing. Their eyes gleam, fixed on each other, happy, daring each other to go further, to be naughtier.

'Smelly bottoms,' says Rosie and they collapse again, convulsed with laughter.

I lean forward and straighten Ella's plate to stop the fish finger taking a nose-dive off the edge.

'Girls!' I say mildly. They can't shock me with their smelly bottoms. I've seen it all. The drunken louts who really do piss on your head if you're sleeping rough. Heaven knows why.

'Smelly bottoms,' repeats Ella.

'Stop copying me!'

'Stop copying me,' parrots Ella. That age-old game of annoyance. I imagine long-dead children, in some ancient land, sitting together, annoying each other in the same way in Greek or Latin.

Rosie sits up, cross now. 'Stop it! I don't like it.'

Then Ella, of course: 'Stop it! I don't like it.'

'That's enough, girls. Eat nicely and I'll tell you a story.'

They both look round, eyes gleaming in the semi-darkness of the den.

'Do you know the story of Peter Pan, the boy who never grew up?'

They shake their heads, interested now.

'Well, you eat and I'll tell you.'

They sit, cross-legged, side by side and munch, dropping crumbs on the carpet, and off we go.

They're very different girls. Rosie is bold and curious, happy to walk up to a smelly lump of homelessness in the street, as I was, and ask my name. Ella is more reserved. Perhaps more complicated. A deep thinker. Or perhaps I just want her to be that. She has her mother's brown eyes and she's turned them on me often today, thoughtful, appraising. Still waters.

I'm careful with them both. Not too affectionate. Not too needy. I don't take Ella on my lap, as I long to do, and hold her, breathe in her youth, her innocence, her faith in the world. I don't bombard her with questions about her life, her home, her mother and father. I don't earnestly ask her if she's happy, if she's kindly treated, if she needs anything, anything at all. I do none of these things. I clown about with them like a galumphing nanny and offer snacks and drinks and play raucous games and tell stories.

But beneath it all, as they giggle and play, I quietly learn her. The curve of her jaw, the puppy roundness of her cheeks, her straight dark hair tied into thin plaits, her way of observing, serious eyes and furrowed brow. The way she tilts her head and says solemnly: 'Let me tell you…' before she speaks. Her way of being in this world. I may never have this time with her again, I know that. I need to remember so the memory will last.

After dinner, we have another game of Hide and Seek. They dash together to crawl into the den or wrap themselves round with a curtain or crouch behind the sofa bed – there aren't that many places to hide – and I make a show of pretending to search in bafflement.

'Well, they can't be in here. They're not behind the chair. Ah! That's it! The curtain!' Theatrical astonishment as stifled giggles come clearly from the opposite side of the room. 'No! My goodness, they're not there either! Where can they be?'

They spend the longest time finding me when I stand poker-still behind the standard lamp, the shade framing my head. Ella sees me at last, right there in front of her, and jumps a mile. For a moment, she almost bursts into tears, then manages to collect herself and laughs. *Strong character*, I think. *Good girl.*

'That,' I say, 'is called hiding in plain sight. Can you say that? Hiding in plain sight?'

They stare back at me with blank faces.

Darkness gathers outside. I heat milk for them and we make our own cocoa, draw the sitting-room curtains at last and remake the sofa bed. We sit, cosy, in a row, my arms loosely round them both. They're sleepy now, getting fractious. I look at the clock. It's turned five. My time's nearly up. Ella will go home very soon.

Ella, frowning, thinking perhaps of her mother, lifts her mouth from her straw and says: 'Did Wendy ever go home?'

I smile at the way she goes straight back to the tale of Peter Pan without preamble, as if the conversation had never paused.

'Oh, yes,' I say. 'Her mother never lost hope, not even after all that time. So she always kept the nursery window open. Just in case. And, one night, when they were ready, Wendy and Michael and John all flew home.'

'Did they get into trouble?'

I look down at Rosie. 'Not at all. Their mother was just pleased to have them back.'

She frowns. 'But why did they need the window open? Why didn't they use the door?'

'That's a very good question,' I say. 'What do you think?'

Ella considers, answers: 'It's because of the magic. They flew in.'

I nod, pleased. 'Exactly,' I say. 'Ella, you are a genius.'

She looks worried. 'What's genius?'

'Very, very clever.'

'Super-duper smart,' adds Rosie. 'Me, too.'

'Quite right,' I say, and we all nod solemnly.

They sip their cocoa. Ella says: 'What about the lost boys?'

'The family looked after them, too. They all went, apart from Peter Pan. He went back to Neverland.'

'On his own?'

I nod. 'He could have stayed. But he didn't want to. He didn't want to grow up.' I pause, considering them. 'Do you want to grow up?'

The doorbell rings.

'Mummy!' Ella jumps up, spilling the dregs of her cocoa down her front.

I brace myself.

SARAH

I haven't had the chance to draw breath all day, it's been non-stop. No lunch break, not so much as a coffee. The first day of the sale is always madness. All I want now is to crawl home, get Ella to bed as soon as possible and veg out in front on the TV. I pick up a family sized bar of chocolate and a bottle of white wine at the corner shop and struggle up the stairs to Becca's flat.

I ring at the door and listen. Silence. I feel a sudden stab of unease, remembering how ill Becca looked this morning, the fact that that homeless woman was left in charge. She's probably been through every drawer. Filled her pockets.

Rosie opens the door, chirpy. She's wearing a cluster of plastic necklaces and a sparkly tiara.

I bend down to whisper. 'Is everything OK? How's Mummy?'

A moment later, that woman's there, blocking the way. She's tied Becca's apron around her waist and it looks wrong on her. I feel myself tense. Who does she think she is? I got Becca this flat. She's my friend. This woman has no right to be here.

She blinks and stands aside. 'Busy day?' Her tone is apologetic, as if she knows at once how much I resent her and the way she's got her feet under the table. 'Quick cup of tea?'

I frown, trying to see past her. 'How's Becca?'

'Not well.' She shakes her head.

I don't trust her. I want Becca well and I want her gone. If Becca hasn't got the balls to boot her out, I will.

Ella appears, hiding behind Rosie in the hallway. She's wearing one of Rosie's party dresses, her feet pushed into play shoes. 'Please, Mummy.' Ella hangs on Rosie's hand, swinging it. 'Can I stay a bit longer? Please?'

I blow out my cheeks and she takes my hesitation as yes. Both girls shout: 'Yay!' and run off towards Rosie's bedroom.

I follow the woman into the kitchen. She moves towards the kettle but I push past and get there first. 'I can do that.' She's not the one in charge here. I have more right to this kitchen than she ever will. 'Do you want one?'

I put my bag down and make tea. She goes to the far counter and gets a plate, then cuts me a slice of chocolate cake. It's a lop-sided cake, home-made, decorated with chocolate buttons. Not pretty enough to be one of Becca's creations.

When I turn around to hand her a mug of tea, she's already set the cake on the table, in front of me. She doesn't look me in the eye. Guilt, I think. Something's not right. She's up to no good.

'Is Becca still in bed?'

She nods.

I go down to see for myself. The room is dark and smells stale.

'Becca?'

No answer. She's lying on her side, huddled and still under the duvet. Sleeping.

Back in the kitchen, I sit down and she pushes the cake a few inches closer to me.

'The girls made it,' she says. 'Try it.'

I pick at it. I'm starving and I'm playing for time, thinking. I want to go home but I don't want to leave this woman here for another night with Becca and Rosie. She sits over her tea, meek, her eyes on her mug.

'How was work?'

'Crazy.' I ease a foot out of its shoe and rub the back of my heel. I haven't sat down all day. 'First day of the sale. And we're one down.'

I don't want to talk but she doesn't stop – she keeps prying. Her eyes dart to my face when she thinks I'm not looking, then back to her mug when I challenge her. She's hiding something.

'Worked there long?'

'Two years. Not much choice. I'm a single parent.'

That hits home. She pulls a face and says: 'That's hard.'

I shrug. She wants to know more, I can feel it. None of her business.

'They're not exactly family friendly, either. If you're late more than once, you lose your job.' I grimace. No point complaining. That's just how it is. 'Anyway, it's easier now she's at school. Becca helps out.' I take another mouthful of cake, grateful for the sugar. 'We look out for each other.'

Her hand is tight around her mug, the fingertips blanching. Her fingers are long but the skin's rough and the nails bitten down.

I look away, out at the darkness. We're reflected in the window, the two of us, her reflection watching mine. I wonder what to do – whether to tell her to leave and stay the night myself, Ella too. I'm just so tired. I won't get much sleep on that old sofa bed.

'What would you like to do?' Her voice is gentle. 'If you could do anything for your job?'

I raise my eyebrows and turn back to her. Stupid question. 'Anything? I don't know.'

The silence stretches. Just the hum of the fridge and the sound of the girls in Rosie's room, giggling, chattering, trying on party dresses and pretending they've already grown up.

She says: 'You might end up as a manager, if you've a knack for it. Or running your own business.'

I laugh and it sounds hard. 'Right.' *Like that's going to happen.*

She persists. 'Why not? You seem smart. Hard-working.'

I shake my head. 'Life's not that simple though, is it?'

She looks away and sits in silence as I finish off the cake and drink my tea. Becca's bedroom door opens and I jump to my feet. She stands there in her dressing gown, leaning heavily against the door frame. I rush down the passage to her and offer an arm.

She blinks at me, dazed. 'Are the girls OK?'

'They're fine.' I help her along to the bathroom and whisper. 'Why don't I stay over tonight? I can look after you.'

She frowns, as if she's struggling to understand what's going on. 'There isn't room. Not with Maddy here, too.'

I tut. 'I'll tell her to leave.'

She gropes her way through the bathroom door. 'What if I'm not well tomorrow? You're working all day. And she's been such a help…'

I glance through to the kitchen. She's sitting in silence, her shoulders hunched. She must have heard.

I hang around outside until the toilet flushes and Becca emerges, her face wan.

'I don't trust her.' I keep my voice to a whisper as I help her back to bed.

'I know.' She sinks back into the pillow and closes her eyes. 'But I do. Rosie likes her. She looked after them all day, and it's not like I'm not here.' She sighs as if she's putting down a heavy weight. Already she seems half-asleep as she murmurs: 'Anyway, you don't trust anyone.'

Maddy looks embarrassed when I go back in to the kitchen. I put my mug in the dishwasher and stand there against the counter for a moment, looking out into the darkness. I'm tempted to kick her out just the same. Becca's in no fit state to make a decision. I grit my teeth. But what if she isn't better tomorrow? She's right, I can't take time off. We'd both be stuck.

I stride through to Rosie's room and tell Ella to get dressed again. Time to go home.

She's about to protest, then sees my face and knows better.

I'm just pushing Ella's arms into her coat at the front door when the homeless woman comes through from the kitchen, carrying the plastic bag with my chocolate and wine. She has a strange look on her face as she hands it over. I struggle to read it: not triumph because Becca has stood up for her, which is what I expected, but something deeper and more troubling. A knowing sadness, almost as if she can read me and is worried about what she sees. It stays with me as I hurry Ella down the stairs to our flat, already thinking about how soon I can open the bottle and have a drink.

BECCA

I lie for a second, testing myself, listening to my head. Quieter. I feel it at once. Better than yesterday. I risk opening my eyes. There's a fresh glass of water on the bedside table. I peer beyond it to the clock. Nearly six o'clock. For a moment, I'm not sure: evening or morning? I manage to turn, slowly, slowly, and raise my eyes to the window. Dark. It could be either. I lie still and listen.

Car engines. Not many. An aeroplane overhead. Then birdsong, faint but optimistic. The start of a new day. I close my eyes and try to remember. Yesterday was Boxing Day. So this must be December 27th. Sarah was here yesterday. And Maddy. Maddy's been looking after Rosie. And Alex? I feel through the fog. Alex is with Mark, staying over after the football as he sometimes does nowadays.

I take time swinging my legs out from under the covers, steadying myself. The heating hasn't clicked on yet and the air in the flat is cold. I palm my way along the wall to Rosie and Alex's room and slowly turn the doorknob, ease it open. It's dark inside, the curtains drawn. My breath stops in my throat. I know, I don't know how, I just sense that she's not there. There's no smell of her, no soft breathing. I flick the light on. Both bunks are empty. Rosie's covers are thrown off, her sheet crumpled and her heap of soft toys in disarray.

The room shifts and sways and I brace myself against the wall. For a moment, I think I'm going to be sick. What was I thinking? Lying in bed while a stranger took over my home, my child?

I stagger back into the hall and look wildly around. The chain is on the front door. Down the hall, the kitchen is in shadow. The whole flat is still and dark with winter.

I open the sitting-room door. A dark shape is slumped in the armchair by the windows. It's her.

'Maddy?' My voice is angry. *Don't play games*, it says. *I know what you are*. 'Where is she?'

She shifts her weight, straightens up in the chair and opens her eyes. For a moment, she seems lost in another time, another place. Then she sees me and smiles.

I raise my voice. A hint of mounting hysteria now. 'Where is she?'

She looks puzzled, then points to the sofa bed.

I rush across. Rosie is cuddled there, tucked up in the spare duvet. Her face is buried in the pillow and her arm flung wide, hair splayed in brown fronds. The sight of her, safe, peaceful, makes my legs wobble.

Maddy is there at my side, taking my arm. She smells stale and I realise she's still in the same clothes she wore when she arrived for Christmas lunch. Of course – she never expected to stay.

I sit like a visitor in my own kitchen and watch her fill the kettle and put it on. It's still black outside. She sits across from me. She averts her eyes and I wonder if I've offended her.

'I'm sorry.' I hesitate. She knew what I thought when I called out just now. When I demanded to know where Rosie was. I saw the hurt in her eyes. She knew that for a moment I thought her capable of harming Rosie, of kidnapping her. When all she'd done was take care of both of us.

I put my head in my hands and suddenly, from nowhere, tears come and I'm crying, sobbing like a baby, foolish, into my fingers. A warm arm goes round my shoulders. A clumsy arm, patting me.

'There, there.' Her voice is gentle. 'It's all right. You're not yourself.'

I lean into her and she tightens her arms around me and lets me weep into her shoulder, making a wet, messy pool on her neck. It's everything. Christmas and the children and Mark and his mother and the misery of feeling so ill, so helpless, so alone.

She rocks me and I cling to her and think of my mother and how much I miss her, now she's gone, and although it's been seven years since she died, in that moment, rocked there in the cold kitchen, it's as raw as it ever was.

Finally, I pull away and find a tissue and wipe off my face, blow my nose. I can't look her in the eye, I'm too embarrassed. 'I'm so sorry.'

'I wish you'd stop saying that.'

The kettle's boiled and she gets up and makes tea.

'She had a bad dream,' she says, as she moves about the kitchen. 'I said she could come and sleep on the sofa bed, if she wanted. Just for fun. So I took the chair.'

I think of the huddled shape, miserable with guilt. 'You can't have had much sleep.'

She grimaces. 'You know the story of *The Princess and the Pea*? Well, I'm the exact opposite now.' A little snort at her own joke. 'I could sleep on spikes and not notice.' She looks down into her tea. 'I never fail to be astonished by the human capacity to adjust. Even my own.'

A silence as she hands me my tea.

'Thank you for looking after me.' I blow out my cheeks. 'I don't know what hit me.'

She considers me for a moment. 'You were exhausted.'

'Well, I can't tell you how grateful I am.' I sip the tea. For the first time since Christmas morning, my stomach feels ready for food. I think about that. 'I feel as if I've lost two days.'

'I've lost whole weeks, even months, sometimes.' She pauses. 'Not lost. That implies they might be recovered, reclaimed from temporal lost property. And that's the tragedy. You never get them back.'

I blink. 'How's Rosie been?'

'Rosie?' She looks surprised. 'Great. We had fun.'

'I should really…' I stop, wondering whether to say what's in my mind. 'I'd be happy to pay you. You know, for babysitting?'

She gives me a strange look and nods at the darkness. 'I'd pay *you*. If I had any money. It's cold out there.'

I look at her as if for the first time. She looks crumpled but very ordinary, sitting across from me, sipping her tea. Her hair is flattened on one side and sticks up in clumps on the other. She'd look so different with a decent haircut. With normal clothes. Even now, she could be my auntie or next-door neighbour. My big sister, even. I know she's odd but she's kind and intelligent and I realise I'm glad she's here, keeping me company.

I think of the girls' voices, giggling yesterday down the hall. How happy Rosie seems with her.

'I should have warned you about Ella coming. I'm sorry. You must have thought—'

She flushes. 'I was glad to meet her.' She gets up from her table and fiddles at the sink with her broad back to me and I sense that she's hiding her face. She says over her shoulder: 'They get on very well, the girls.'

'A bit too well. School says they're inseparable.'

'And you see her mum a lot?'

Her tone is stiff. I wonder what Sarah said to her. If she was rude to Maddy. She can be, if she doesn't take to someone – I've seen it.

I say: 'Sarah's a single mum, too. We've been friends for a while now, since the girls started school and wanted playdates together. She's been very good to me. I try to help out when I can.'

The water cascades into the sink. She's busying herself with washing a plate which already looks perfectly clean. 'She was worried about you.' She pauses as if she's trying to decide how much to say. Finally, she turns back to face me and says pointedly: 'I wasn't sure how much she knows about me. How much you'd told her.'

I look into my cup, embarrassed. What can I say? *She knows you're homeless and doesn't trust you?*

'I suppose Ella might have said something after seeing you in the park.' I'm floundering, avoiding her eye. 'And I think I did say you were coming for Christmas lunch.'

She looks deflated and turns away, back to the washing up.

I take a deep breath. 'What happened to you, Maddy? What exactly' – I hesitate, trying to find the courage to ask – 'well, what went wrong? Why did you end up on the streets, without anywhere to live?'

She doesn't answer. For a moment, I wonder if she didn't hear or didn't understand what I meant. Then I see how rigid her shoulders are. Maybe it was too much. Maybe I've no right to ask something so personal.

She turns, scrapes back the chair and sits down with a bump.

'A magic mirror,' she says. 'Those windows and the way they reflect us back at ourselves. That's what they remind me of.'

'Pardon?'

'You know. The magic mirror. It's a common device in fairy tales. *Beauty and the Beast. The Snow Queen.*' She scans my face for a sign of recognition and seems to find none. 'The magic of the reflected self. It goes right back to Narcissus. You do know who Narcissus was? Yes?'

She peers at me and I remember what an oddball she is.

'Don't they teach people anything nowadays?' She looks irritated.

We face off across the table. She seems irritated but anxious at the same time, as if she realises her behaviour is strange and doesn't know how to be normal.

I say: 'Why do you do that?'

She looks away. 'Do what?'

'You're always referring to books. It feels like a put-down.'

'A put-down?' She looks genuinely startled. 'Why?'

I shrug. 'It makes me feel ignorant. You're pointing out that you know something I don't know.'

'No!' She frowns and says, almost to herself: 'Is that what people think? It's not that. Not at all.'

'What is it then?'

'They're just in my head,' she says. 'So, it's what comes out. Isn't it the same for everyone?'

I shake my head and wonder about her, about what did happen in her past, about why she's just avoided my questions and changed the subject. Then an image comes to me of Rosie romping around the kitchen with a colander on her head, brandishing a wooden spoon, skating on the tea towels. Of Ella with her face in the mixing bowl. Of the den she said she made for them out of cushions.

I soften and smile. 'Oh, Maddy. Whatever you are, I am glad I met you.'

'Likewise.' She smiles, too. I have the sense that she doesn't understand what's happening between us but is relieved that it's suddenly all right, that she isn't getting it wrong. Not at that precise moment, at least.

'Are you better, Mummy?' Suddenly Rosie is there, stumbling into the kitchen, dwarfish in her nightshirt, hair tangled.

I open my arms to her and she traipses across, still half-asleep, and climbs onto my lap. I hold her close and rock her. She smells of sleep and stale breath. My baby, already growing up too fast.

'Much better, thank you.' I plant kisses on her ear, her hair and she squirms.

'Can we make pancakes again, Maddy?'

Maddy glances at me. 'That's up to your mother, Rosie. She's back at the helm now.'

'If you like.'

I give Rosie a final squeeze, then let her scramble free and pad across to the fridge. It takes all the strength in her thin arms for her to pull the door open with a rubbery thwack. She lifts out the eggs. Maddy is reaching for my blue apron, limp on the back of a chair.

'Are you sure, Maddy?'

I watch the two of them move easily around each other. Maddy pulls out a wooden spoon and a mixing bowl and Rosie kneels up on the chair beside her, ready to help.

There it is again, that easy chemistry they seem to share.

'I might have a shower, if that's OK?' I kiss Rosie on the top of her head before I go. 'Thanks so much, Maddy.'

My phone rings just as I'm stripping off in the bathroom. Jane from the wine bar.

'Can you talk?'

I switch the shower off, perch on the edge of the bath and pull a towel around my shoulders as she continues. No 'How was your Christmas?' where Jane's concerned. She likes to cut straight to the chase.

'Just wanted to check in,' she says, 'to see if you've decided about the job? Don't want to rush you but if you don't want it, I need to advertise.'

I hesitate. Water droplets, gathering on the tiled wall beside me, fall into each other and expand, then spill out into tiny, meandering rivulets. I stretch out a finger and disperse one.

'I'm working on it,' I lie. What chance have I had?

A moment's silence. I sense her disapproval.

'Jane, can you just give me another couple of days? I'll let you know for sure on Saturday. I'm just figuring out the childcare.'

'OK.' She doesn't sound pleased. 'Saturday. But I do need to know.'

She hangs up.

In the shower, I tip back my head and feel the water explode on my face, cascade down my shoulders. I feel well again, flooded with well-being. *I've survived. I can do this.* And I realise how much I want this job. It's a real break. More money, of course. But it's more than that. It's a chance to develop proper cooking skills, in a great team. Dennis won't stay forever. He's always talking about retiring. Maybe I'd be ready to run the kitchen by then, if I work hard. Despite her impatience on the phone earlier, Jane clearly believes in me.

I massage shampoo through my hair and lean backwards under the water to rinse it off. I think of Maddy, clumsily putting her arms around me when I cried. Of the warmth in her face when she saw Rosie and the fun they've been having together. Maybe we could help each other? I could see her through the winter, give her somewhere warm and dry to sleep. In return, she could cover some evenings at home, while I did the extra shifts.

I step onto the bathmat and reach for the towel. What was it Maddy said when she came out of the bathroom that very first night, smelling of bubble bath? *Behold, Venus is risen!*

I smile as I start to rub my hair. Rosie would be thrilled. Alex might be more of a challenge but he'll just have to put up with her, if she agrees. I imagine bumping into David downstairs, next time he's polishing his car. *I'm a trainee chef at Jane's wine bar now – have you been there?* He's bound to have been. Everyone knows Jane's. He'll know there's more to me than just being a mum.

I rub the end of the towel over the steamed-up mirror and look at myself. My eyes gleam with excitement. I look more alive than I have for a long time, just thinking about saying yes to Jane. Slowly, even as I look, the mirror mists again.

Then my shoulders sag. I think how little I really know about Maddy, how cagey she is about her life. My spirits deflate. Maybe Sarah's right not to trust her. I just don't know.

*

'Why's she still here?'

'Keep your voice down. She'll hear.'

'I don't care. What the hell are you thinking?'

Mark's been in the flat all of five minutes. We've barely got beyond hello before he catches sight of Maddy pottering in the kitchen. She's teaching Rosie and Ella how to make an omelette for lunch. A jam omelette, apparently. She seems happiest in the kitchen. Perhaps that's what she missed most, when she lived under a bush.

Alex, his bag dumped in the hall, retreats to his bedroom at once and shuts the door.

I take a deep breath and try to change the subject. 'How was the match? Alex has been OK?'

He shakes his head. His tone is crisp. 'I'm sorry, Becca, but it's unacceptable—'

'Unacceptable?'

'All right, let me spell it out, if that's what you need. That woman must leave. Now. And not come back. Get it? You have no idea what you're dealing with. She's dangerous.'

'You don't know the first thing about her.'

'Do you?' His eyes stray down the hall to the kitchen as if he's watching for Maddy to do something outrageous. His face is a mask of contempt. 'I mean it, Becca. She needs to leave. If you can't throw her out, I will.'

I take a deep breath. 'She's fallen on hard times. That's all. You don't know her.' I think of the way she cared for me. 'She's really kind. I couldn't get out of bed. You weren't here.'

'I could be. If you stopped all this nonsense and came home.'

I shake my head. 'This is my home now.' I turn away and stride through to the sitting room, as far from the kitchen as we can be. He follows me through. It's the nearest we can get to a private conversation in this tiny flat.

'Why didn't you call me?' His voice is hard. 'I mean, if you were so ill.'

'What's that supposed to mean?' I manage not to add: *Are you calling me a liar?*

His shoulders are hard and set. 'Great example for the kids, Becca. What is she – a druggie? Ex-con?'

'Neither, actually.' I feel myself flush. The more he seems to despise Maddy, the more I want to defend her. 'Rosie adores her.'

'She's five. She adores everyone.'

'No, she doesn't.' I take a breath. 'Ella was here, too. They had fun.'

'Right. Ella.' He and Sarah hate each other, they have from the start. He blows out his cheeks, pushes past me and crosses the room. He puts his hands squarely on the bottom of the window frame and closes the sash, then slides the catch to lock it. It's a proprietorial gesture which only makes me feel more undermined.

'She's playing you, Becca. You just can't see it. She's smelt kindness on you and she's playing you like a fiddle.'

I don't reply. I've wondered the same, of course I have, but, from him, it sounds downright patronising. I'm tired of his belittling me, telling me what to do. This is my home, not his. He can't lay down the law here.

'What was wrong with you, anyway?' He turns back to face me, his eyes suspicious.

'Vomiting, dizzy, cracking headache.' I hesitate. 'A virus, I suppose?'

'Funny virus.' He narrows his eyes. 'How do you know it wasn't her?'

I stare at him in disbelief. 'How could it be her?'

'Maybe she spiked your food. Knowing what would happen.'

'Don't be ridiculous.'

'Why not?' He's getting more forceful now, working himself up, trying to push his point home. 'Like a date-rape drug. And it worked. She's worked her way in. Made you dependent on her.' He shook his head. 'Like it or not, Becca, she's leaving.'

I look at his tight expression, the conviction in his eyes that I'm naïve and he knows best – not just about this but about everything. His belief that, if ever I disagree with him, the best solution is to batter away at me until I give in.

I think about every time I've tried to tell him, in the past year, that I want to live my own life, that I want to be my own person again, that I want to leave. Every time he's either mocked me or tried to shout me down, as he's doing now.

I take a deep breath. I am listening. I'm worried too about what's right, about keeping the children safe. But he can't bully me. Not any more.

'I'll think about it.' I force myself to stay calm, to nod at him. 'I will. Thank you. But I'll make my own decision.' I cross to the door and open it, stand there. 'I think you'd better go.'

He hesitates and I wonder if he'll make a scene, if he'll refuse to leave, if he'll carry out his threat and try to throw Maddy out, despite me.

'You're not yourself, Becca.' His face changes, from anger to a sickly sympathy, which is far worse. 'You're not properly well. I think, when you are, you'll see I'm right about this.'

I don't answer. Time stretches. I stand there, my knuckles white where I grip the door handle, my legs trembling.

'You're all heart, Becca, I know that.' He simpers. 'But it's a tough world out there. It's clear more than ever that you need looking after.'

I can't look at him. Finally, he sighs and walks out, calls goodbye to Alex and Rosie and heads for the front door. The moment after it slams is very quiet.

The only sounds are voices from the kitchen, Maddy's, Rosie's and Ella's, chanting an old-fashioned poem: '*Never go down to the end of the town without consulting me!*'

I find the sofa and sink into it, grateful that Mark has gone but praying to God that he isn't right about Maddy.

MADDY

I know something's up when Becca comes through into the sitting room later that evening and shuts the door behind her. I don't like closed doors, they make me feel trapped.

'Can I have a word?' She looks stressed.

Theatrically, I set down my book. Well, her book, actually. She doesn't have much of a library. Even so, I'd like the chance to finish reading my way through it, to suck up the little black words like a famished anteater. And already, looking at her sober face, I'm thinking: *Ha, time's up. Just as I was getting comfortable. Time, gentlemen, please. The old heave-ho.*

I sit down on the sofa bed and face her as she settles in the armchair. *Called to the headmistress's study for a dressing-down. Worse than that. Expulsion.*

'I'm so grateful,' she says. Her hands twist around each other in her lap. Wringing her hands. *Will these hands ne'er be clean?* I haven't opened my mouth, not this time, but she seems to sense that I'm rambling inside my head and a fleeting look of annoyance crosses her face. *Stop it, Maddy. Why do I do that? Why can't my mind be calm?*

I sit on my hands as if I'm sitting on my brain too and try to focus. To listen.

She takes a deep breath and starts again. 'I'm really grateful for the way you looked after me. And the girls.'

I open my mouth to interrupt and she gives me a look. I close it again.

'I like you, Maddy. I want to help you. We don't have much room. You know that.'

I keep my lips pressed together, struggling not to interrupt while she gets it out.

'But if you'd like to carry on spending the night here, just for a while, I'm OK with that.' She looks awkward but also embarrassed.

By the pricking of my thumbs. There's more to this! '… And?'

Her eyes slide away from me to the blank wall. 'I've been offered a promotion at work. I work in a wine bar and, well, I've always loved cooking. Always wondered if I could make a go of it, professionally.'

I nod. I'm not surprised. I've seen all the kitchen equipment, the cupboards full of obscure ingredients, the spice drawer.

She says: 'They've offered me some evenings, helping to run the kitchen. Proper cooking, not just lunches.'

Her voice changes as she talks about it. A little faster, a little breathier. She really wants this, I can tell.

'I wouldn't leave until nearly seven. But it's all evening. I need someone to be here, with Alex and Rosie.'

'Of course you do.'

She ploughs on. 'So, I was wondering… if you like, you can sleep here at night, on the sofa bed, free of charge, and in return, keep an eye on them. Just when I'm out.'

I consider. I may be homeless but I'm not a fool. 'Free babysitting.'

She has the grace to flush. 'Well, it's not free, is it?'

'It's certainly not paid.'

She juts out her chin. 'I can't give you cash. But it's in return for somewhere to live.'

'Sleep,' I put in.

'And food. And hot water. All that.' She looks exasperated. 'Surely you'd rather be here than sleeping under a bush?'

I narrow my eyes. 'Nothing wrong with a good bush.'

She looks taken aback. 'You don't want to stay?'

I shrug. 'Not on those terms. Would you?'

She glares at me, annoyed now. 'Well, yes, actually. I think I would. I'd rather help out in a family than be on the street. It's not exactly difficult work.'

I bend forward and clasp my knees with my forearms and rock myself, thinking. *Why, Maddy? Why are you doing this? Isn't this what you wanted? Isn't this your chance? You can do this.* But can I? What if I ruin it? What if I let them down? I have never liked being trapped by arrangements and contracts and expectations. I could go back to teaching if I wanted that. Then: *No, you couldn't, you liar. You know you can't teach again. Never, never, never, never, never.*

I take a breath and force myself to say, meekly for me: 'Maybe I was a little hasty. Maybe we could work something out. To mutual advantage.'

She's watching me closely, her face sterner than before. 'There's something else,' she says. 'If we're going to do this, I need to know a bit more about you.' She sees my face and lifts her hand. 'I don't want to pry. It's not that. I just need to understand a few things.'

The silence stretches. I say warily: 'Like what?'

'Well.' She steels herself. 'Why did you lose your home?'

'That's complicated. A long story.'

She sighs. 'OK. Let's get specific. Maddy, you said you're not on drugs. Was that really true?'

I nod. That's easy. 'Never even smoked.'

'Good.' She looks relieved. 'And no trouble with the police?'

My eyes slide away from hers as I shake my head.

'What about drinking?'

Ah. Drinking. What can I say? How can she possibly understand?

I try to find the words. 'Everyone likes a drink now and then…'

She frowns. I think how I must have stank when she first met me, when she put my clothes in the wash and helped me clean up.

'Look, there's lots of booze on the street.' My heart's pounding. 'It's not a problem, I don't drink now.'

I hold out my hand. Pretty steady.

'I love Rosie. And Ella. I'd take good care of them. You've seen that. I'll try not to get in the way. Not to be a nuisance.' I hesitate, embarrassed at how desperate I suddenly sound. 'I won't let you down. I really won't.'

She sits quietly for some moments, watching me. I can't tell what she's thinking but she's figuring it out, trying to make a decision. Then her face softens. 'OK.' She comes across and stretches out her hand. 'Shall we give it a go? Maybe I'm crazy, but I like you, Maddy. And I believe in second chances.'

Her fingers are soft and I feel the calluses on my own as we shake.

I can't sleep that night. I lie, unblinking, staring at the patterns of light and shadow on the ceiling. *I don't know if I can do this. I don't think I have the strength.*

It's a struggle. If you haven't been through it, you can't know. I have. Already, in these past few days, I've suffered. I wake every morning with a dry mouth, shaking, frightened, thinking about the prospect of getting through the day without a drink. I don't just want one. It isn't as simple as that. I need one. A searing, physical need. An itch that can only be eased by a shot of the hard stuff. *Liquor. Hooch. Moonshine.*

In the hospital, through those first days of hell, they forced me to dry out, cold turkey, but at least they gave me medicine to dull the pain. I don't know what – something in the drip that calmed my nerves and helped me to keep on top of the shaking. Some elixir that scared away the demons that swarmed through my head and tried to drag me under. Now I'm stronger, healthier than that.

But I'm also on my own.

I pour myself a glass of water. Sometimes, when it's getting too strong, I sip it, pretending it's vodka. Gin. Whisky. I'm not much fooled.

There are good moments. Here I am, lying on the sofa bed, my body at full stretch, listening to the hums and clicks of the central heating as it quietens for the night, to the creaks of floorboards. I can feel it, a second or two of physical well-being. The pure pleasure of a cool, clean sheet and a pillow under clean hair and the heavy warmth of the duvet on my bones. The light breath of air blowing in through the open sash. It's a blessing to be here, I know so.

Becca is kind and Rosie too, and Alex, well, he's his father's son. I know that man poured poison into Becca's ear when he visited today. I'm not a fool. I know *Hamlet*.

But he miscalculated. He showed himself to her for what he was, suspicious and cold-hearted and a bully. She'll keep me here because she's kind, but also because she needs me. She's spelled that out. We need each other. I'm the childminder she can't afford to pay.

She's handing me the chance I longed for, the hope that brought me to this part of London, to this street, to this block of flats. But can I do this? Have I got the strength?

Already, there've been bad moments, even here. There are times, at night, when the silence is deep, when I start thinking. About what I've done, what I've lost, about the letter which is always with me, always in my pocket. Those are times when all I crave is oblivion.

Once I even got up, changed out of Becca's cast-off pyjamas into her cast-off clothes and stood at the front door, my clammy forehead pressed hard against the paintwork, trembling, willing myself not to do this, not to go out there to search out Mick or some other boozer and beg for a drink.

That time, I held firm. I crept back to lie, shaking, underneath the covers. But it wasn't strength that dragged me back. It was fear. Fear of the shame and self-loathing that would come with being unable to control myself. With messing up my only chance. My one and only. But there'll be more times, more tests.

What if I fail? How will I live then?

I put on the light and reach under my pillow and take out the letter, smooth out the folds, read it over, touch the ink with my fingertips, as if it had the power to heal me. *This is the real fear, isn't it, Maddy?* Not the closed door or the fear of being exploited or any other such nonsense. I touch my lips to the corner of the letter to say goodnight and fold it carefully away.

Darkness again. My heart races. *What if I stay here, if I take my chance, and it ends in disaster? In heartbreak? What then would I have left to live for?*

I press my eyelids tightly together until the darkness spangles.

Nothing and again nothing.

SARAH

'Hey! Alex? I've got something for you.'

He hesitates, his foot already on the bottom stair, ready to run up, two at a time, to their flat. He twists to look back at me, uncertain, as I stand there in the half-open doorway to my own flat.

I laugh. 'Don't worry, Rosie's here. Your mum's made a dash to the shops.'

He shrugs, turns around clumsily, weighed down by adolescent awkwardness, and slouches across to head inside the flat with me. *Caught you.*

Alex stands on the entrance rug, looking ahead at the mis-matched second-hand furniture. It's cheap stuff. There are some things even I can't pinch. He catches sight of himself in the mirror and stops to look, then sees me watching him and reddens.

'Come on through.'

I lead him in. Ella and Rosie are hunched together at the kitchen table, colouring and sticking. They had their dinner at Becca's after school while I finished work. Now I'm doing a bit of payback by bringing the girls down here and giving Becca the chance to dash to the supermarket.

It's strategic, too – that homeless woman, Maddy, has got her feet firmly under the table now, taking charge every time Becca goes to work. I want to keep my foot in the door and stop her taking over completely.

'Cup of tea? Coke?'

He shakes his head, ill at ease. The girls raise their heads to check him out, then go straight back to their colouring.

I direct him sideways into my room with a nod and he follows. He stands in the doorway and keeps his eyes on the carpet, avoiding looking at my bed which dominates the room with its mess of pillows and tousled sheets.

I stand on the bed and lift a bag from the top cupboard, hand it down to him.

'Picked up a new computer game a few days ago. You got this one?'

He pulls it out and his eyes glisten at once. 'Cool!' He turns it over to read the back. 'Series five.'

'Want to borrow it? You could figure it out for me.'

'Really?'

'Sure,' I smile. 'Why not?' I hesitate, choosing my words with care. 'But it needs to be our secret, OK? I don't want grief from your mum. Deal?'

He grins. 'Deal.'

He's about to leave when I sit on the bed and pat the covers beside me. 'Alex, can I ask you something?'

His face clouds again, worried.

'What do you make of Maddy? I mean, the way she's started staying over with you guys and all that? How long's it been now? Several weeks, right?'

He grimaces. 'She's a bag lady. Did you know?'

I nod and pull a sympathetic face.

'She's weird. She hangs out in the park all day. She used to live on the high street. Gross.'

I make a non-committal grunt. 'I worry about your mum, you know? She's so kind. She's not as streetwise as you and me.'

He considers this.

'I'd hate to see anyone take advantage of her.' I pause, sensing his reaction. 'I'm not sure I trust Maddy. Do you?'

He shakes his head. 'That's what my dad says. He thinks Mum's gone bonkers, letting her stay in the flat. Says he'll come round and send her packing soon, if Mum doesn't.'

'Hmm.' I can just imagine Mark foaming at the mouth. He's not used to Becca making her own decisions although, on this one, he and I are oddly on the same side.

I nod at Alex. 'Keep an eye on her, would you? Let me know if she does anything strange. If anything goes missing, you know?' I point to the game in his hand, still in its cellophane wrapping. 'And I'll look out for another one of those.'

His eyes dip to his shoes, trainers with worn toes, and he shuffles, then looks up at me again with resolution: 'OK.'

BECCA

These things always happen when you least expect them. I've got enough on my plate. Getting on top of the new job. Keeping an eye on Maddy and the way she's running things when I'm out. And Mark. He's back to sending volleys of bullying texts and letters again, about Maddy mostly. He can't handle the fact I didn't take his advice and throw her out and of course he's vicious about the fact I'm working full-time now. Sarah says he's just threatened because I'm getting on my feet. Maybe that's right. I'm trying hard to ignore him but it isn't easy.

Friday night comes round again and I head to work knowing exactly what to expect from the busiest shift of the week. Dennis and I are flat-out all evening, serving up endless tables of chicken risotto and beef bourguignon, the dishes of the day.

These hectic evening shifts have a completely different rhythm from lunches. Tonight, as usual, there's a warm-up period when the first tables arrive and the pace is steady and controlled. Then suddenly, in a matter of minutes, the wooden strut above the serving hatch is fluttering with orders and the race is on, a battle to keep afloat or drown in demands. For several hours, Dennis and I run back and forth, barking numbers at each other as we fill plates and line them up along the hatch for the waitresses to take out. We're still developing our mutual radar, a way of navigating swiftly around each other in the small kitchen, a dance of dishes that can be flawless if we're both fully focused and in sync.

The tide retreats as quickly as it rolled in. Suddenly, it's all desserts which only need plating and garnishing. The waitresses do coffees. Dennis starts to organise leftovers and wipe down surfaces, clearing the pots and pans and casseroles for the washing-up lad and, last of all, bringing out the iPad and totting up remaining stock.

I finally get the chance to race to the toilet. I see my face in the mirror there, flushed and sweaty but alive, triumphant, surging with adrenalin and the sense of a job well done, of money honestly earned. It's a new feeling and I love it. In that kitchen, in the middle of the whirlwind, I forget Mark and Alex and Rosie and Maddy and bills and shopping and laundry and even more, I forget myself.

I'm heading back to the kitchen through the bar where they're still serving brandies and port, the mood languid now, when I see David, my landlord. My neighbour. He's sitting quietly at the far end, leaning forward, a glass of white wine in front of him, looking right at me. I blush, I'm sure. The sight of him is so unexpected and I'm suddenly conscious of how wild and sweaty I look, of the way my hair's plastered to my head. He, by contrast, looks calm and composed. He doesn't speak or move, just smiles.

I rush back to the kitchen to hide and help Dennis clear away. A few minutes later, Jane comes through.

'A message from David.' She looked amused, watching for my reaction. 'He says do you want a lift home?'

I lower my face to the leftover beef I'm spooning into a plastic container. 'That's OK. We're not done yet.'

'Sure you are.' Jane looks at the surfaces. Most are already clear. 'I'll finish up if you want to get away.' She comes a little closer and says: 'I didn't know you knew David. Lucky you.'

I twist sideways to see her face. She isn't mocking me – she's smiling, a kind smile.

'I don't, really. He's my landlord.'

Jane nods. 'That figures. I'd heard he's loaded. Bit of an investment whizz.' She pauses. 'He's a regular but he hasn't been in for a while. He's only had one glass, by the way, don't worry. That's all he ever has. Mr Responsible.'

I stack the last dish for washing and peel off my rubber gloves. It isn't far to walk but my feet are aching. I'd like to be taken home, to be looked after, just for once.

'Tell him I'm on my way.'

So instead of slipping out of the kitchen door, the staff exit, I find myself escorted through the wine bar and out through the front, with the dispersing customers.

David's manner is easy and confident, as if he's always done this – appeared at closing time and driven me home. As if we both expected it. He keeps the chat light-hearted as he holds open the car door and settles me inside, then slips into the driver's seat beside me and pulls out into the deserted road. He's wearing his cashmere coat and jeans which look expensive. I feel all too aware of the baggy jumper I've thrown over my work shirt and battered jeans and the flat, worn shoes which are comfortable in the kitchen.

It's only as he's seeing me safely inside the apartment block, hitting the hallway button to light me up the stairs, that he says, so casually I almost miss it: 'I don't suppose you'd fancy dinner one evening?'

It takes a moment to register. Did he really just say that? About taking me out for dinner?

The pause is embarrassing and we both pitch in at once, talking over each other:

'Of course, if you'd rather not—'

'That would be lovely. I mean, well—'

And then he's smiling and saying straightaway, as if he's worried I might change my mind: 'How about Tuesday?' and I find myself nodding and the hallway light times out and he presses it back on again and says: 'Great – see you Tuesday evening then – seven thirty?' and suddenly I'm on my way up the stairs, wondering what just happened but excited, exhilarated and my fingers are still shaking as I put my key in the lock.

*

When Tuesday comes, I take time getting ready.

I need several tries to get my eyeliner straight. I twist around in front of the mirror, trying to see my outfit from the back. Black trousers – the same ones I wear for work – freshly washed and dressed up with a sparkly black and silver top. I've got my best bra on, the one that gives me cleavage. It's been in the back of a drawer for months. I fiddle with it, squirming, anxious. The face in the mirror looks so tense that its mouth crumples and I turn away, sit down on the bed and sink my head in my hands. *What am I doing?*

Maddy looks me over at the door. For a moment, she seems about to tell me off and I take a deep breath, bracing myself. I haven't told her where I'm going tonight, but I wonder if she suspects it might be a date.

'*Full royally apparelled*,' she mutters to herself, then catches my eye and has the grace to look embarrassed.

I pull a face. 'I'm taking that as a compliment, whatever it means.'

Rosie comes running out from the sitting room in her night-shirt and clasps me around the thighs. 'You look very pretty, Mummy.'

I stroke her hair, strands still damp from her bath. 'You be good for Maddy, OK? I won't be late.'

'OK.' She kisses my fingers, one by one. 'Love you more than you love me.'

'No way.' It's a new game of hers, this competition to love each other more. 'Love you more.'

'No, you don't.'

'Yes, I do.'

'Don't! Don't! Don't!'

'See you later, Alex!' No answer from his room. He'll move to the kitchen with his homework, his computer games, once Maddy puts Rosie to bed. He doesn't like her but he's tolerating her presence, just for the moment. 'Bye, Maddy.'

David is waiting outside on the pavement as I emerge from the block. Bang on time. He's wearing grey chinos and a jacket with gold buttons. He smiles as he looks up, then opens the passenger door of his car and holds it, acting the gentleman, as I climb in. He smells of soap and a hint of aftershave. Expensive. Sexy.

As he revs up and slides the car out into the road, I'm so self-conscious, I don't know where to put my legs, my hands, how to sit. He keeps his eyes on the road and I take the chance to look at him. Handsome. Strong featured. Calm.

'Do you know The Old Mill?' he says. 'It's a bit of a drive but I like getting out of London, once in a while. The mill isn't working nowadays but it's a very atmospheric building. They've turned it into a rather good restaurant. Hope you're hungry.'

'Always.' I sound lame. 'That sounds great.' *I don't know how to do this. It's been too long.* I turn away to look out of the window, watch the lit shop windows and coffee shops. Lines of hurrying commuters blur as the lights change and he picks up speed.

The Old Mill is charming. David parks and leads me across a cobbled courtyard and he's right, it's only half an hour's drive away but suddenly it feels a world away from London. Away from the light pollution, the darkness is intense, the stars bright overhead. The quietness presses around us. As we walk, all I hear is our footsteps and our breath and the rush of flowing water from nearby.

We head for the faux lantern hanging over the arched doorway and into the dimly lit interior, its Victorian features – stone floors and exposed wooden beams – still intact. Our table, tucked away in a corner, overlooks a weir. The insulation cuts the sound of the water but an exterior spotlight shows the churn so close to where we're sitting. Black and turbulent.

The waiter hands us the menus and withdraws.

'You've been here before?' I wonder with whom.

David nods. 'Once or twice.'

'And this was a real mill?'

'That's what I love about this place. The sense of history. Of all the people, long dead, who sweated it out right here. The backbone of Victorian England.' He stops, laughs. 'I'm sorry. I'm getting a bit carried away, aren't I?' He leans forward and points to the specials page inside my menu. His arm is so close to mine, I can feel the rising warmth. 'The duck's good. And the steak.'

It's been a long time since anyone took me out to dinner. And even longer since they showed any interest in me. Not Mark or the children, but me. David asks so many questions, not in a probing way but gently, as if he really wants to know. About my job at Jane's and how it's working out, now I've been doing evening shifts for a month. The restaurant I'd like to open for myself someday. About my childhood and then what I studied, what I did before having children, where I've travelled, what films and books I love. Even about losing Mum when Alex was little, and how much I miss her, even now. The conversation is easy and relaxed, more so as the wine flows, and never falters.

I have the sense, as I consider how to answer, of excavating myself, of chipping away at the layers of everyday sediment that have built up since Alex was born and finding the person buried deep inside. The person I'd almost lost and am pleased to meet again.

His phone's on silent but keeps flashing, there on the table. Sometimes, he just checks it for a second and leaves it be. Finally, once we've finished our main courses, he gets up.

'Would you mind? Work. Won't be a moment.'

When he comes back, I pluck up courage and ask: 'What do you do, exactly?'

'It's very boring.' He smiles. 'I'm a financial advisor. I manage people's money. Very rich people's money, basically.'

I nod. 'And you work for yourself?'

'I do. I started off working for a company, then set up on my own.'

I consider. 'And that's how you came to buy property?'

'Absolutely. I started with next to nothing and every time I saved up enough, I bought another place.'

The waiter appears and hands us dessert menus. He has a quick look, then adds: 'The kind of clients I've got now, they're the yacht-owning, country-house type. They're great but I really have to earn my commission. That means weird hours. Late-night calls to the US. Early morning and Tokyo's waking up. I never really switch off.'

We share a raspberry pavlova and finish with coffee. When David pays the bill, I murmur a protest, offer to pay my share, but I know he won't let me. I'm grateful. I've seen the prices. And somehow, it would spoil the romance of the evening if I started fumbling in my bag and working out my share. My head buzzes with the wine and the exhilaration of being out, of feeling desirable. I think about Jane's sly glance when she asked me about David and the fact she's clearly impressed that I know him. About how easy life with a wealthy banker might be.

'What's that smile?' David leans forward, smiling himself.

I flush. 'Just thinking what a lovely place this is,' I lie.

I turn to the window and put my face close to the glass to see through the reflection of the restaurant and out into the night. The tumbling rush of water is just visible in the darkness, racing endlessly from the dirty, clogged city of London towards the sea.

As we leave, the cold air comes as a slap in the face. David takes my arm and I'm grateful for it, my legs unsteady on the cobbles. He guides me back to the car.

The headlights swing down the narrow road, picking out hedges and farm gates at first, then, gradually, houses and side roads as we drive back into the suburbs. He drives steadily but the speed of the rushing fences and walls, the sharp bends in the road leave me dizzy. The after-taste of the rich food makes me nauseous. I grip the door handle with one hand to steady myself.

I remember what Jane said – *Don't worry, he never has more than one glass* – and think more carefully about the bottle we shared. She was right. He barely touched his wine. It was my glass the waiter kept refilling, over and over, my voice that did all the talking, all the disclosing. *What had I really learned about him?* Hardly a thing.

I lift my spare hand to my face and run it down my cheek, my neck, realising how numb I feel and how tired.

When we reach home, we stand for a moment on the pavement outside the blocks of flats. David jangles his keys in his hand and nods towards the next block where he lives.

'Quick nightcap?'

I hesitate. I want to see his place, to learn more about him from the way it's furnished and decorated but I'm also dropping with tiredness.

'Come on.' He smiles. 'You're practically home. And I know for a fact you don't have to relieve the babysitter.'

He's right, of course. Maddy will already be asleep on the sofa bed. I could stay out all night and it wouldn't really matter. Then I blink, wondering how he knows about her. I haven't mentioned it. I feel a moment's awkwardness. He's my landlord, after all. Maybe I should have asked permission.

'You've heard about Maddy?'

He shrugs, non-committal.

'She's only staying a while,' I say. 'Just until she's back on her feet.'

He doesn't answer, just turns and leads the way towards the adjacent block. It looks the same on the outside but his ground-floor flat is far more spacious than mine or Sarah's. I stand just inside the door for a moment, trying to get my bearings. The box room, which I use as the children's bedroom, has been knocked through completely, making a single, huge sitting room. There's a modern dining table in one corner, with a low-hanging pendulum light. One corner has been converted into a wooden drinks bar, mirrored, set about with tall bar stools. At the far end, a pair of cream leather sofas face towards a wall, which is dominated by a large plasma screen. Instead of carpet, the floors are polished wood, scattered with oriental rugs.

The lighting is low. Hidden spotlights send dim cones down the walls and soft pools along the top of the bar. He helps me out of my coat and leads me across to the sofas. The cushions let out a long, steady breath when I sink into them.

He points to the bar. 'What's your poison?'

I shake my head. 'I couldn't. Really. Thank you.'

He looks thoughtful, then sits heavily, too close beside me. His weight on the cushion tips me sideways towards him and I lean away, reaching for the arm of the sofa to keep myself upright.

'I like you, Becca.' His face is so near to mine that I struggle to focus. His breath smells of coffee and, distantly, of stale wine. He reaches out to touch my face. His fingers are slow and gentle as they stroke my cheek. Mesmerising.

I tense. *I'm not sure. I'm not sure I can do this.*

He smiles. 'It's all right. Just relax.' His fingertips slip down my top and trace the curve of my breast. I feel them, warm, through the material. He runs his other hand round the back of the sofa to my back and draws me towards him, his mouth searching for mine.

'David.' I pull away in a sudden rush of panic. *Too much. I'm too drunk, too queasy.* 'I don't know.'

He sits very still. 'That's OK.' His voice is low. 'I don't want to rush you.'

I push his hand away and manage to get to my feet.

'I'm sorry.' The room sways and comes back again. 'I've had a lovely evening. I really like you, David. I do.'

He doesn't answer, just stands up and reaches for my hand.

I say: 'I ought to get back. Check on the kids.'

'Of course,' he says. 'I'm sorry. I just thought…' He hesitates, his face shy. 'I've had such a great evening. I thought you had too.'

'I have.' I pick up my bag and start to move towards the door, feeling stupid, embarrassed, clumsy with alcohol. 'It's not that. I'm just, well, it's just…'

He nods, all gentleman again. 'Don't say a word. It's fine.'

I stumble out and along the street to my own block, then hurry up the stairs, desperate to be in my own bed, feeling a fool.

The flat is shadowy and silent. I drink a glass of water and fall into bed. The room lightly sways and I close my eyes and sink back into the mattress, my head buzzing in the quiet, my body still feeling the cautious, gentle stroke of his hand.

At lunch the next day, Jane waits until Dennis leaves the kitchen, then leans through the hatch and raises her eyebrows.

'So,' she says. 'How was it?'

'Great.' My face must give me away.

Jane's expression clouds. 'What happened?'

'Nothing.' I keep my eyes on my hands as they make up a side salad, fanning the pieces of lettuce in the shallow dish. 'I mean, dinner was lovely. He's great.'

'And?'

'And what?' I add some halved baby tomatoes and sliced peppers.

She tuts. 'Well, what happened afterwards?'

'Don't be silly.' My embarrassment makes me sound more irritated than I am. 'Nothing. I'm not a teenager. I went home to bed, that's all.'

'Right.'

'Sorry to disappoint you.'

'Not just me, by the sound of it.' She grins.

Dennis comes back into the kitchen from the cellar carrying a crate of vegetables and Jane withdraws her head. I finish off the salad and start on the next one, feeling defensive and slightly sick.

The next time I have an evening shift, I dress with care. I've been practising some of the things I might say to David if he offers to take me out again. Sorry, maybe.

For the last hour of the evening, I glance whenever I can at the corner of the bar, looking for him. It stays empty.

The next evening is the same. And the next. Slowly, I start to realise that the excuses I'm making to myself – *He's just busy, he's being thoughtful, he's giving me space* – are nonsense.

Whatever happened, I think I've blown it. It's over as quickly as it began.

MADDY

Home. There are times I feel at home here now.

Not in the sitting room, where I sleep. Not in the bathroom, where – every other day, because heat costs money – I lie semi-submerged and look down the mounds of breast, the risen island of broad stomach, the coral reefs of toes and am grateful for soap and clean water.

It's here in the kitchen I have learned to feel comfortable. I stand here now at the window, a cup of tea warming my palms, and look down. The flat is quiet and empty and I relish the silence.

The trees will start to bud soon. Already I can imagine the scrawls of bare black branch softening and ripening and shining with new life. Another year rolls out at my feet, my fifty-fifth. How the time passes.

I'm getting better. Slowly and unevenly, but there are moments now that I feel myself, my old self. Hopeful, even. My appetite's coming back. My head's clearer.

I see it in my face when I catch a glimpse in the bathroom mirror. The woman there is still hollow-cheeked but her eyes are brighter. She's coming back to life, at last. I can't think yet about what that means. Whether, one day soon, I might find the courage to speak out. I'm too frightened. Because if I try and fail, there will be no hope left, and what will sustain me then?

Far below, a man comes out of the back door of the flats and heads round to the bins with a sack. I peer more closely. He's smartly dressed in slacks and jacket. Dark hair. Quick, purposeful walk. I nod. *I know you.* The man from the flat across the way who washes his fancy car. Quiet but always watching. It takes one to know one. I purse my lips and sip my tea as he reappears and crosses back along the back of the building, then disappears. *I know you. I know where you go, late at night, when you think no one can see. I know who you visit in the dark.*

I look at the clock. Becca will be home soon with Rosie. I'll be gone by then, giving them space, back only in time to let Becca get away to the wine bar for the evening.

I wash up the cup by hand. It's Saturday tomorrow. The day I long for. Becca is working the lunch shift. She hardly leaves that place, now I'm here. Alex will be off with the school, playing football, as he always does. And Ella is coming. I smile to myself as I reach to put the cup away.

We go to the park on Saturday morning. The same park which used to be my home. Already, it seems another life. As we enter the gates, I let go of Rosie and Ella's hands and, like puppies let off the lead, they career, shrieking, down the path towards the play area, jostling and tugging at each other's coats in the battle to win the race. I glance to the side as I pass the bushes where I once lay. The grass is tramped down to one side and for a moment, I feel panic that I've lost my spot, that when I'm turned out again, and it can't be long, I'll have nowhere to go.

The cold air burns our cheeks. I push the girls on the swings and pretend to be a shark, then a crocodile, biting their toes. They scream and think it's a game and it is – but they need to know. too. Beware. Dangers lurk everywhere.

Later, at home, we make jam omelettes and toast and they sit in the kitchen, short legs swinging, munching and talking, always talking, these girls.

'D'you know, Sebbie is five and he's lost two teeth.' Rosie sets down her fork and shifts her lip to show. 'Here. And here.'

Ella considers with solemn eyes. 'Arthur's got a dog called Hector. It's brown.'

They nod, eat.

'More toast?'

Neither answers so I sit between them and eat it myself. Ella's looking pale today. She's a slight child at the best of times, an elf, but today the hollows in her cheeks seem more defined than usual.

'Good girl, Ella.' She seldom has much appetite. 'Try some more omelette.'

Rosie says: 'D'you know, if you dig a really, really big hole and keep digging and keep digging, you can make a tunnel right through the world.'

Ella says: 'Why?'

Rosie shrugs, forks another piece of omelette. 'You just can.'

'It would get very hot,' I say. It's the teacher in me. 'The middle of the earth is so hot, all the rocks have melted.'

They don't answer.

'That's what happens with volcanoes,' I say. 'Melted rock called lava bursts out.'

Ella says: 'I know that.'

Rosie says: 'D'you know, the most fastest animal of all the animals is a chimpanzee.'

Ella blinks across at her.

I consider and then decide to say: 'Actually, I think it's a cheetah.'

Rosie rolls her eyes, her newly discovered scornful look. 'That's what I said. Silly.'

I let it go.

Later, in the sitting room, we sit together on the sofa bed and watch one of Rosie's DVDs. I don't usually approve of television but Ella seems particularly subdued and I sit close to her, my arm around her narrow shoulders. She cuddles into me and rests her head on my shoulder. She smells of the park. Of outdoors and fresh grass and the winter's remnants of leaf mulch. I touch my cheek to her hair and close my eyes, just for a second, drinking her in.

A sound in the hall. The rattle of Becca's key in the lock, the click of the opening door. I get to my feet and stride through to the kitchen to put the kettle on, jolly and matronly, playing my part.

That evening, Becca heads out at half-past six for the Saturday night shift. Best money of the week, she says. They're fully booked. She gets ready in a flurry of movement. As she says goodbye, Rosie clings to her thigh: 'Don't, Mummy! Don't go!'

Becca hesitates, looking stricken.

I put my hands on Rosie's shoulders, hard and bony under her thin nightshirt. I say over her head: 'Off you go. She's fine. We're having baths and then stories, aren't we, Rosie?'

Becca leaves but her eyes are miserable with guilt. I want to say to her: *This? You think this makes you a bad mother? This is nothing. Believe me. You have no idea.*

But I can't. She must never know.

Later, when Rosie is asleep, I go through to the kitchen where Alex is slumped over his homework. His books are open but his games console is on his knee, hidden under the counter. As if I didn't know.

I run the tap until the water comes hot and fill the bowl, add the washing-up liquid and see the bubbles rise. One of life's small pleasures.

'Just put them in the dishwasher.' His weary, superior tone. How he hates me, this boy. How he hates everyone.

I don't answer. I pull on Becca's rubber gloves, pick up the sponge and start to clean. Plates and bowls. Spoons and forks. What great writer ever wrote about washing up? I dredge through the sludge in my head for a quote. Nothing found. But why not?

I rinse off a plate and put it to drain. Not enough women in the annals, maybe. For all his understanding of the fairer sex, did Shakespeare ever crouch over a bucket to wash out a flagon or two? I suspect not.

'Gross. They're not for washing up,' Alex says, from behind me. He means the gloves. I know. He's right. I've seen her wear them and not at the sink. But my hands are calloused enough. 'They're for cleaning the bathroom.' *Pick, pick.*

I fall into a new rhythm of sploshing water and soap and try to escape him. *Toad, dressed absurdly as a washerwoman, up to his elbows in suds.* I had that book, as a child. *The Wind in the Willows.* I should tell Rosie and Ella that story. They might like it.

'Why are you still here, anyway?'

I sigh. I glance up at the dark square of window and see the room reflected back at me, the shape of the boy seated at his homework, his head raised, staring at my back. He's a teenager. He's cross, not just with me but with the whole world.

'You'd better ask your mother that, not me.'

Spoon and knife. Bowl and plate. Pots to come. Almost done.

'We don't need you. Anyway, I'm too old for a babysitter.' He's spoiling for a fight. I don't answer. I just wait for him to let it out.

He hesitates, uncertain how far to push me.

'My dad says you're mental. He says a normal person wouldn't end up on the street.'

I let the plate fall and turn to face him, not angry, just sad for him.

'Lots of people end up on the street. Life doesn't always work out the way you expect. However hard you try.'

He pulls his eyes away from mine and his cheeks redden.

For a while, neither of us speaks. I say: 'I am not mental. I've just had some problems along the way.'

He bites his lip, staring fixedly at the wall. 'Why don't you get a proper job, then?'

I breathe deeply. 'I used to be a teacher. An English teacher. But I made a mistake and I can't do that any more.'

He slides his eyes to my face. 'What mistake?'

'I'm afraid I can't tell you that.' I pause. I want to be honest with him, to help him understand how complicated the world is, even for adults. Finally, I say: 'Do you know why I can't tell you? It's because I feel ashamed.'

I turn back to the dishes and he turns his eyes to his books and we don't speak of it again.

The next morning, I make up sandwiches from the fridge, pull on my old boots and coat and head out early, before even Becca has stirred. The morning is damp and chill and the street outside is deserted.

I head down the high street. Somewhere along the river, church bells are tolling, signalling the start of an early morning service. Calling worshippers to prayer. It's an eternal sound, old-fashioned somehow, in the high street which is strewn with plastic beer glasses and burger wrappers and, here and there in the corners, the stain of vomit.

Low light shines from the windows of the café at the back of the park. The first flowers are poking through, down the edge of the path. Crocuses. Mini daffodils. The first sign of spring. Steam rises from the vents along the back of the roof, over the small kitchen. Dark shapes move to and fro behind the opaque side windows. I move stealthily to the back door and hover there.

'Professor. What're you doing here?'

I swing round. Mick's voice. I sense him in the shadows.

'Mick? That you?'

He steps out of the darkness and the falling light from the back window catches his face. I frown. He's changed. His cheeks look hollow, his chin dark with stubble. His skin, stretched tight over his nose, distorting his features, has a grey pallor. His forehead is beaded with sweat.

He just looks at me. I try to shift my expression, to look pleased to see him, but too late. He seems to read my shock.

'Not in good nick, Professor,' he says. 'Just one of them things.'

His voice is slower than I remember, as if he has to think to form the words. His eyes, usually so sharp, look dull. His injured arm hangs limp at his side, the plaster cast grey and peeling now.

I gesture to it. 'About time they got that off, isn't it? Is it all right?'

He shrugs. 'No, it bloody hurts. I'm not going back there again.'

I bring the sandwiches out of my pocket and hand them to him. 'Brought you these.'

'Ta.' He shrugs and his good arm reaches for them without enthusiasm. He nods towards the back door of the café. 'Get me a coffee, would you? Latte. Three sugars.'

I hesitate, wondering for a moment why he doesn't go inside himself, why he was skulking in the darkness when I arrived. His pride, I think. He knows how he looks. He doesn't want his friends, who've given so much, so often, to realise how far he's fallen.

When I come out with his free coffee, we skirt the park and walk down to the embankment, sit side by side on a bench there and look out over the water. There's the first hint of dawn on the horizon. No sign of a sunrise, just a broad lightening of the thick cloud. I take the lid off the coffee and put it in his good hand, take the sandwiches and open them out on my knee for him to take.

'No offence, Professor,' he says, grimacing over the first sandwich. Cream cheese and lettuce. 'But you're no chef. Stick to the books, you know?'

'Offence taken.' I shrug and add, to make him smile: 'You shouldn't be so damn picky.'

We're both trying too hard. He pretends not to see the difference between us now. That I'm clean and dressed in Becca's decent cast-offs, that safe, warm sleep at night has helped the scabs and cuts on my hands, my feet, my face, to heal, and that a diet of regular meals shows itself in my cheeks. He nods to my hand which is holding the sandwiches steadily. No shakes today.

'You off the booze then?'

I nod. I pretend not to notice the tremors in his good hand and the smell he gives off: stale urine and dried sweat. His fingers, poking out from the plaster, are pasty and swollen.

'Shame.' He sighs. 'Because I'm out at the minute. Keep running dry, God help me.'

'That's not like you.'

He gives me a wry, sideways look. 'I'm not me, any more. That's the truth.'

A duck scrabbles along the surface of the water, then takes off, wings flapping, soaring along the length of the water. On the far side, a man calls to his dog. The name isn't clear but the low notes of his voice skim the surface of the river.

'Can't they sort you out?' I nod at his arm. 'The doctors?'

He pulls a face and doesn't answer. 'I'm done, Professor. You know what?' He looks out at the water. 'I've a mind to head back up north. Back home.'

I blink. I can't believe he's serious. 'Really?'

'It's time.' He stares out vacantly at the water, avoiding my eyes. 'Sometimes you just know.'

He falls silent. I try to push another sandwich on him, but he waves it away and sips the cooling coffee.

I say, trying to sound cheerful: 'That all sounds a bit morbid.'

He shakes his head. 'It's those thugs that did my arm – they've got it in for me. They don't mess about. I might not make it, next time.'

We sit for a while, two shabby old friends side by side in the quiet of the early morning. The light grows, drawing the outlines of the bridge, the trees, the buildings along the opposite shore.

Two young women jog along the path behind us, looking fitter than I think I ever was. A young man pushes a baby buggy.

'Can I ask you something?'

He inclines his head without answering.

'What about your kids?'

He frowns. 'How'd you mean?'

'Well.' I hesitate. 'Will you go and see them, if you go back home?'

He blows out his cheeks. 'I'd like to. I miss them. You know? But their mum wouldn't be too pleased. And anyway, they don't need an old wreck like me pitching up, do they?' He pauses, thinking. 'I'm not all bad. You know that, don't you, Professor? Just keeping my head above water. Bit of fencing here, bit of trading there. Never did anyone any harm.'

'So why are those men after you?'

Mick drains his coffee cup. 'I couldn't mind my own business, could I? I saw a kid one day in the mall. They'd set him up, carrying drugs. He only looked about ten. Shaking like a bloody leaf. I took his rucksack off him, emptied the crap in a bin and sent him home. Told him to stay close to his mum and dad for a few weeks, everywhere he went, and sing like a canary if they came after him.' He blows out his cheeks. 'Don't know if he did. Anyway, one way or another, they figured out it was me.' He hesitates. His eyes, puffy and red-rimmed, struggle to focus on me. 'Look, Professor, listen to an old bloke – I know you've done stuff. Stuff you don't want to own up to.'

I open my mouth to interrupt and he stops me with a look and carries on.

'I don't want to know. That's your business, see? But you've got another chance, see? God knows why. Don't screw it up. Grab it with both hands. Set things right, whatever you did. Sort it out.'

I swallow hard. I can't answer.

The effort seems to cost him. He sinks back into his seat and seems at once tired and diminished. He sits very still, looking out at the river. All around us, the day's beginning. The rhythm of traffic crossing the bridge picks up to reach a steady, distant hum. Behind us, rowers and joggers and dog-walkers hurry along the path.

He says: 'I'm going to miss all this.'

Something in his tone frightens me. I say: 'It'll always be here, Mick.'

He narrows his eyes without looking at me. 'Yes, but I won't.'

His head sags. I thread my arm along the back of the seat and grasp his far shoulder and pull him towards me. I expect him to resist, to shake me off and tell me not to be daft. But he doesn't. He topples towards me as if his strength has ebbed and I lean his cheek against the soft worn pad of my coat and stroke his hair, matted and filthy but still human, still Mick, and feel the heat of the fever rising from his skin.

His muscles slacken and I raise my other arm to make a circle round him and hug him tightly to me, this broken man, holding him as he shudders and sobs, the same way I held my girl when she needed me, when she crawled on my lap all those years ago and pressed her face in my neck, the same way I would like to be held someday, if there is ever anyone to love me again.

*

I had so much love, once. So much, I bathed in it. I thought I knew how lucky I was, but when it's engulfing you, you can't see it. You breathe it in, swallow it every day and become accustomed. You can't stand back and see it for what it is: extraordinary and priceless – and fragile, too.

It was my fault. All of it. I destroyed it. No one else. That's the pain of it. How can I tell you? How can I ever tell? Whatever misery I suffer, whatever hardness life gives, I deserve it. I have sinned. *All the perfumes of Arabia.*

I didn't see much of John when we were growing up. Christy and I hung out together but John – her passionate, brilliant twin

– was seldom around. Football, rugby, guitar, drums, karate. He had wild crazes, one after another. It was always the best thing ever and we watched from a distance, marvelling at his energy.

All I knew was that Christy would nod knowingly to me, when I was round at their house and he swept through, a whirlwind, slamming the door behind him. 'It's rock-climbing now,' she'd say. She didn't have to explain. I knew that, whatever it was, he'd be intent, saving up for all the gear, training all hours, pushing himself to excel. He was a force of nature. I was too shy even to talk to him.

And then we all left school and Christy disappeared to the south coast to study and John and I found ourselves at the same college in the north. He made a point of seeking me out. I didn't even think he'd remember who I was. And suddenly the new craze was me. Maddy. I've never been happier. And he was, too, for a while.

He whirled into my life like a hurricane and swept me up, dizzy and crazy and, yes, destructive too but it was worth it, just to be with him. We were young then. I was passionate about English and a solid, hard-working student until he burst in. He was passionate about everything, in his own chaotic, untutored way. He used to tease me for loving studying more than I loved him. Absurd. I set down my books in a heartbeat when he appeared at the door, his hair messed up, his shirt crumpled, his eyes shining.

'Let's go, Maddy. Come on.' He seemed always on fire, reaching for me, tugging me out of my corner, out at a gallop. 'Life's too short.'

My tutor wasn't pleased. He called me in at the end of my second year. The year John claimed me as his own.

'I have high hopes for you,' he said. He was a thin man with large eyebrows who wore leather waistcoats. 'You're top-student material. You're capable, Madeleine. But you've got to focus.'

John laughed when I told him. I knew he would. It became a catchphrase for him – '*You're capable, Madeleine.*' He'd put on his stern face, balanced on his elbow at my side in my single bed. 'Just *focus*.'

He turned life from black and white to colour. Plays. Parties. Day trips. Knocks on the door at one in the morning and there he was, madness in his eyes, urging me out with him to some all-night bar, drinking, dancing, messing about.

I'd always liked a drink or two when I was nervous: a shot of Dutch courage to get me through a party, a disco when we were teens. I could never afford more than that. He was the one who really gave me the taste for it, who taught me how to keep drinking until the bottle was empty, as he did, how to let go of all my doubts and insecurities and inhibitions and fly. He was Icarus, my brightly shining candle. On fire. Casting everything else, everyone else, into shadow. Oh, my John.

We didn't tell Christy. Maybe that was wrong of me, keeping it a secret. I just remembered how much she mocked his girlfriends, when we were younger. They worshipped him, she said, laughing about this one's hair or that one's make-up, but they'd never keep him. None of them was ever smart enough, pretty enough, worthy of her brilliant twin. I saw it, even then – she didn't want to share him. Not even with me.

It was still a secret when we graduated. John got a job in advertising. He was heading for great things, they told him as much. His flair, his creativity, his boundless energy. They loved him then. I was happy to put my career second to us. My degree was only mediocre, but I didn't mind. I was too happy. Too much in love. John was all-consuming.

So we moved into a bedsit and I found somewhere local to do teacher training. He earned enough to cover the rent. We ate beans on toast and spent the little money we had left on booze, on partying. I did my best to make something of our place, cramped as it was. I had some old-fashioned idea of giving it a woman's touch with throws and unusual vases and bowls I dug out of second-hand shops. I'm not sure he even noticed. I just wanted to please him. To make him happy. To make sure I wasn't just another passing craze.

Then he announced that he had a surprise. He was bringing an old friend round for dinner on Saturday night. Someone he wanted me to meet. He was impish, his eyes full of glee.

'Who?' I thought of the trail of teenage girlfriends, the school friends who played in the same sports team or joined his rock band.

'Someone special.' He took my hand and whirled me around on the thin carpet. '*Super* special.'

My stomach fluttered. I tried to sound jokey. 'What? Special-er than me?'

He kissed me on the tip of my nose. 'Who could be special-er than you, love of my life?'

I had essays and lesson plans to do that week but even as I worked, sitting at our shabby table, I planned. On Saturday, John dashed off to play football. He was gleaming with excitement.

'Darling!' He bent me backwards over his arm for a movie star kiss. 'Don't you love surprises?'

I did my best. I walked round the shops finding the best cuts of meat I could afford and made a casserole. I grated my knuckles raw making a lemon cake. I picked wild flowers and arranged them in a jar. I vacuumed and scoured.

Finally, once the table was set with our mismatched crockery, I had a shower and dressed with care in the least shabby of my charity shop clothes. I studied myself in the mirror, then went to find an old shawl and tied it round my shoulders, then looked again. Whoever it was, I wanted to impress them. To look grown up and sophisticated. I wanted John to be proud.

Seven o'clock. He said they'd be here about seven. I sat by the table, the window ajar, looking down at the street, several floors below. My stomach was tight with nerves. At seven thirty, I opened one of the cheap bottles of wine I'd bought and drank off a glass, then a second. I was going for a third when I heard voices.

John, loud on the stairs. 'Come on! Wait and see!' He sounded drunk.

Then, as they came up the stairs, a woman's voice, low and indistinct. I should open the door, greet them as they came up the final flight, act the hostess. Instead, I froze, paralysed with nerves. I pulled the shawl closer round my shoulders and waited.

John's key rattled in the lock and the door was flung open.

'Ta-dah!' He was laughing. 'Surprise! Behold, my mystery lover!'

Christy walked in, stopped dead. Our eyes locked. 'You!' She looked furious.

I stared back at her, too shocked to speak.

She turned back to John. 'Is this one of your bad jokes?'

He pulled a comical, sad face. 'Aw, that's not nice, sis. Be kind.'

She turned back to me. 'You bitch. How could you?'

I didn't move. She walked round the room, picking holes in it all with her eyes. She picked up a faux crystal vase, a small china ornament, fingered the crocheted mats and the cheap throws. Her eyes were hard with disdain. She didn't need to say anything. I knew her too well.

She turned to John as if I weren't even there. 'What's with all the crap? I thought you had better taste.'

I flushed. John looked sheepish. If he'd failed to notice my pathetic home touches before, he was seeing them now and in the worst possible light.

'Don't be like that.' He put a hand on her arm.

She stopped at the table and looked at the bunch of wilting flowers.

'Funny how you both forgot to mention it, your little romance,' she said. 'How long's this been going on?'

John shrugged. He picked up the half-empty bottle of wine and poured us all generous glasses.

'Have a drink.' He handed one to Christy. 'Maybe we should have told you. Sorry.' He hesitated, meek. 'I thought you'd be pleased.'

She drank it off, her face sour. 'Pleased? I'm ecstatic.'

It was excruciating. She punished me for the rest of the evening. She didn't have to say very much – I felt every blow. She made a point of dominating the conversation, of laughing with John about times they'd had together as children, experiences only they shared. She sat close to him, touching his arm now and then, stroking his hair.

'My twin brother,' she kept saying. 'My other half.'

He didn't demure.

She made fun of me every chance she got. Through her eyes, it was all ridiculous. My sad little outfit. My cheap casserole – 'Goodness, how terribly bourgeois!' The lemon cake – 'Fancy! What a little homebody you are now, Madeleine.'

I sat and bore it all in miserable silence. A guest at my own execution. It was worse that the scorn she heaped on his earlier girlfriends. She was cruel in a way I'd never thought her capable.

I could see why. I'd hurt her to the core. I was her closest friend and I'd deceived her, I'd betrayed her. I'd secretly stolen away the man who mattered most to her, the one person no one else was ever good enough to have. I understood that. I didn't blame her. I knew how much she adored him. I always had.

The biggest shock for me was John's reaction. I saw with horror how he fawned on her. He laughed when she made mean-spirited jokes at my expense. He clasped her hand and patted her. He piled his scorn on hers, outdoing each other to ridicule the bedsit, the food, me. I hadn't seen them together much before. I hadn't realised that if she adored him, he worshipped her.

When we'd finished eating, she turned to him. 'Let's get out of this shithole and party like the good old days.'

He grinned, already drunk, emptied the rent-pot on the sideboard into his pocket and took her hand.

'Madam. Come away with me, into the cruel night!'

I didn't move. I focused my eyes on his back, willing him to turn, imploring him in my head not to abandon me.

They were at the door when he finally seemed to remember me.

'Coming?' He seemed surprised to see me still sitting there.

I hesitated. I wanted reassurance, some warmth or kind gesture that could make me feel welcome.

Christy narrowed her eyes. 'Yes, what about it, Maddy? Fancy playing gooseberry? Of course, you might want to change before you go out in public.'

I shook my head. I was shaking. 'You go.'

Please, John, please don't leave me here, all alone. Say you'll stay.

He pulled a face. 'Don't be so bloody boring, darling.'

Christy laughed. 'A leopard can't change its spots, John. She's always been boring.'

The door slammed and they were gone. Laughter echoed in the stairwell, then faded to silence.

I sat alone at the table and drank the rest of the wine. The bedsit stank of congealing lemon glaze. When the wine ran out, I ransacked the cupboards. A bottle of cooking sherry was stashed away at the back. I drank the lot.

I blamed myself. I'd known all along. Deep down, I'd known she mustn't find out. That she'd feel betrayed. She was as intense as he was, in her way. Two sides of the same coin.

I made it to the bathroom before I was sick, then drank as much water as I could hold and crawled into bed.

He and Christy came back in the small hours, so drunk they could barely walk. I hunched on my side, head splitting, as they crashed around, knocking over a table, sending a lamp hurtling to the floor, giggling.

The next morning, I got up before them and sought refuge in a local café. I sat there much of the day, drinking pots of tea and eating toasted teacakes, with my coat wrapped around my legs. When I finally went home, Christy had gone.

I wrote to her. I said I was sorry, that we should have told her, that I hadn't mean to hurt her, not for the world.

She didn't answer.

But from then on, something changed. I hadn't only lost Christy, I'd lost part of John, too. It wasn't anything he said or did but a sense I had that something between us had broken and although it appeared to heal, it mended crookedly.

About six months later, as winter set in, John came home from work in a foul mood and wouldn't speak to me. He kicked off his shoes and lay on the bed in his suit, his face in the pillow.

'What's wrong?' I tried to stroke his hair but he shook me off. 'Has something happened?'

He wouldn't talk to me.

It went on. Angry silence. Lethargy.

For several days, he seemed sunken. He was barely able to drag himself out of bed in the morning, wash and get himself to work. He came back early, drew the curtains and crawled into bed without a look, without a word. Was he ill?

I sat beside him in the dark. He didn't sleep. He lay motionless under the covers, curled round on his side like a child. When I touched him, he pushed me away. When I asked him how he was, he didn't answer. He didn't eat.

I went to the phone box on the corner and called Christy. It was all I could think to do.

When I told her what was happening, there was a long silence on the line. Then she said: 'He's just hit a bad patch, that's all.

Everyone has them. Just with John, they're more, you know, intense.'

I was stunned. He'd been like this before, then? She didn't sound surprised or even concerned.

She said, her voice sharp: 'You took the good times, didn't you? If you can't handle the bad ones, get the hell out. He's not like other people. I thought you knew that by now.'

I stuttered: 'Of course.'

'Well, then.' She paused and her breath came hard on the line: 'And I'll tell you for nothing, if you try to change him, if you bleat on about medication and doctors, he'll leave you. He's special. He needs a bit of love and understanding sometimes, that's all.'

Of course, I stayed. I loved him. I learned to deal with his dark days, his depressions, his self-destruction. They didn't come often. Most of his life, John burned bright and I revelled in it. The darkness was just the payment.

From the start, I had known I wanted to be with him. It wasn't romance. It was a need. He was a life force, such an energy that I wanted to be near it always, in its glow, fired by his schemes and passions and raw bursts of energy.

It took us a few years to start a family. I was twenty-five when I found out I was pregnant, and I was thrilled. He was, too. He loved children, he always said so. He talked about having ten and schooling them himself, at home, about converting an old bus and driving them around Europe in the summers, about mammoth sleepovers at weekends and cooking everyone sausages and pancakes. He'd be an amazing dad, I was sure. And he was, in his own crazy way.

I gave up drinking the day I realised I was pregnant. It was all or nothing with me, I knew that. I couldn't risk damaging the baby. Besides, we needed all the money we could get. We still didn't have much but John moved us into a bizarre, one-bedroom flat in a converted candle factory. Heaven knows how he found it. Apart from the elevated bedroom, it was all open plan and a barn of a place. Lofty ceilings and industrial windows with thick sills and bricked-up alcoves and an unwieldy range for a kitchen.

On the day he signed the lease, he bounced around, showing me the views – the quaint iron staircase, open tread, which wound from the main room to the mezzanine bedroom above.

'She'll love it!' He ran around the space as if it were a race track. 'We can play football in here. Build the biggest train track in the world. The biggest fort.'

He sped across to me, skidded to his knees and slid the final few feet towards me. He wrapped his hands around my waist and kissed my large stomach.

'You're gonna love it,' he told the baby inside. 'I can't wait.'

I cast a wary eye over the staircase, wondering how safe it would be for a crawling child. I opened the rusty range and peered inside. It smelt of charred wood.

'Oh, come on!' He grabbed my hand. 'Isn't it perfect? What kid wouldn't love this!'

His grin was infectious.

'How will we afford it?'

He turned away. 'Leave all that to me. It's fine.'

We didn't own any furniture. John started scratching around the city dump on Saturdays and salvaged scrap, hammered it together to make wobbly tables and a lop-sided bed. It didn't matter. I remember them as happy days, sitting on a badly mended chair, plumped up with cushions, my hands resting on the mound of my stomach, feeling for kicks, surveying the empty factory where once women had dipped wicks into vats of molten wax and shaped candles.

John was the only man to come to all the community antenatal classes. He lay on the floor at my side, holding my hand and practising breathing exercises. He bathed the plastic doll and winded it. He studied the stages of labour and asked more questions than anyone else.

The other women smiled indulgently. 'What a love!'

He charmed their socks off. Their own husbands seem indifferent by comparison.

At night, he lay on the rickety bed with a hand warm on my stomach. Sometimes, he put his mouth to my stomach and sang to her. Soft, low songs. I didn't hear them, I just felt them as hot breath on my skin and vibrations through my body.

'She can hear me,' he'd say. 'The midwife said so. She knows my voice.'

He had such plans to attend the birth, to cut the cord, but in the end, his courage failed him. When the contractions came, he descended into such a panicked state that instead of driving me to hospital, as he'd promised, he ordered a taxi for me, kissed me goodbye with terror in his eyes and left me to it.

Afterwards, he appeared on the ward, loud and drunk, his arms wild with flowers and a bunch of garish, pink balloons. He hung back at the foot of bed, afraid.

'It's all right.' I smiled, dizzy with hormones. 'Come and meet your daughter.'

He crept forward and gazed down at the tiny scrunched face, wrapped round in a muslin, sleeping in my arms. His eyes filled with wonder, then with tears.

'Princess! She's perfect!'

I nodded. 'Isn't she just?'

I was settled in a teaching job by then and the school had let me arrange six months' maternity leave, much of it paid. At first, John sulked and said he wanted time at home with us, too. He tried, but within a week he had returned to the office. I was glad. We needed the money.

I made friends with a group of mums, a bus ride away from the old industrial estate where we lived, and we did the usual round of playgroups and coffee mornings. But mostly, I was happy to be at home, sober again, in our crazy, draughty factory with the spluttering range, spending time with our beautiful daughter and waiting for John to come home.

I wondered sometimes what it might be like to live with someone else, someone more conventional. The baby didn't sleep at night and neither did I, those first months. John wanted to help but he didn't know how. He seemed frightened of his own exuberant clumsiness, of hurting her. He wasn't like the other fathers I met. But I had known from the beginning that he wasn't the solid, dependable sort.

And I never knew when to expect him. Some nights, he didn't appear until the small hours and crept in drunk, making a comic performance out of climbing up the spiral staircase on his hands and knees. He was the one who started calling her by her middle name, Charlotte, or his version of it: Charley. I didn't mind. It was part of the fun, part of the specialness.

Sometimes, he turned up in the middle of the day, hiding presents behind his back.

'Hey, Charley! Look what Daddy's doing!'

He clowned about to make us both laugh.

'Surprise! Close your eyes, Charley!'

He brought squeaky bath toys that made Charley squeal and gurgle. He bounded in wearing a tiger mask or plastic spectacles with a stuck-on nose. He popped streamers and showered the floor with scraps of coloured paper. I swept them up. I didn't really mind. He brought life with him, when he was happy. A good life.

And on the bad days, well, we learned to let him be. I walked miles that winter, pushing Charley in her buggy, wrapped up in her snowsuit, her little face poking out at the grey, just to give him peace and quiet when he needed it, to let him sleep. I didn't talk about it. There was no one really to tell. Besides, I'd made my choice. I'd made my bed. And I was happy to lie in it.

Christy sent a parcel of baby clothes soon after the birth, but she never visited. We'd agreed a truce, a superficial peace, for John's sake. But she never truly forgave me, I knew that. We were never friends again, like before. It was partly because I took her brother from her. But mostly it was because I kept it secret from her for so long, for making it clear that my first loyalty was to him, not to her. To her, that was an act of betrayal.

And that was the way we lived, in our old candle factory, stuffy in summer, freezing in winter, cavernous and echoing. I went back to work, part-time, and found day-care. Charley learned to crawl, then walk, then scoot, then cycle, all across our vast vault of a floor.

Each evening, when John was increasingly out drinking with his friends, we cuddled in the double bed together and I told stories about magic kingdoms and castles and bears. We always ended, as her eyes grew heavy, with our favourite, *Peter Pan*. The story of the boy who never grows up and the girl who flies away with him into the dark night and the mother, left behind, who waits with hope by the open window, waiting for her daughter to come home.

Four years. Four sleepless, chaotic, intense crazy years, flying too close to the sun.

How could I not have realised how dangerously low John sank that final month, how bleak his thoughts were, how hard he struggled just to get through the day? How did I not see?

I did know he'd hit darkness, that fourth winter.

There was a week, not long after Christmas, when it poured with rain every day. The sun never seemed to break through the cloud. All week, he drank late with clients and staggered up the iron staircase, clanking and cursing, in the small hours. Charley lay asleep on her child-sized mattress in the corner of our loft bedroom. Usually, if he came home drunk, he crouched beside her, sentimental, stroked her hair and kissed her cheek and watched over her, his eyes wet with tears.

This time, he barely looked. He fell into bed beside me and hunched on his side. It was cold drunkenness, mean-spirited. He smelt of stale sweat and spilt booze. For days, he hadn't bothered to shave.

That morning, and those that followed, I tiptoed round him as he lay, snoring, and tried not to disturb him as we crept downstairs and got ready for the day. When we came back in the evening, he was always gone again.

I thought it was just another bad episode. I thought it would pass. I thought that if I loved him hard enough and gave him space to recover, he'd come back to us and burn brightly again. Do what he did best: bring life and light back into our lives.

In class, at school, I was teaching *King Lear*. I remember. The head teacher came to the classroom door, sober-faced, and beckoned me to come out and I told the children to keep quiet or I'd hear them, to read on without me for a little while.

All she said as she walked me to her office was: 'I'm sorry. Let's hope it's a mistake.'

There were two police officers there, a man and a woman. The woman wasn't much older than I was. I thought: *Oh God, John, what've you done now? Got into a fight? Smashed something up?*

I wish.

They'd found him dead on the railway tracks, wallet in his pocket. The driver said he was just lying there, waiting. He didn't move. Seconds before the train hit, he opened his eyes and looked back at the driver in his cab, clear as anything.

I wish he'd left me a note. Said he'd loved me. Said he didn't blame me.

I wish he'd talked to me.

I wish he hadn't done it.

I wish I'd been different, been there, done something, saved him. I wish I hadn't loved him so much.

*

Afterwards, I wasn't much interested in the world. It didn't seem to matter, without John. A light had gone out and it would never be lit again and there was no way to stand the darkness.

For the years since we met, everything I was, everything I did, had been for him. Without him, a pit opened up and swallowed me whole. A pit full of whisky and gin and vodka. My old loyal friends, back at once, opening their arms to me.

I remember waiting to pay at the local store and the woman in front of me twisting to look over my trolley, stacked with bottles of cheap, own-brand spirits with a packet of frozen fish fingers, a pint of milk and some chocolate biscuits for Charley on top. The way her shocked eyes travelled from the groceries to my face, then jumped away as if they'd been burned.

Mostly I remember lying on the floor. Drinking. Shaking with shock, with grief. The drumming of rain on the windows. The drumming of my heels on the hard floor.

I raged and screamed and cursed him. *How could you? How could you be so selfish? How could you leave me here, all alone?* Later, I sobbed and told him I was sorry, I forgave him, I understood. So please now would he come back to me?

I buttered whole loaves of bread and left the stack of slices on the counter so Charley could help herself. Opened endless packets of biscuits and left them within reach for her to snack. She brought one to me, sometimes. She found me out where I lay, eyes closed.

'You can have one, Mummy. Here.'

I couldn't bear to look at her. She was too like John. Those were his eyes gazing back at me, his uncertain smile. I lay as still as I could, head throbbing, the room tilting and spinning, and tracked her by sound. The rumble of her scooter wheels circuiting the room. Her high-pitched voice, singing and chattering to herself. Sometimes, the bright music and voices of children's programmes on our small television.

A neighbour had a key. She'd collected her from day-care once or twice in the past when she had a fever and I was stuck at work. Mrs Peabody. She was a motherly type, middle-aged, widowed, who lived near the bus stop. *Widowed.* I never truly understood before what it meant.

Now, she kept appearing, there in the flat. No point ringing the bell. I never answered the door or the phone.

Her moon face hung over me. 'Do you want anything, lovey? Cup of tea?'

Charley pushed in at her side and I moved my eyes to her. 'If you could maybe get Charley dressed. Take her to day-care. I'm not feeling too well.'

She nodded, wrinkled her nose. 'Maybe she could stay with me for a while. Just until you're back on your feet?'

I lost track of time. Mrs Peabody came and went with her padding feet, her low, anxious voice, offering water, tea. She brought me fish-paste sandwiches and left them covered with a cereal bowl. The smell grew more foul as the day wore on. Sometimes, my girl curled briefly against me. I knew her smell, the warm press of her small body against mine, no matter how much I'd drunk.

Mostly, I was alone. The weight of the silence was crushing. John was in it. His face. His laugh. Later, his sobbing.

Every day or two, I put a coat over my dressing gown and staggered to the local store. I didn't buy food. I wasn't hungry for food. Just bottles of cheap spirits. Then I crawled back and lay again on the joyless floor, thinking about John, aching for him. I dissected it all, every memory of every day. From the first until the last.

I tortured myself by imagining his despair when he stumbled down the embankment, on that final journey, and lay down, weary in body and soul, on the cold, hard metal of the tracks. I imagined the vibrations down the rails of the on-coming train, as real as the vibrations of his singing through my pregnant body. I saw his eyes, calm and knowing, finding the face of the driver as the train emerged from the tunnel and bore down, too late to brake.

John wouldn't let me be. I couldn't see him, however quickly I turned. But I heard him, there by my side, just out of sight, sobbing as if his heart was breaking. It was too much to bear.

So I drank until I passed out. I welcomed the escape. When I came to, vomiting and head splitting, I welcomed the pain. It was punishment, that's how it felt. Punishment for failing to protect him from himself, to keep him safe, to save him. Christy was right, all these years. I was never worthy of him. I tried, God knows, I tried. But I was never enough.

Mrs Peabody threaded through the days. Her voice changed, from gentle to chivvying.

'Come on, now, lovey. Don't let the little one see you like this. How about a cup of tea? How about a shower?'

She tutted over the uneaten sandwiches. She made me hot drinks which stagnated on the table. She cleaned up the vomit like a trooper. And, all the time, Charley stood wide-eyed, apart from me, and watched.

She blamed me too. I felt it. I'd let her daddy die. I'd let her wonderful, funny, brilliant daddy take his life. She knew as well as I did that it was my fault. That I didn't deserve to go on living without him. That without him, I was nothing.

And then she came. Christy. Mrs P must have looked through my desk and called the numbers in the address book there until she found someone who was obliged to come.

Christy was hard-faced and tight-lipped. She didn't need to say a word. I'd taken John from her and failed him. It was my fault. It was in her face. But what more could she do to hurt me? I was already hurting enough for both of us.

She squatted down by my side on the floor and waved a sheaf of papers at me. Envelopes.

'This can't go on. You've got to move out. You hear? There's no money. Nothing.'

My head was a fog of pain. All I wanted was to be left alone. To be left alone to die.

I think I said as much: 'Go away, Christy. Leave me alone.' Maybe I did. Maybe I just thought it. I don't know.

She was there again. Another day, I think. The day had died. It was all shadows. Her eyes gleamed in the half-light as she tried to make me drink water, tried to make me understand.

'You've got to leave here. They're sending the bailiffs round. No one's paid the bills for months, didn't you know?'

She had a red suitcase. A hard shell on wheels. It wasn't ours. She filled it with Charley's things. Maybe she brought her round too, to say goodbye. Was she there? I don't remember.

Christy said: 'You can come, too. Now, with me. But no more drink. You hear? That's the deal. Sober or not at all.'

Then what happened? I don't know. How can I remember? My time for living was done. She was no longer there and, later, strangers came, burly men in heavy boots.

'You can't stay here, sweetheart. Sorry. Just following orders.'

And so it began. Handouts from strangers. Booze where I could get it. Sleeping in parks, in bus shelters, in doorways. John's weeping always in my head. I went under. I went under for a very long time.

SARAH

Alex takes refuge with me more than ever. He's unhappy with himself. He can't settle at home and he doesn't like Maddy, the bag lady nanny. But he's too young to be out alone. I remember that age. I hated it too.

I like nicking stuff for him. He loves me for it. I see the thrill in his eyes when I hand him the latest game or electronic gadget. He longs for these things, without even understanding why his longing is so desperate and so intense. I think I know. I feel something of myself in him. It's not just the games but what they represent for him. Status. Style. A sense of belonging, for a moment, to a cool, exciting world out there that he can't yet join and that he's afraid will never accept him.

I watch him now, sitting in a corner of my settee, his shoes kicked off, already lost in a computer game. A second game, still shiny and new in its plastic wrapping, sits on the table in front of him. He's got a Coke at his elbow, a bowl of crisps. He couldn't be happier. I sip my glass of white wine, watching him, and smile to myself. I did that.

Later, when it's dinner time, Maddy appears, bringing Ella home and ready to collect Alex. The girls race through to Ella's bedroom and pull out stuffed toys, making the most of whatever time they're allowed here.

'Five minutes!' I warn them from the doorway. Neither head turns. 'Then it's dinner time, Ella, and Rosie needs to go home.'

Maddy stands awkwardly in the middle of the sitting room, looking across at Alex, who ignores her. I hesitate, still outside Ella's room, and take a moment to observe her. She looks different. Her hair's clean and neater and her face is softer. She's put weight on. Her trousers – Becca's old trousers – are less bunched at the waist. She's starting to look almost normal.

Her expression's strained. She looks at Alex, his snacks, then at my half-empty glass of wine. Her eyes jump away from the wine as if it burned her. I know that look. I smell her need.

'Want a glass of wine?' I shouldn't, I know. It's cruel. I can't help myself.

'No, thanks.' She answers too quickly. She doesn't fool me. Her breath is shallow and quick.

I sit down beside Alex and pick up my wine, swirl it around the glass so it rises and falls in waves around the sides, spilling its fragrance, then I dip my lips to the rim. The taste explodes in my mouth and spreads slow heat through my stomach and I savour the glow, the slow dissolve of tight muscles and sinews.

Her face is troubled as she watches my performance. Her hands are fists at her sides.

I smile. 'Take a seat.'

She perches on the edge of a chair, across the room from me.

She says in a low, slow voice: 'Be careful. It takes over, if you let it.'

I say, annoyed: 'What does?' But I know, of course. I know exactly what she means. Alex hinted as much. His father said she had a drink problem, that, at Christmas, her eyes never left the bottle. And she thinks I'm as weak as she is, that I can't handle it? I purse my lips and glare at her as she sits there, looking mournfully across at me, as if she thinks she's so wise, so superior.

'You're looking well.' I say it as a challenge, not a compliment. 'Isn't it time you moved on? You can't stay with Becca forever.'

She doesn't answer.

I press on. 'How long's it been now?'

Her face clouds. 'I haven't been counting.'

I don't know why she bothers me so much. There's something watchful about her, always. Something needy, as if she's biding her time, looking for a chance to question me. It disturbs me, brings out the worst in me. I drink off my wine.

Between us, Alex breaks into a new level in his game and pumps the air: 'Yeah!'

He doesn't lift his eyes from the screen and a second later his thumbs are flashing again. She says with sudden brightness: 'Anyway, why don't you and Ella join us for dinner? There's plenty. We'd love that, wouldn't we, Alex?'

He isn't listening and of course doesn't answer and it's such an abrupt invitation, that it takes me a moment to catch up. I stare. She looks anxious and pathetically eager, as if she's willing me to say yes, but is also afraid of being rejected.

I think: *My god, she's planned this.* I imagine her huddled over recipe books, then making sad little lists and shopping with Becca's money and cooking, all in the hope I'll go upstairs and keep her company, using Ella as bait. Something twists in my stomach, something sharp that makes me want to hurt her, to push her away and stop her from trying so hard with me.

I tug at the gold necklace round my neck, a new one I lifted a few weeks ago, and shake my head.

'How very kind. But I think not. Thanks all the same.'

She deflates at once.

I hesitate but already she's gathering herself together and getting briskly to her feet, saying to Alex: 'Come on, young man. Dinner's ready.'

Alex sighs and blows out his cheeks.

I hand him the brand-new game from the table. 'Take that, if you want. Let me know what it's like.'

His eyes shine. 'Really? Cool. Thanks.'

We head towards the door, stopping to prise Rosie out of Ella's room. Ella jumps up as soon as she sees they're leaving and wraps her arms around Maddy's waist.

'No! You can't go!'

Maddy ruffles her hair and plants a kiss on the top of her head. My breath quickens.

Maddy says: 'I'm afraid we've got to, sweetheart. We'll see you again soon.'

Ella twists back to me. 'Can't I, Mummy? Can't I go with them?'

I tut, embarrassed. 'You've only just come home.'

'But I want to.'

As Maddy ushers Alex and Rosie out of the door, Ella stamps her foot and pouts and I put my hands on her shoulders to hold her back.

As soon as they've gone, Ella twists out of my grasp and storms off to her bedroom.

I follow her. 'Ella! What's the matter with you?'

She lies on the bed, banging the pillow with her fists.

I say: 'You've been up there for hours. I've hardly seen you.'

She won't look at me.

'I'm your mother.' Anger bubbles up from nowhere. Anger about Maddy and the influence she has now on Becca and the girls. The way she's insinuating herself into their lives, into their affections. 'Why do you want to be with her? She's a tramp. A bag lady. She's nothing.'

'You're mean.' She twists around and glares at me, her small face contorted. 'She's my friend. I like her.'

I turn on my heel and go through to the kitchen to heat up her dinner, hands shaking. When I open the fridge, the open bottle of white wine, there in the fridge door, calls to me. *Just one glass. Just one more*. Then maybe the rest later, once Ella's asleep in bed.

MADDY

I can't sleep. It's late. Becca's home from work and already in bed.

I lie on my back on the sofa bed and stare blankly at the ceiling, thinking about her.

She drinks too much. I don't know how to help. She won't listen to anything I say. She despises me. She wants me gone. But why? What have I done to her?

I turn onto my front and bury my face in the pillow. Jealousy. I sense that. She holds the people she loves close, too close. Becca. Rosie. And Ella, of course. The harder I try, the more threatened she seems. I sigh, breathing heat into the hollows around my mouth.

It's hopeless. It doesn't matter what I do. Even if I keep going, stay sober, get on my feet, she'll always see me as a down and out. A loser.

I sit up and peer into the shadows, too restless to sleep. I need a drink.

I can't, I mustn't, I've come too far for that. I lie down again and straighten the duvet. Light flickers across the ceiling and I twist, following the patterns.

No good. I can't sleep. I get up and dress, find my shoes and coat at the door in the darkness and start to feel my way downstairs, hand on the smooth wooden banister. I'm not sure where I'm going. Just out. A brisk walk. Twenty minutes, down the high street, along the river and back, long enough to clear my head.

I've nearly reached the final stairs when the buzzer sounds at the heavy front door to the block and someone pushes it open. I hesitate and duck down to peer through the banister rails. Sarah's door opens too and she steps out in her dressing gown. I narrow my eyes and watch.

A man steps inside and meets her in the entrance hall, kisses her cheek, embraces her. They don't speak. A handsome man in a cashmere coat. I recognise him at once. He's the same man as before, the one I've seen creeping through the shadows to her door, collar raised, and seen him again as he left, much later, saying goodbye by holding her tight. A clandestine visitor who never stays the night.

Sarah glances around and I shrink back into the darkness of the stairwell, heart beating hard. Her door clicks shut.

When I look again, they've disappeared together into her flat, silent and furtive.

SARAH

'Turn around and let me see.'

I'm sitting on a stool in the corner of the changing rooms. Becca wobbles down towards the full-length mirrors at the end, her legs hobbled by the tight skirt and high heels.

She's put weight on, since she started the job. Across her stomach and thighs. Must be all that extra cooking and tasting. I wonder what I can say honestly that might sound encouraging.

'Your legs look amazing, Becca. It's just that skirt... maybe a bit tight?'

She pauses in front of her reflection. I can't see her face from here but her shoulders droop. That's never good.

'How about a dress?'

She bends over and slips off the heels, then comes back in her stockinged feet. She goes straight into the cubicle again without replying. I creep to the curtain and peep around the edge. She's peeling off the skirt and reaching for her black trousers. The same pair she wears everywhere.

I say: 'Let's grab a coffee. We've got time.'

Maddy's taken the girls to the pictures to see the new Disney film. Becca's paying, of course, but at least it gives the two of us a chance to hang out together. She needs cheering up. I just thought some retail therapy might help. It always helps me but, then again, I rarely pay for anything.

In the café, she stirs her cappuccino in a never-ending circle, drawing the chocolate powder on the surface into fading brown spirals.

I say: 'Cheer up. Think how much money you've saved by not buying anything.'

It's a feeble joke and she doesn't even smile.

'Sorry.' Stir, stir.

'What is it, Becca?'

She shrugs. 'Oh, I don't know.'

I know her better than that. 'Yes, you do. Come on. Tell Auntie Sarah.'

She sighs. 'It's Alex. He seems so distant all the time. So moody.'

'Teenagers are supposed to be moody, aren't they?'

'I know but…' She pulls a face. 'I just hate it. He hardly talks to me at the moment. Or Maddy.'

'Everything OK at school?'

'As far as I know. They haven't said anything.' She raises her eyes, imploring. 'I keep finding new stuff in his room. I don't mean to pry, but I've got to clean and he doesn't have much space.'

I try to look surprised. 'Like what?'

'Well, some new trainers, really expensive ones. Computer games. Gadgets. He doesn't get much money from me, I can't afford it. So where's it all coming from?'

'Mark?'

She shakes her head. 'I've asked him. And I've tried asking Alex but he just clams up. He hasn't said anything to you, has he?'

I shake my head and try to look sincere. I'm kicking myself. I thought Alex would do a better job of hiding the stuff I give him but as least he hasn't grassed on me. Yet. I'm very fond of Becca but she knows I don't earn much and I don't want her to get suspicious. She just wouldn't understand my shopping scam, she's too squeaky clean. And, after all, I'm only trying to help.

'I'm sure it's nothing to worry about. He's a good kid.'

She nods and sips her coffee but doesn't look very reassured. We sit in silence for a moment, surrounded by the chatter and bustle of the café.

I lean in towards her and lower my voice. 'You don't think Maddy could have anything to do with it? I mean, you know so little about her, let's face it.'

'Maddy?' Becca frowns. 'I know she can be odd sometimes but she's not dishonest.'

The foam leaves a white moustache on Becca's upper lip and she licks it clean.

I pull a face. 'Well, I hope you're right.'

We're almost ready to leave when she says suddenly: 'I really miss my mum.' She stops and looks me full in the face, embarrassed. 'Silly, isn't it? It's years now, I know. But recently, what with all the upset with Mark and now worrying about Alex, I just really miss her. I just keep thinking maybe she'd know what to do.'

I nod but inside I'm thinking: *Well, at least you knew your mother, at least she loved you. You don't know how lucky you are.*

I always knew I was adopted. The Parents didn't dwell on it, they just fed me some corny story from the start about the fact they loved children so much, they decided to look for a little girl who needed a new mummy and daddy and then they found me and they were so happy, they brought me home to keep. Some crap like that. All about them, in other words.

I just knew not to ask about my birth parents. I don't even know how I knew, just an understanding that it would be ungrateful and hurt them. So, I tried not to think about it. Not to dwell on the fact I never felt I belonged in their home, in their family. They weren't bad people – far from it. It would have been easier if they were. They were fine upstanding members of the local church, known in the community. People were always telling me how lucky I was, as if I was indebted and would have to pay them back in some way. That's a hell of a burden to place on a little girl.

It wasn't their fault that I went off the rails as a teenager. But their priggishness didn't help either. They were so easy to shock. So easy to offend. It was child's play. And whatever I did, they always forgave me and even found excuses. Bailed me out. Drove to strange places in the middle of the night and brought me safely home, sad and disappointed but without reproach, Father with his overcoat buttoned over his pyjamas, his hair thinning and grey at the temples as he hunched over the steering wheel and I sat in ungrateful silence beside him. Mother sitting up in the cold sitting room, waiting, wrapped round in her padded dressing gown and felt slippers, ready to greet me with forgiveness and hot milk. I was usually drunk by that stage.

Did they love me? I suppose so. They seemed frightened of me, too. Frightened of this monster they'd taken on and, because they were so pure and had sought me out as their own, could never bring themselves to desert. Maybe it would have worked better if they had. If they'd once turned round and said: *That's it, one more scene of that sort and you're on your own!* I think I'd have respected them more. Maybe even toed the line.

I was the one who deserted them, in the end. I went wild once I left school, living hand to mouth, sleeping on strangers' floors, in strangers' beds. You can get by when you're young.

I turned up on their doorstep with a stomach swollen with Ella. Little idea who the father was, I could barely remember the names of the men I'd slept with. I didn't go back to tell them because I wanted help, although I did need it. I went because I wanted to upset them. To shock them. To see if I could finally stretch their love to breaking point, after all this time.

It was a Sunday afternoon. I was sure they'd be in, they always were, doing the crossword or reading after Sunday lunch. But it was just Mother that day.

She opened the front door and just stood there for the longest time, looking at me, blinking, as if she couldn't quite believe I'd materialised again after several years of silence. She'd aged. Her cheeks sagged and she'd changed her hair, cut it short as she grew out a lifetime of colour and let it turn silvery grey, and there was a premature tiredness about the way she held herself.

Finally, she said: 'How lovely to see you. Are you coming in?'

I sat on the settee and looked at the photographs along the mantelpiece – I was in most of them – while she boiled the kettle and made tea. She opened a packet of biscuits and put them out on a plate. It made me feel like a visitor, that formality, not a member of the family after all.

I blurted it out at once. 'I'm pregnant. I thought you ought to know.'

Her hand, pouring the tea from the pot, stayed steady.

'Yes, so I see,' she said, and I realised she'd known from the moment she opened the door. 'Are you keeping well?'

And so the love stretched, even there, even after all that time.

Later, after we'd sat for a while in silence, listening to the ticking clock, I started to accuse her. I felt driven. I wanted to get at her, to upset her.

'Why didn't you tell me about my real mum?

She shrugged. 'You never asked.'

I pulled a face. 'How could I? You never let me talk about it, either of you. I always knew it was a closed subject. Out of bounds.'

She looked genuinely surprised. 'Really? How funny. I kept trying to talk to you about her, about the little we knew. You never wanted to hear it.'

I put my hand on my stomach and imagined the baby inside. 'Tell me then. Tell me now.'

She leaned forward and spoke slowly and deliberately, her eyes on my face. 'There's not a lot to tell. I'm afraid your father wasn't very well, I mean, I gather there were emotional problems. He took his own life when you were very little. I'm sorry.' She stopped, her eyes on my face, watching my reaction. 'Are you OK?'

I swallowed. 'What about my mother?'

'She disappeared when he died. There was some talk about her being an alcoholic – I don't know all the details. But in the end, you were made a ward of court, then put up for adoption.' She shrugged. 'That's it, really. You're an adult. You'll be a mother yourself soon. You're perfectly free to find out more if that's what you want.'

I don't remember what else we said that afternoon, just how calm she was. All those years, I thought she'd scream or rail or weep if I tried to find my birth mother, but it seemed I was the one who was frightened of the truth, not her.

'Your father always said you'd ask about it in your own time, when you were ready to hear it,' she said as I got up to leave. 'He's usually right.'

That night, I sat up late in the darkness, alone, trying to remember. Memories lay just below the surface, shimmering, out of sight. They'd settled there, undisturbed, since I was a small child. I'd never tried so hard before to stir them.

A low voice, telling stories, always stories, and when I rested my ear against her chest, listening, the sound of her voice changed, reaching me not just through the air but through our bodies, straight from her bones into mine. And she sang to me. A slow, lilting song. Late at night, if I had a fever or a frightening dream and cried out, she lifted me out of bed and cradled me in her arms and rocked me, her body bent around mine, keeping me safe, her softly singing voice lulling me back to sleep.

There was a vast, echoing room, as lofty as a church and carrying the same scent as one, with thick walls and high windows without blinds. Light poured through the glass, slanting columns of sunshine in which dust danced. It threw puddles across the floor and I scooted in and out of them, skimming along the hard floor. Alone. How could I scoot in church without being caught? I didn't understand.

In the end, as Ella grew inside me and the deadline of her birth loomed, I wrote letters and went online and tried to do my own research and unearthed at last my birth family's last known address, documented on the court records which confirmed that I was made a ward.

My father worried for me. 'You won't reach her there,' he warned. 'It was never her address, just a relative's. She'd already disappeared by that point, love.'

'I know.'

Then later: 'You won't get your hopes up, will you? You know what I mean. She might have died, years ago.' My father paused, feeling his way. 'And even if she's still alive, are you really sure you want to make contact? What if you don't like what you find?'

'I want to find her. Whatever she's like. I really do.'

And so I finally sat down, just weeks before Ella joined this world, after months of doubt and years of wondering, and wrote the letter I'd waited all my life to write. The one that started: 'Dear Mum.'

Time passed. There was no reply.

BECCA

We're so busy at work that for whole periods, half an hour here, an hour there, I block out everything apart from orders and dishes and the race to replenish stock. We peak at some time after nine o'clock and then suddenly we come back to ourselves, the wave has crashed all around us and broken and we shake ourselves off, look around again, garnishing desserts and starting the slow process of consolidating, clearing up and making lists for Monday.

That's when the worry about Alex and the mess of breaking up with Mark come rushing back to fill the vacuum and for a second, I don't want to surface to real life, I want to stay under in the world of work.

'Red or white?' Jane pokes her head through the serving hatch. It's another feature of these mad evening shifts – a drink on the house towards the end. I drink so little nowadays that it's a treat.

She comes through a moment later with glasses in hand. Red for me. Generous measures. I've barely eaten since lunch and it hits my stomach at once.

'How's she done tonight?' Jane calls across the tiny kitchen to Dennis.

He's scraping dollops of leftover beef bourguignon into a plastic box.

He grunts and says: 'Not bad,' over his shoulder.

Jane smiles at me and raises her glass. 'That's high praise, trust me.'

When I get home, the flat is quiet. The door to the sitting room is ajar and I peer into the shadows to make out the large, prone shape of Maddy, asleep on the sofa bed. Her breathing is heavy. The curtains are parted and the sash window raised a few inches, letting in a low, cool current of air.

In their room, Alex and Rosie are both asleep in bed. As I pull their door gently closed, I see the shiny case of another new computer game, gleaming in the thread of light through the curtains. I cross to my own room and lie in bed, a knot in my stomach, wondering what on earth is going on.

I stare into the gloom, sickened. I don't know my son any more. I'm not sure what to think, what to believe him capable of doing. I twist onto my side and curl up my knees and try to think of the last time he and I did something alone together: watched a film or went shopping or even just had a quiet, relaxed chat in the kitchen. I shake my head. There just isn't time. Mark takes Alex out alone once in a while – his soccer buddy. But when Alex is at home with me, I always have so much else to do, and Rosie demands constant attention.

I twist onto my back and kick off the covers, suddenly too hot. I've lost touch with my son. My Alex. How could I have let that happen?

He was such a loving little boy. We were happier then, Mark and I. Alex seemed a miracle to us both. In those early months, soon after his birth, I felt so heavy with happiness that time seemed to stop. All the rush and bustle of the world of work seemed ridiculous. Nothing else mattered but holding him, feeling his small body cuddled into mine, gazing at him asleep in my arms, milk-drunk after a breastfeed, his pale skin almost translucent, his eyelashes dark and delicate.

I remember getting up in the middle of the night just to stand in the half-light in my bare feet and stare down into his cot while he slept. We made this boy, Mark and I. We created this beautiful, clever child. As the years passed, every time Mark hinted at the idea of trying for a second, I said no. Too early. Too soon. What's the rush? We're still young.

I couldn't tell him the real reason, that I didn't want another child barging in and disrupting what I had with Alex. He was my joy and I was the centre of his world and it was perfect. How could I hope to have another child as amazing as him? How could I be as besotted?

It was a foolish fear, of course. When Rosie finally came all those years later, she was just as wonderful to me and I fell head over heels in love all over again. But in one way, I had been right. She did prise me away from Alex. Suddenly Mark became the one who had time to talk to him, to play with him, to spend time with him while Rosie clung to me.

I sit up in bed and wrap my arms round my body and suddenly I long for the days when he was a small boy again and came running if he lost sight of me for a moment, his hands outstretched, his eyes shining, calling for me.

Where did he go, that sweet, open-armed boy? How did I lose him?

MADDY

An awkward week. Suddenly the flat seems to have shrunk even further, and Becca and I practically bump into each other whenever we're both there. When she isn't working, I pull on my patched blue coat and take myself out. Walking, mostly. Revisiting a few familiar doorways, the embankment down by the river where Mick and I sometimes drank, a deep, dry bush or two. There's no trace of him. I wonder if he really has gone back home, if he's found the courage to seek out his children and, if so, how they treated him.

Already I wonder how I ever survived out here, on the streets, in the cold. That's dangerous in itself. Far worse to soften up from a short stay back in bricks and then be pitched back into outdoor life. Vulnerable in body, vulnerable in spirit. And for the moment, I'm still sober, clutching on to my one chance. Frightened of the abyss if hope abandons me.

Becca doesn't need to say a word. She's tense and I sense that something's recently changed between us, that whatever thread grew between us has torn. I don't know why. I try to stay invisible for a while. Fortunately, that's my forte.

Alex keeps to his room, out of my way. I stay out of Becca's hair. Rosie and I? Well, we rub along much the same as before. When I take charge, in her mother's absence, I'm happy to play schools – her new obsession – to act the schoolgirl to her Miss Lily. It suits us both very well.

Saturday is an Ella day. Becca goes out early to prep and cook for the lunchtime service. Alex is going out to see a school friend.

He says he wants to do homework with him, that they need to work together on some project. I very much doubt that but Becca seems willing to believe what she wants to believe and lets him go. I'm glad to see the back of him. He's been sulking in his room all week, like Achilles in his tent.

We paint unicorn pictures today, Rosie's choice. Ella gives me a hug when she arrives and I sit next to her, across the table from Rosie. Ella's hair smells of traffic fumes and, somewhere deep underneath the pollution of the outside world, of camomile shampoo. Her forehead creases as she works, the tip of her tongue sticking out of the corner of her mouth. When Rosie messes about, Ella looks up and laughs and shows the dimple in her cheek. Despite my forebodings and all the warnings I give my old, battered heart, it melts to a puddle at the sight.

Then Rosie starts getting silly and before long, she gets paint everywhere. One minute, they're kneeling up at the kitchen table which is covered in sheets of old newspaper; the next, red and yellow paints are sploshing in arcs of colour through the air and leaving splatter marks down the kitchen cupboard doors.

'Oh.' Rosie holds her fat paintbrush and looks worried.

Ella lifts her forearm – her hands are too daubed in paint to use – and awkwardly tries to wipe the bridge of her nose. I look more closely. Her nose and one cheek are sprayed with droplets of colour.

'How did that happen?'

'Like this.' Rosie waves her brush to demonstrate. She looks happier already, realising I'm not cross. More paint spins through space and lands on Ella's face.

'That's enough now.' I take Rosie's brush. 'Ella, go and wash that off in the sink.'

I untie the strings of her apron and slip it over her head. She trots off obediently towards the bathroom.

'Right.' I stand back and survey the cupboard doors. 'Can you help?'

Rosie jumps down and tears off a piece of kitchen paper. She strains to reach the tap and wet it, then comes to help me to wipe the surface clean. It takes us a while. At first, the paint just spreads and it looks worse than ever and it takes us several sheets of paper and a floor cloth to make headway. By then, Rosie's hands, her fingernails especially, are rimmed with red and yellow. I bring a kitchen chair to the sink so she can kneel up and reach and fill the washing-up bowl with warm, soapy water.

She's almost the right colour again when Ella re-appears. Her face glistens. Her top and trousers are dripping wet.

'I'm freezing.' She wraps her arms around her body and pulls a miserable face.

I hand Rosie a towel and start on Ella.

'Take off those wet clothes. Can you do that? I'll see if your mummy sent us any clean ones.'

Her backpack, which came carrying her water-bottle, snack and favourite bear, sits in the hall, close to the front door. I start to rummage through it. There are stripy trousers inside and clean pants, but no sign of a fresh top.

I take the bag into the sitting room where the light's better and go through the pockets. Zipped pouches on the front and down the sides. Not much. A broken crayon. A few torn bits of paper. A printed card which came with a chocolate bar and shows a cartoon sheep.

I'm about to give up when my fingers close on something else, something hard and irregular inside the lining, along the back near the bag's small, padded straps. I tug the zip open a bit further and search.

Something's stuck at the back there. It moves when I reach for it with my fingertips, sticking my fingers into the jagged side of the lining. A chain. I manage to hook it at last with my little finger and draw it out. A gold necklace, the price tag still attached. At the side, the remains of a security tag, prised away.

When I lift it and let it turn, the light streaming in through the window sets it sparkling. It's delicate, finely worked, and has the weight of gold. It coils in my palm.

I reach into the bag again and prise out more. A second necklace, also gold, but this one lightly studded with pearls. Finally, an amber ring. I frown, trying to make sense of what I've found. I think of Sarah's flashy jewellery and the brand-new computer games she lent Alex the other day, and all of Ella's shiny, expensive toys and I feel a sudden chill.

'Maddy!' Rosie's voice, hollering from the kitchen. She'll be through in a second, looking for me. 'Where are you?'

I thrust the jewellery back into the hiding place and leave Ella's bag by the front door, and go into the children's room to get one of Rosie's tops.

'Here. You can borrow this.'

Ella stands in the same spot, her wet clothes in a heap on the floor at her feet, her thin arms wrapped around her ribs. I hurry to dress her, then take her on my knee to hug her warm.

BECCA

The lunch shift has been steady but not too bad – a lot of quiches and salads – and because of all the prep I did during the morning, we're still well stocked for the evening.

Jane comes back into the kitchen to ask what we'd like to drink.

'Should be able to get you out early,' she says. 'Tables three and seven might need dessert but otherwise it's just coffees. I can finish up.'

I bend down and stack the dishwasher, pass the worst pots and pans through to the back. My mind is already moving on, shifting from orders and cooking to the things I need to do for home. Shopping. I can swing by the supermarket on the way back. I could cook shepherd's pie for supper. Bake some chocolate cupcakes, for a treat.

A gentle male voice at the bar asks for another glass of water and for a moment I think it's David and my heart quickens. I look up and peer through the hatch, wondering how I look, flushed with the heat of the kitchen and probably dishevelled. But it's not him at all. There's some middle-aged man talking to Jane, one I haven't seen before. Part of the quiche and salad brigade.

My phone rings in my bag and I rush to answer it, just get there in time. Number withheld. I frown. A cold call, perhaps. I've had a few of those recently.

A man's voice. Official. 'Is this Rebecca Williams?'

'Yes. Who's speaking please?'

'This is Jonathan Marshall, head of security at Clary's in the mall.'

'Clary's?' I struggle to catch up. The big electronics shop. I haven't been in there for years.

'Are you able to come down here please? To the store?'

My knees start to buckle and I lean heavily on the kitchen counter. 'Why? What's happened?'

The voice is impassive. 'There's been an incident at the store, I'm afraid. I'd rather discuss it face to face, if you could come down—?'

'An incident?' I shake my head. I think of Rosie, of some awful accident. 'What do you mean?'

'Theft, Mrs Williams. Ask for me by name. Jonathan Marshall. They'll know what it's about.'

As we end the call, I close my eyes and the kitchen swims.

Jonathan Marshall is a tall, thin-faced man. His expression is stern. He doesn't shake my hand, just gives a grim nod and leads me through the store towards the back. Everything we pass looks suddenly different. Darker. The shoppers seem so carefree, so innocent. The brightly coloured signs, the brimming shelves with their offers, their specials, make me feel physically sick with worry.

Mr Marshall leads me through an unmarked door and down a short, shabby corridor, lined with cupboards and lockers. He holds open the door to a side room.

'Alex!'

He's alone inside, sitting hunched forward, his elbows on the table, his face in his hands. His shoulders shake. His rucksack is open on the table. A computer game lies beside it.

I want to put my arms round my boy, to hold him to me and say: *It'll be ok, buddy, whatever you've done, we'll work it out.* But I'm out of my depth and trembling and Mr Marshall presses into the room with us, closing the door, watching everything.

'What happened?'

Mr Marshall says: 'He was with two other boys. Sixteen-year-olds. They tried to prise the security tag off a pair of noise-cancelling headphones and leave the store with them. It's all on CCTV.'

I stare at Alex in disbelief. He doesn't lift his head, doesn't look at me.

'I'm so sorry.' I'm desperate. I pull out my wallet. My voice runs on, garbled. 'I'll pay. Whatever they cost. Of course. I don't know who those other boys are but Alex has never done anything like this before. Never. He's only fourteen.'

Mr Marshall's eyes bore into me and I bite my lip, trying not to cry. I mean nothing to him. He must do this every Saturday. Just another teenage shoplifter. Another shocked mum.

'The other boys are known to us.' He nods at the wall. 'They're next door. I've called the police this time. I'm afraid they've left me with little choice.'

'The police?' I stare at him, aghast. 'I mean, are you sure Alex really took something? He wasn't just watching?'

Mr Marshall looks down his long nose at me. 'We've reviewed the CCTV footage. It shows the other two stealing the item between them. Your son was clearly with them but at the back. He's guilty by association.' He moves past me and lifts the computer game, brandishes it. 'This was in his bag, Mrs Williams. I can't be certain it came from this store. But we have had several similar items stolen in the past week.'

Alex lifts his face at last and gazes at me. His eyes are red and swollen with crying. His nose is stringy with mucus. I've never seen him look so afraid.

'Alex says you purchased this for him some time ago, as a gift. Can you confirm that?'

I steady myself and take a deep breath, pull my eyes away from Alex's beseeching look.

'That's right,' I lie. 'I bought it online. As a present.'

I take a step towards Alex, partly to hide my burning face from Mr Marshall, and stand against him, put my hands on his shoulders.

'Thank you, Mrs Williams.' Mr Marshall's voice carries a hint of sarcasm. Panic rises through my chest. He's going to ask for evidence. An online receipt. A record of the order in my emails. I'm trapped.

The room seems to hold its breath, waiting for him to decide what will happen next. My hands are trembling and I don't know which of us is shaking more, me or Alex.

Finally, Mr Marshall says: 'I suggest you take Alex home and the two of you have a good long talk. You might wish to explain to him that once his so-called friends have criminal records, it's going to make it very hard for them to get jobs in the future.' He stoops and turns directly to Alex. 'As for you, I don't ever want to see you in this shop again. Understand? Count yourself lucky that your mother's backing you up. I'm tempted to hand you over to the police with the other two and see what they make of it. You've had a very narrow escape.'

Alex shrinks into himself, petrified and slight.

Mr Marshall escorts us out, through the entire store. A long walk of shame. Alex, red-faced and sniffing. I watch our moving feet along the floor tiles, feeling the eyes of other shoppers turning on us, praying we're not seen by anyone we know.

I wait until we walk further through the mall and are around the corner from Clary's, then stop and put my arms around him and pull him tight. I don't know whether to hold him or shake him, whether to soothe or scream.

'I lied, Alex,' I say. I'm weak with shock. 'I lied to get you out of trouble. I don't ever, EVER want to do that again.'

We manage to move a few more steps through the shops, then again stop. We both seem to have forgotten why we're there or how to get home again.

I take his face in my hands. 'Did you steal that game?'

He shakes his head, emphatic. 'I didn't, Mum. I really didn't. I just brought it to show them. I swear.'

I glare down at him. 'So where did it come from?'

He twists away his eyes at once. 'I can't tell you. I'm sorry. I promised. But I didn't nick it. I honestly, honestly didn't do that.'

MADDY

Alex and Becca arrive home together. As soon as I hear her key in the lock, I know something's up. She always shouts a cheery hello from the front door, however tired she is. This time, she's silent.

Rosie, Ella and I are cutting and sticking at the kitchen table. I go to the kitchen doorway and look.

Alex's eyes are red-rimmed, his cheeks pale. He slinks through the hall without a word and goes straight into the sitting room. None of the usual kicking off of shoes and slouching to his bedroom to play his computer games.

Becca follows him. Her face is strained.

I go back to the girls and keep them busy. It's all I can do, for now.

Later, Alex slips back to his bedroom and the door closes. I give the girls some milk and biscuits and find a children's programme on the iPad. They sit side by side at the table and watch, happily absorbed. I boil the kettle and take Becca a cup of tea.

She's sitting on the sofa bed, her head in her hands, shoulders shaking.

I set the tea on the coffee table in front of her, sit beside her and thread my arm around her back. She collapses sideways onto me at once and sobs into my neck.

I stroke her hair. 'There, there.' I don't ask. I don't want to intrude. I just wait and rock her as she cries until she becomes calm again. She finds a tissue and blows her nose, wipes off her face.

'I lied to the security man at Clary's.' She looks distraught, her face blotchy and red. 'I lied to protect Alex. What if he's been stealing? How could he? Mark will go crazy. He'll blame me, I know he will. And maybe he's right. Maybe it's all because I moved out. Because I've gone back to work. Oh, Maddy, what have I done?'

I hold her hands in mine and look her hard in the face. 'Take a deep breath and tell me. OK? Tell me what happened.'

'He was with some boys; some older boys and they were caught shoplifting.' Her eyes are wild with distress. 'He says he didn't do it. He just tagged along. But this was in his bag.' She reaches behind her on the sofa bed and pulls out a new computer game. I recognise it, of course. It's the one Sarah lent him. 'Store security says it's probably stolen. I covered for him to get him off the hook and said I'd bought it. But I didn't. Oh, Maddy, all that stuff he's got. What if he has been stealing? What do I do?'

She dissolves again into tears.

I sit there, shocked, looking miserably at the game, thinking about Sarah and the jewellery hidden in Ella's bag, the computer gadgets, the new toys. Wondering what to say.

'What's Alex said?'

She blurts out through the tears. 'He keeps denying it. He says someone gave him the stuff but he won't say who. It's not like him. He was always such a good boy. He knows not to steal. It's all my fault.'

I feel sick. He's covering for Sarah, of course he is. He's a loyal boy and she told him not to tell. Oh, Sarah, what have you done? I hand Becca the tea and sit close beside her while she drinks it. She's struggling to steady her breathing, to compose herself. When she's finished, I put my hands on her shoulders and turn her to face me.

'Now, you listen to me,' I say. 'You are a kind, strong woman and a great mother. You know Alex, don't you? You trust him?

Focus on that. If he's looked you in the eye and said someone gave him this stuff, let's assume he's telling the truth. Right?'

She sniffs and manages to nod.

'This has nothing to do with your job. It's not your fault. It's a mess but we're going to get to the bottom of it.'

Her eyes are on mine, wretched but drawing strength from me.

I say: 'Let me have a think. Right now, you are going to give your boy a big hug. He's a good boy and he needs his mum. Tell him it's going to be fine.'

She nods, uncertain, then blows her nose again and gets wearily to her feet to go to him. I sit alone in the quietness for a moment, thinking, struggling to breathe.

Back in the kitchen, the girls are fighting.

'It's mine!'

'It isn't! Smelly Elly.'

'She called me Smelly Elly!'

I weigh in at once but only half hear them as they bicker, too distracted to concentrate.

Sarah arrives soon after five. Becca answers the door and they speak in low voices in the hall.

'Maybe he's telling the truth,' Sarah says. 'Maybe he just fell in with a bad crowd?'

Ella, hearing her mother's voice, scrambles down from her chair and runs through with her picture. 'Look, Mummy! Look what I did!'

I follow behind, lift down Ella's coat from the peg and guide her arms into the sleeves.

Becca shakes her head. 'Thank God I'm not working tonight.'

'Just a minute, Ella.' Sarah looks thoughtful, her eyes on Becca. 'I'll come back later, if you like? After dinner. We could let the girls watch a film if you want to talk.'

'Can we?' Ella beams.

'*Aladdin*. Can we watch *Aladdin*? Please?' Rosie, close behind her, jumps up and down and waves her arms.

Becca nods wearily.

Sarah says: 'Let's have something to eat at home first, Ella, and get ready for bed, then pop back up in your pyjamas and dressing gown. OK?'

'Yay!' The girls jig around in a victory dance together.

I pick up Ella's backpack and hand it to Sarah. 'I'm afraid she got a bit wet, earlier. I found dry trousers but I couldn't find a spare top in here.' I pause, my eyes on her face. 'Even though I had a really good rummage.'

Her eyes flick to mine, snake-like.

'You want to give that a good clean out,' I carry on. 'You don't know what you might find in its nooks and crannies.'

'Thanks.' She takes the backpack from me and turns on her heel to usher Ella out of the door.

She moves quickly but I catch her look. She knows exactly what I'm talking about, exactly what I've found in Ella's bag. Jewellery, with torn price tags still attached. And she's calculating, trying to figure out what I mean to do about it.

I go through to the kitchen to start on Rosie's dinner. As I move from fridge to cupboard to counter, slotting bread into the toaster, reaching down a plate, spooning baked beans into a pan, I think about Sarah. I picture her in her own kitchen, preparing Ella's meal. I imagine her pouring herself a glass of wine, her hands trembling. I feel her thinking about me, about what I said.

When Ella isn't looking, she'll slip her hands into the backpack and feel for the stolen jewellery hidden inside. She'll stare at it, guilty and calculating, figuring out what else I know. Wondering if I've remembered where I saw that computer game, the one Alex is so desperately trying to keep a secret between the two of them, despite Becca's pleas. Wondering if I noticed that it's the one she handed him as we left her flat. She's wondering if I'm smart enough to put two and two together. And, if I am, whether I'll tell Becca what I know.

BECCA

I can't sit still. I pace up and down the kitchen, driving Sarah mad. The sound of the television drifts down the passageway from the sitting room where the girls are watching their film.

'I mean, even if he did nick it…' Sarah sits at the kitchen table. The bottle of red wine she brought with her is open and both our glasses are filled. 'I know it's naughty but it's not the end of the world.'

I try not to look shocked. 'Sarah! It's stealing!'

She shrugs. 'Well, it's shoplifting. That's not really stealing.'

I stop for a moment and stare at her. 'Of course it is.'

She shrugs, reaches for her glass and sips her wine.

'I don't know what to think.' I pace back towards the window. 'Maddy seems to believe him. That someone gave him this stupid game and he's covering for them. But why would he?'

She waves her arm, dismissing me. 'Let it go. Kid's stuff, that's all. He's had a shock. You all have. He's learned from it. Now, move on.'

I shake my head.

She says: 'It must be one of his school friends and he doesn't want to get him into trouble. That's all.'

I come to an abrupt stop at the table. 'Most of his friends are so sensible, though. I know them. I've never heard of him hanging out with older kids before. That's new.'

'Well, he won't hang out with them again. He gets it. For heaven's sake, sit down. You're wearing out the floor.'

I stand there, leaning against the table, worrying. 'I keep thinking, maybe it's my fault. Is this because I left Mark? Because I'm working so much? Is it a cry for help?'

'Oh, please.' She takes another drink.

'It just feels as if he's changed. You know?'

Sarah points to my untouched glass of wine. 'Sit down and have a drink and stop being so dramatic.'

I force myself to sit opposite her. I make a show of lifting the glass but I can't drink. I feel too sick. 'He's been like this since Maddy came.' I pause. 'What you said about Maddy before, that maybe she's not honest, did you really mean that?'

Sarah shrugs. 'Well… you don't know much about her, do you?'

I consider. 'She looked after all that money for me, when I walked off without it. Remember? The night I met her. Why would she do that if she's a thief?'

Sarah shrugs. 'To make you think you could trust her, I suppose. To see what else she could get out of you.'

I shake my head. 'That's too far-fetched. She couldn't know I'd end up giving her a place to sleep. She's not a mind-reader.'

'Well, if you aren't going to listen to me, why did you ask?'

I hesitate. The truth is, something *is* bothering me. Something about Maddy.

'I keep thinking. About when I showed her the computer game. The way she looked at it.'

Sarah looks at me sharply. 'What do you mean?'

'I don't know. Just a feeling. She sort of reacted as if she recognised it and then covered it up.' I hesitate, trying to put it into words. 'I just got the feeling she was hiding something.'

For a moment, the kitchen falls silent. The strains of the television bleed through from the sitting room, the relentless upbeat music of the children's film. Alex, shut inside his room, is quiet.

'If that's how you feel,' Sarah says carefully, 'maybe you should ask her to leave? You don't have to say why. She'd only deny it, wouldn't she? Whether she's got something to do with it or not.'

I can't answer. Throw her out, back onto the streets? I think of Rosie and how much she loves her. Of the way she's held me when I've cried on her, almost like a mother. I scrape back my chair and start pacing again, up and down the kitchen, thinking about Maddy and wondering what to do.

Sarah says: 'Where's she gone, anyway?'

I don't know. That's something else that bothers me. Where does she go for hours at a time? In the afternoons, after I get home from work. In the evening, if I'm here. She doesn't have money. Who does she go to see? How does she manage? Something doesn't add up.

'Would you stay for a bit? Until she gets back?'

Sarah smiles and nods at once. 'Course. If you like.'

'Ella can sleep in Rosie's bed, can't she? They've done it before.' I hesitate. I feel suddenly very alone. 'I think you're right. I think I do have to confront her about what she knows. And I'd like someone else here. Just in case.'

MADDY

I creep back late. My hands and feet are frozen from walking along the river, waiting until it's late enough to go back to the flat without intruding on their evening. I slope along the towpath from one bridge to the next and back again, marking time. On the move. Watching my back.

All my thoughts are of her. Foolish girl. How could you? How could you steal and lie and let the boy take the punishment, that boy who clearly adores you and stays so stupidly loyal to you? The hardness in you makes me weep. There is an emptiness at the heart of you, I see that. It's my fault, of course. Mine and your father's, for what we did to you.

But didn't they love you enough, those adoptive parents of yours? You think it's your right to take what you can, I see it in you. You think the world owes you. Oh, child, how can I make you see that all the clothes and games and jewels in the world can never fill that emptiness?

The heat comforts me as soon as I enter the communal hallway and start up the stairs, forcing my numb feet to move from step to step towards the top. My thoughts focus on getting warm. Too late for a bath – don't want to make a noise, Becca might be in bed by now – but I can run a basin of hot water and sink my hands into it. That will get the blood flowing again.

Already, I think about the sofa bed, of the simple joy of stretching out on a sheet, safe and sheltered and clean, shoes off, and the feel of a blanket over my body. Maybe a cup of tea, before I turn in. Get warm on the inside. I put my key in the lock and sneak inside, soundless.

I stop. The kitchen lights are on. An ambush. I sense it at once.

Becca appears in the kitchen doorway, looking down towards the front door, waiting. She looks wretched. I walk slowly down the hall towards her, dragging my feet. Getting warm will have to wait.

And there's Sarah. Sitting at the kitchen table, settled, an empty bottle of red wine on the table beside two empty glasses. The smell of the wine, lush in the air, tightens my stomach at once with need.

'Maddy, I'm sorry. I need to talk to you.' Becca's trying to sound tough but she looks frightened and I'm the one who feels sorry. She sounds as if she's practised what to say to me, either aloud with Sarah or in the silence, inside her head.

I stand there, leaning against the kitchen counter in my patched blue coat, suddenly very weary.

Becca glances at me, then looks past me into the air and steels herself to carry on. 'This business with Alex,' she says. 'I have to believe him. He isn't a thief. I think he's protecting someone.'

I stare at the floor and purse my lips. I feel already condemned. *More sinned again than sinning.*

She says: 'I just get the feeling you know something, Maddy.'

I lift my head. Of course I do. *You know that, don't you, Sarah, sitting there quietly, your eyes on your glass?* One of us is going down for this. You or me. We both know it.

But you're wrong about me. You think I'll fight back and protest my innocence. That I'll tell Becca that you're the real thief. You're ready to sound outraged, if you need to. To say I'm a liar. Maybe even cry a few crocodile tears. That's why you needed to drink this evening, to drown your guilt and bolster your courage. That's why your knuckles are white where your hands are gripping each other on the table-top. I know you, my child. How could I not?

Why do you think I came to this part of London, to this street, to seek out a filthy doorway opposite this block of flats? I came to find you. I came to watch and wait and learn you. I thought, maybe, if I got sober again, I could tell you who I really am, that I could take out the letter you wrote me, the one I carry everywhere, and prove it to you and try to explain and then to beg forgiveness.

You don't want that. I know. You want me gone. But I can at least do this for you, do this as a final act of love, from mother to daughter. It's all I have to give.

I take a deep breath. 'It's true. I stole those things. All of them. I made Alex promise not to tell. You mustn't blame him.'

'Oh, Maddy!' Becca's face collapses. She reaches behind her for a kitchen chair and sits heavily. 'How could you?'

I swallow. 'I'm sorry, Becca.'

Becca's eyes brim with tears. 'So it was you? But why?'

I can't look her in the face. She trusted me. She opened her home to me, shared everything, even her children. Now she thinks I betrayed her. I look at Becca's shabby, fluffy slippers, bleeding stuffing at the toe and, poking out from under the table, Sarah's shiny new boots. Becca shakes her head, distraught.

She says again: 'How could you, Maddy? How could you do that? I treated you like family. I can't believe it.'

Her voice falters. The two of them sit there, staring now at the table, rigid and silent. I bite my lip.

After a while, Becca says: 'We'll miss you, Maddy. We all will.' She hesitates. 'What can I tell Rosie? She'll be heartbroken.' She lifts her eyes to mine and I see the hurt there. 'Oh, Maddy. I thought you were more than that.'

I turn away, go through to the sitting room and stuff my few belongings into shabby carrier bags. I take Becca's spare key from my pocket and leave it on the table. It's done. Nothing more to say. *Never look back.*

Sarah's waiting there by the front door when I go to leave. I can't look at her. So, this is it.

The end of my long journey to find you.

All the things I longed to tell you, to explain. About your father, who burned so brightly. How much he loved you. He didn't want to leave us, you must never think that. He just couldn't help the way he was made.

And how can I explain the things I did? I've loved you too, Sarah. More than life itself. You were the only reason I kept going at all. It might have been so different. If I'd known before that you'd thought of me, if I'd known you wanted to see me, if I'd known about your letter… But Christy kept it from me because she needed to punish me, you see? It tore her in two when your father died. Her twin, her other half.

I didn't come searching for you because I wanted to upset you. I just needed to find out for certain, to see if you really meant the words you wrote in your letter. If you longed to meet me too, whoever I might be, however battered and bruised.

Now I know. I don't think you do want the truth. I couldn't bear it if you were ashamed of me, after all these years. So perhaps this is the only gift I can give you, after all. This small thing. Perhaps it's the best I can do.

All this passes through my head as I stand there, carrier bags in my hands, eyes turned down, looking at the worn bristles on the mat. Sarah reaches out and pushes a wad of notes into my pocket. I tense but don't move. Hush money. We both know what I'll spend it on. It's one of the few truths we understand about each other.

I lift my eyes to her face and try to read her expression. Her eyes, John's eyes, are full of guilt, and also confusion. She doesn't understand why I'm doing this. *Oh, my child. My little Charley. If only you knew. You'd do it for Ella too, if you ever had to.*

I try to smile but my lips are too tight. There's so much I need to say but I can't.

'Live well,' I whisper. 'Be the best you can be.'

She frowns, not understanding, as I pull open the door, walk out past her, and am gone.

SARAH

When I go back to the kitchen, Becca's sitting at the table with her head in her hands, sobbing. I touch her shoulder.

'How could I be such an idiot!' She can hardly get the words out. 'I really trusted her. I liked her. You were right, all along.'

I can't talk about it. I just say: 'Go to bed, Becca. You're done in.'

In the bedroom, I ease Ella away from Rosie, both fast asleep in her bed, and scoop her into my arms. She presses her face into my jacket in her sleep as I head downstairs, stumbling a little on the bends. Her body is warm and bony and getting steadily heavier. I carried her everywhere, once, with ease. Soon I won't be able to lift her at all.

I balance her on my thigh as I open the door to our flat and she stirs and groans until we're safely inside and I can lay her horizontal again, tucking her into her own cold sheets. I put her bear in her arms and she settles at once.

I sit for a moment on the edge of her bed, watching her sleep. She's beautiful, my daughter. Perfect. I think of the way she threw her arms around Maddy's waist, the way Maddy kissed her hair. Rosie isn't the only one who'll be hurt when she finds out Maddy's gone.

What did Maddy say, before she left? *Be the best you can be.* I sit in the shadows and frown. The wine buzzes in my ears. I thought she'd fight back when Becca accused her. I thought she'd deny everything, maybe accuse me instead. I was all ready for a display of righteous indignation, my look of hurt and horror.

But instead she confessed to something she didn't do. Why would she do that?

Ella kicks out a leg and shifts the duvet and I reach out to cover her again.

Later, I retrieve the jewellery from Ella's backpack. I don't know why I took it now. It suddenly looks gaudy. I hide it all in the back of a drawer, embarrassed by it.

I think of Maddy's face as she handed the backpack to me. She knew. I'm sure of it. She was warning me to stop it, before I get caught. She was giving me another chance.

I go to bed feeling unsettled. I lie on my side and watch the patterns of light and shadow skitter across the curtains as cars pass and think of Maddy, outside in the darkness, sleeping who knows where. I can hardly imagine it. She'd be tucked up on the sofa bed upstairs if she'd told Becca the truth.

I turn over, restless. I'm glad I gave her that cash. I wish I'd had more.

MADDY

I sit, huddled against the window, right at the back of the coach. It's an old coach which bounces and heaves as it gathers speed. The back of the seat in front is scribbled with black graffiti. A name, scrawled in badly formed letters. *Handwriting. They don't teach it properly, nowadays.*

Car lights and street lights flash by as we drive, stretching, one to the other, into a continuous line, leading me north, leading me home. My knees are drawn up and I rock from side to side, agitated, my coat wrapped close around my body.

It's late. After midnight. I've blagged my way onto the last bus north out of Victoria with a sob story about a sick husband. The driver says no until just before he pulls out, then gives in, worn down, and lets me creep onto his half-empty coach without a ticket. I can't buy a ticket. The ticket office has already closed. I can't even bribe him. I've nothing left to give.

We career through London in the darkness, this reluctant driver with his handful of paying passengers and me, a stowaway. It's a regal goodbye, through the heart of the capital. Tourist London, shining with rain. Marble Arch. Piccadilly Circus. The length of the Edgware Road. Not long now until the start of the M1 and London will fall away from us all, sloughed off like a dead skin.

He slows down at the lights. I rest my forehead on the cold glass and peer out. A row of darkened shop doorways, peopled by lumpen sleepers, huddled figures, padded and bagged against the cold. I close my eyes. I can almost smell it. The stinking puddles in the corners. Spilt beer. The thickening grease on wrappers, discarded from burgers or chips.

In six or seven hours, the bustle will begin again. The stream of hurrying people, with cartons of coffee and croissants in paper bags and free newspapers and briefcases, heels click-clacking, will become a meaningless blur as they pass by the invisible sleepers.

The bus slides on and the shadowy people are gone forever. My hands tremble. I look round. A young man, a student perhaps, sits a few rows ahead of me, headphones on, collar raised, slumped low in his seat. The other passengers are in the front half of the coach, grouped together for safety.

I reach into my carrier bag and lift out the bottle. A cheap own brand from the late-night supermarket. The biggest I could find. A shaft of passing light catches the liquid, turns the amber to gold. The hard stuff. My tipple. My own.

Saliva swells in my mouth. My palms sweat. A full 75cl bottle. *Drink me!* Yes, Lewis Carroll. You understood it all. I will drink and fall, fall, fall through the rabbit hole to another world.

Just a nip then, to start me off. I cut the soft flesh of my hand tugging at the screw top. I see the blood without feeling it. The smell finds me at once, as soon as the cap is free. Dizzying. *Hello, dear friend. Welcome home.*

Then the taste explodes in my mouth, filling my throat, sending fire through my insides. I shudder and tears come to my eyes. Already, a few greedy swallows in, and my hands and feet are becoming numb, the tension in my spine is easing. Taking the edge off. I mumble to myself as I tip back the bottle again, closing my eyes.

I let go at last, as my body relaxes, and start to cry. I curl into a ball, rocking the bottle in my arms as if it's a glass baby, head down, weeping.

I had my chance. Nothing ahead now but to go home, to join John, right where he left us, there on the railway tracks. *The long day's task is done. And we must sleep.*

I let the whisky take me back. It loosens my mind and sets my thoughts adrift, back to the past, to that terrible time after John's death, when I lost first him and then myself and then, finally, my daughter too.

*

'Maddy?'

Christy didn't recognise me at first. I saw myself reflected in her face, in her horror. I was filthy, I knew that. Smelly too, probably. I'd lost a lot of weight.

I couldn't answer. I just sat there, curled in their doorway, struggling to focus on her.

She reached past me and opened her front door, helped me inside.

'Sorry.' I didn't know what else to say.

She warmed milk for me. I remember the thick, sweet taste of it and the weight of it in my stomach. I sat on the linen basket in her bathroom, sipping hot milk, watching her run me a bath.

In the bath, I drew up my bony legs. She soaped me down with a sponge as if I were a child again. We didn't speak, not yet. It was too much. The warm water. The smell of musk. The soft, steady stroke of the sponge. She didn't flinch when I started to sob, just kept on washing me, massaging shampoo into my matted hair and rinsing it off.

Later, when I was clean and starting to sober up, she dressed me in her own old clothes, settled me in an armchair and brought through a tray of coffee and biscuits.

She shook her head. 'Where were you?'

I didn't know how to answer. I wasn't even sure. It was months since John's death and since they'd thrown me out of the flat. Months since I'd seen Charley. I knew only because I'd seen the seasons change. Frost turning to rain and slowly back to warmth again.

Where was I? In gutters. In outhouses. Under bridges. Eating when someone fed me. Drinking where I could. Wishing myself dead. Wishing myself with John. His sobbing was always in my head. His torment.

No one can ever know how much I hated myself for what had happened, for not realising, for not stopping him. It was all my fault. I was an unfit wife, an unfit mother. Lord knows, I came close to joining him in the darkest days.

The only thing that stopped me, however drunk I was, however sick in body and soul, was that one day, when I could bear to come back to the world, I'd be her mother again.

I looked around. There was an array of framed photographs along the mantelpiece. Tom and Christy on their wedding day; Andrew and Jeremy posing together in school uniform, both giving wide, toothless grins. And John. A faded snapshot of John and Christy together on a beach as children, wearing matching straw hats. They were holding hands, radiant with life, looking out with the same brown eyes, the same grins, each balancing the other as only twins can. And beside it, in a small silver frame, a photograph of John with Charley riding high on his shoulders. My beautiful girl. Her hair in bunches, her mouth wide with laughter. A snapshot we took when she was barely three.

'Is she here?' There were toys stacked against the wall. Construction sets. Jigsaws.

'Here?' She stared at me, her eyes incredulous. 'Maddy, you disappeared. You abandoned her. You were too drunk to know whether she was around or not. You couldn't look after her. What did you expect me to do?'

'I know. I can explain.' I pushed my shaggy hair out of my face. Her eyes were on my hand, seeing how it shook. I hid it quickly. 'I wasn't well. But I'm better now. I've come to take her back.'

She shook her head. 'Maddy. Not a word. All these months. I thought you were dead.'

I blinked and stuttered at her, panic rising. 'Where is she? I'll make it up to her. I will. I'll go back to teaching. I'll rent somewhere. We'll get by.' I paused, looked around the room for some trace of her. 'So, where is she?'

The house seemed suddenly desolate. No Charley, then. Just Christy and Tom and their two young boys.

She pushed the cup of coffee towards me. 'I'm sorry, Maddy. Really. They made her a ward of court. She's being adopted.'

'Adopted!' I screamed. 'But she's mine! They can't do that. I'll stop it. I'll fight.'

'Calm down.' She sat very still and looked at me with a steady, sad gaze. 'I did what seemed best. We struggle to feed our two. And you weren't here.'

I shouted: 'I was ill!'

She said very quietly: 'You still are, Maddy. You need help.'

Pain flared in my stomach, in my chest. I needed a drink, that was all. I glared at her. 'You wanted to hurt me, didn't you? You never wanted me to be with him. I took him from you and you never forgave me.'

'That's not true.' She sighed. 'I was upset at first. I admit that. You betrayed me, getting involved with him, moving in with him and not even telling me.' She paused and her eyes strayed to the photograph of the two of them as children, holding hands in the summer sunshine. 'But we stayed close, John and I. We did meet. He came to see us, when he could. He just didn't tell you. You were so wrapped up in Charley, you didn't seem to care.'

'That's not true. You're just saying that. You blame me, don't you? You think it's my fault he died.'

She shook her head. 'No, Maddy. I've never thought that.'

I got to my feet. Christy's clothes hung on me, baggy and soft. 'I'll go to court. I'll get her back.'

She sighed. 'You can try. But be careful. I've done my homework. You go to the authorities and you know what will happen?

They may charge you.' She listed my crimes on her fingers, one by one. 'Child neglect. Child cruelty. Child abuse.'

I couldn't speak. I leaned heavily on the arm of the chair. Could she be right? Was this it? Something tightened in my chest. This was the only thought that had dragged me back from the edge of hell, that had saved me from following John into the darkness – the thought of getting her back, of being her mother again.

She narrowed her eyes, watching me.

'Think about Charley, Maddy. Please. What can you offer her now? You're not well. You don't have a job. You can't even give her somewhere to live. Don't you think I'd have taken her in, if I'd thought we could give her what she needs? She's found a loving family. They can give her the chance to put all this behind her and start again. Don't you want that for her?'

I couldn't listen. I staggered past her to the door and fumbled my way outside, onto the empty road.

She was right. I went back to the bottle, to the street. I nearly didn't make it.

I'd never teach again. I knew that now. How could I? The first background check and the truth would out. The only jobs I would ever be able to do now were the unskilled ones, cash in hand, no questions asked. It was only because of the kindness of strangers that I ever got cleaned up and dried out while I was still young enough to recover.

And so I found myself a hole. Dark and deep. I hid myself away in that mouldering trailer in the caravan park. Sober and anonymous. Living and partly living. Year on year.

I might have played out the rest of my life there if it hadn't been for that letter from my nephew, Jeremy, telling me that Christy had died. I didn't expect anything from them when I went to the funeral. It just seemed right. Respectful. A way of laying something finally to rest. John would have wanted it. They were twins, after all.

I had a chance of happiness, more than many people are lucky to have, and I destroyed it. I let down my husband and my daughter, both of the people I should have loved and cherished. She didn't despise me any more than I've despised myself, all these years.

But the letter he gave me? That knocked me to the ground.

Now, all these years later, as I head through the night at the back of the long-distance bus, I remember and, sentimental with whisky and tears, I push my hand into the pocket of my coat and take it out. This letter I carry with me everywhere. The letter to me from Charley, written five years ago when she was twenty-five.

The bus is dark and the thin strains of light from the road flick like flames over the words. It doesn't matter. I've read it a hundred times. I have it by heart.

Dear Mum,

I hope this letter reaches you, wherever you may be and finds you well. If it does, I hope it's not too much of a shock to hear from me. I've thought long and hard about whether to write to you. I found the address in the court papers and thought I'd try. If you don't answer, I'll try to understand.

You may wonder why I'm trying to make contact with you after all these years. I'm expecting my own baby now, you see – a little girl – and the thought of becoming a mother myself has made me think such a lot about my own childhood and about you and why you gave me up the way you did.

I always knew I was adopted. My parents have been kind and generous and have given me everything they could but I've always felt there was something missing. I never really fit in. They are very conventional people and I suppose I'm not. I think I've disappointed them, over the years.

I've just moved into my own flat in London, ready for the baby. The address is at the top of this letter. You can write to me there, if you want to.

I only have a few memories of you. I think I remember your voice and a song you used to sing me. It comes to me at night sometimes in my sleep but disappears again as soon as I wake up. And I remember a cavernous room which smelt of wax, with high, bare windows which let in columns of sunlight and a large hard floor where I used to scoot. Was it a church?

And I remember the stories you used to tell me. Perhaps that's my strongest memory. Sitting on your knee, late at night, listening to you tell me about Peter Pan and the Lost Boys.

I hope to hear from you but, if I don't, please know that I wish you well, Mum, whoever you are.

Your daughter,
Sarah

I don't blame them, the people who adopted you. They just saw your names on the forms, *Sarah Charlotte,* and called you Sarah. Just as you'd expect. They weren't to know you were always Charley to us. Maybe at four, after all that had happened, you wanted to keep that secret. Or maybe, in your new life, with your new parents, you didn't want to remember.

I run my fingers over the surface of the paper in the darkness, reading it with my fingertips as if it were Braille. The paper is furred now with age and falling into pieces along the folds.

I think about the flats where I went to find her and which became so familiar to me. About the times I watched her from the shadows of shop doorways, marvelling at how beautiful she was, how smartly dressed, watching her take little Ella to school, caring for her daughter as I had failed to care for her. I'll miss her too, my little granddaughter. I'll miss her frown as she puzzles about the world, her high voice, earnest, saying: 'Maddy, let me tell you…' and the warmth of her small arms around my neck when she gave me a hug. *Be brave, lovely girl. Live your life well.*

Charley wanted to make contact, she said. Perhaps even to meet me. She wanted to hear my side of the story. To know from me what really happened and how I came to give her up with such finality. To find out who I was.

I lift the bottle and drink. That was what sent me over the edge again, after Christy's funeral. The knowledge that Charley had reached out to me and had been met with nothing more than silence. And then, once I'd fallen back again on drink, once I'd lost the meagre job I'd had and my home with it, how then could I present myself to her, to my wonderful daughter, and say: *Here I am, your mother. A tramp. A wreck. A soak. Mad Maddy*. How could I, when she so clearly despised me?

BECCA

With Maddy gone, the sofa bed stays folded away under neat cushions. I rush through the sitting room now, looking for my bag, getting ready to go out. I'd got used to the clutter that came with Maddy: the piles of cast-off clothes and soggy plastic bags, the half-read books balanced on chair arms and tables, her place held by a piece of biscuit wrapper or torn shred of paper. And she seemed always to be talking, telling Rosie some story or other, or intoning those strange musical quotes of her, an echo of someone long dead. I shake my head. She was always strange, I know that. But I miss her.

I check through my bag and go in search of my shoes. Alex still won't admit that it was Maddy who stole those wretched games and told him not to tell. Perhaps it doesn't matter. However awful it was at Clary's that Saturday, at least we're doing better now. We make a point of spending time together, just Alex and me, when Rosie goes off to see her father. Alex is talking to me again about his problems, his worries, about what's going on in his life. And, all in all, he seems happier. He only hangs out with his old mates, the ones his own age.

I'm nearly ready when Rosie comes thumping through from the kitchen, her mouth stained with chocolate.

'I want to play schools,' she whines. 'I want to be Miss Lily.'

'I know you do. But what did I say?'

She pulls a face. 'It's not fair. Maddy played schools with me.'

'I asked you to wash your face. We need to go. I'll be late for work.'

I reach for our coats.

'I don't want you to go to work.'

'I know. I understand that. But we need the money, Rosie. Everyone has to work.'

I zip up the backpack with her pyjamas and toothbrush, her bear. 'Come on. You like going to Ella's, don't you?'

'Why does Alex always get to go to Daddy's?'

I keep my voice level as we head down the stairs to Sarah's flat. 'It's your turn next time, remember? And this way, I can carry you home when I get back. How cool is that! You go to sleep in Ella's room and wake up in your own!'

Rosie cheers up as soon as Sarah opens the door and Ella looks around her, bouncing on her toes with excitement. The girls run off together, giggling, to play in her room.

Childcare hasn't been easy since Maddy left but I'm making it work – with a network of babysitters, and Sarah and Mark plugging the gaps. I'm getting by.

It's pouring with rain outside and I pause in the doorway, turn up my collar and pull on my woolly hat.

'Need a lift?'

I look up. David is sitting in his car a hundred yards from me, calling out of the window.

I run over in the wet. 'That's OK, thanks. I'm only going to Jane's. Not far.'

He smiles. 'Go on. You'll get soaked.'

I hesitate, then smile back and climb in next to him. The smell of the leather hits me at once. My stomach tightens. It brings back memories of the night we went for dinner, the two of us. The edge of his hand brushes my leg as he puts the car into gear and moves out into the road and I tilt my knees away, embarrassed. The car smells of him. Soap and wet wool and a hint of spicy aftershave. His eyes are on the road and I take the chance to look at him. A kind face, as well as handsome.

He says: 'How's work?'

Safe territory. 'Great, thanks. I'm in charge of the kitchen tonight. First time.' I hesitate and wish I hadn't put my woolly hat on. I must look ridiculous.

He gives me a quick sideways look. 'Nervous?'

'A bit.'

We sit in silence for a moment. The traffic lights change and he swings the car forward, moving left into the high street.

We're almost at the turn-off for Jane's when he says: 'I hear your guest moved on. Are you doing OK on your own?'

I blink, taken aback. Where does he get his information about me?

'It all went a bit pear-shaped.' I wonder how much he knows. 'But it was always going to be short-term, you know.'

He pulls up at the side of the road, near the cobbled path that leads down to the staff entrance at the back of the wine bar. He leans his arm on the steering wheel and twists to face me. His smile shines in his eyes.

'Well, good luck. Try not to poison anyone.'

'Thanks for the lift.' I fumble with the handle.

I climb out into the rain. As I move to shut the car door, he calls: 'I'll come by later, if you like. Give you a lift home?'

I nod, trying not to show how pleased I am. 'Sure. Why not? That would be great.' I stand for a moment in the rain, smiling to myself, as he pulls away.

I'm just starting down the path when a woman's voice comes from the shadows.

'Any spare change, love?'

My heart clenches. I stop, turn and take a few steps back to look.

A woman sits huddled in a shop doorway, the bottom half of her body inside a grubby sleeping bag, a blanket wrapped round her shoulders. She stares back at me, then holds out her hand. The lines criss-crossing her palm are black with ingrained dirt.

I can hardly look her in the eye. Her face is thin and pinched with cold, her hair prematurely streaked with grey and hanging in loose tails round her cheeks. Her eyes are bright. She tips her head to one side as I look her over and smiles, showing a broken tooth.

I rummage through my pockets and dig out a £5 note, then push it into her hand with as little physical contact as possible. I turn and hurry away down the path, rushing along the wet and uneven stones, embarrassed, heading for the wine bar to spend my evening cooking expensive food.

SARAH

The girls take a while to get to sleep.

Later, after it's gone quiet, I go to check on them.

I feel the cold air as soon as I walk in. A night draught, blowing right into the room, whipping away the heat.

'Ella?'

The girls are either asleep or pretending to be. Ella lies in bed, curled round, her head poking out from under the sheet. Beside her, Rosie is sprawled asleep on her back on the camp bed.

I creep to the window and shut it with a bang, then slide across the metal window catch.

I'm tired of arguing about it. She's doing this every night. It's never open much, just a few inches, hidden by the curtain. But it's enough for a passer-by to get his hands under and open it, if he felt like it. Enough to freeze the room.

The next morning, over breakfast, when Ella and I are alone together, I take her to task.

'Why did you open the bedroom window again last night?'

She sits slouched over her bowl of cereal, eyes half-closed with sleep, spoon in hand.

'Ella?'

She lifts her eyes. I check the kitchen clock. She needs to eat her cereal and get on with cleaning her teeth. We're going to be late.

'Please. We've been through this a hundred times. Your room was freezing. You don't want to be ill, do you?'

'I'm not ill.'

I sigh, put my own cereal bowl in the dishwasher and close it up.

'It's not safe. Don't you see? What if someone climbed in? We're on the ground floor. It's possible.'

She considers. 'Like a burglar?'

'Maybe.' I haven't gone this far before. I hadn't wanted to frighten her. But maybe I need to, to ram the message home. 'A bad person. That's why we keep the window closed and locked.'

'I like it open.' She spoons another mound of cereal into her mouth.

I sit down beside her at the kitchen table and try hard to listen. I can't help feeling there's something here I'm missing. It isn't like her to be so stubborn.

'Why?' I take a deep breath. 'Why do you keep opening it? Don't you like being warm and cosy?'

She hesitates and mumbles something into her cereal.

'Say that again, Ella. I didn't catch you.'

She says, more clearly: 'So she can come home.'

I blink. 'So who can come home?'

She turns her eyes on me, doleful. 'Maddy.'

I shake my head. 'Maddy isn't coming back, Ella. I thought I'd explained that. She's gone away, remember?'

She frowns and turns away from me. 'You've got to leave the window open so the magic can work. So she can fly home.' She sticks out her lip, cross. 'It's true, Mummy.'

I tut. 'What's she been telling you? That's just a story, Ella. There's no such thing as magic, not really. You know that.' I shake my head.

'There is! Maddy said she and her own little girl used to live in the factory where they made wax for the lost children's wings. They stuck feathers together so they could fly, like this. But Peter Pan flew too close to the sun and the wax melted.'

I stare at her. I can't believe Maddy filled the girls' heads with such nonsense. Peter Pan didn't have wax wings, anyway. That was another story. A myth.

Ella presses on, her face red: 'And it's true about the windows. Maddy does it, too. Every night. Rosie told me.'

'Ella!' I don't know what to say. 'She lived on the streets for a long time. You know that. If she did leave the window open, it wasn't to let lost children fly in. Maybe she just likes fresh air.'

Ella pushes away her bowl and jumps down from her chair. 'You don't understand anything. You've just grown up and forgotten. She said that's what happens.' Her small face is red with frustration as she blurts out: 'She *will* come back. People do if you love them enough. She said so.'

She runs from the kitchen towards her bedroom, leaving me sitting there, stunned, looking at the congealing bowl of half-finished cereal.

Ella stays upset all the way to school, her face closed and angry. I say no more about it.

That night, I go into her room on my way to bed to check on her. I know as soon as I walk in, just from the temperature, that she's managed to slip the catch and push the window open again.

I shake my head and go to shut it, weary but not surprised. I grip the edge of the top sash with my hands, ready to press it down into place. Then I stop. My knuckles blanch, my fingers tighten. A memory passes through me like an electric current. Intense and instant but half-formed.

My mother. Crossing the room to shut a window, all those years ago. I'm little, three or four, curled in bed, pretending to sleep but secretly watching her. A creak and then a clatter as the window fell into position. High, industrial windows without curtains. She needed a long pole to close them. The noises sent panic through me. *What about Wendy*, I thought, *how will she fly home now?*

I had sat up in bed and she saw me at once, as soon as she turned around.

'Sweetheart, what are you doing awake?'

She came to sit on my bed and put her arms round me. She started to sing, that song I hear in my dreams and can never remember, and I relaxed into her, closed my eyes, drowsy again. Happy. Safe.

'I love you, little Charley.' Did she really say that or am I imagining things? And why Charley, not Sarah? 'I'll always love you. No matter what.'

She was warm and soft and I nestled into her, breathing in her special smell. And the other smell is there too, in the background, the smell of molten wax that suffuses the very fabric of the building.

Now, in Ella's shadowy room, I turn and creep across to her. What had she said? *Maddy said she and her own little girl used to live in the factory where they made wax for the lost children's wings.* I sit down heavily on the edge of the bed and my breathing is shallow and fast.

Maddy? I think of her stooping to kiss Ella's hair with such tenderness, such reverence. Of the sad, knowing look on her face when she handed me Ella's rucksack. She knew exactly who the real thief was – but she still took the blame herself. She gave me a second chance. Why would anyone do that for someone else? Why would anyone show that much love?

Live well, she'd said. *Be the best you can be*. It was her blessing. Her goodbye.

Ella twists onto her back in her sleep. Her arms are thrown wide, her hair splayed across the pillow. Her breathing is slow and even. My hands are shaking as I pull the covers free and tuck her in, then touch my lips to her forehead.

No, I think. *It can't be that. No.*

*

David comes around to the flat at once, just as I knew he would, just as he always has.

He looks tired. He works too hard. I pour him a drink and he settles in a chair, his eyes on my face. He doesn't speak. He just waits. He knows me too well.

I take a deep breath. 'This is really stupid.'

He doesn't move a muscle.

'Maddy told the girls the same story my mum used to tell me. My birth mum. I remember.'

'Which story?'

'*Peter Pan*. About leaving the window open so Wendy can find her way home. She does it, too. Rosie told Ella.'

He frowns. 'Everyone knows *Peter Pan*, Sarah. That doesn't mean anything.'

'But leaving the window open? Isn't that weird? Who does that?'

'Lots of people like to sleep with the window open.' He looks worried. 'What is it, Sarah?'

'It made me remember a time. Late at night. That same thing with the window.' I pause. 'Her voice. Calling me Charley.'

He says: 'Charley?'

'Charlotte. My middle name. Right? Charley. Maybe they called me that?'

He shrugs. 'I don't remember. You were just Sarah.'

'And that's not all. Maddy told her she used to live with her little girl in an old wax factory.'

'A wax factory?'

'The smell. David, I remember the smell of wax. I thought maybe it was a church. High, vast windows and an open floor. I used to scoot round it, in and out of the sunlight.'

I get to my feet, agitated, and pace down to Ella's room to check on her, to make sure she's safe and fast asleep.

When I come back, David's sitting forward, his hands clasped.

He says quietly: 'You think that maybe that's why she came here in the first place? She was looking for you?'

I nod and press my lips tightly together, trying not to cry. When I'm composed again, I blow out my cheeks. 'There's something else.'

Of all the people in the world, David is the one person I trust not to judge me. He's always stuck up for me, right from the start, when he was still a little boy. Since those first tense weekends when his parents drove me back to meet him and to visit their home and showed me the bedroom, right next to his, all pink and pretty, which would later become mine. All through those first difficult months when I first came to live with them as his adopted little sister.

I take a deep breath. 'You know all that trouble with Alex? It wasn't Maddy at all. I stole that stuff.'

He looks shocked. I almost stop there, frightened. But something in me wants him to know. Something wants him to be horrified, to shout and tell me I disgust him. That I've disappointed him, just as I always disappointed our parents.

'It's just a thing I do.' I shrug my shoulders as if I don't care. 'I only nick stuff from big stores. Those bosses are multi-millionaires. You know that. They don't even notice. And what have I got?' I wave a hand around the flat. 'This is all yours, all of it. I wouldn't have anywhere to live at all if it weren't for you.'

He doesn't shout. His face crumples and for a moment, he looks as if he's about to cry. 'Oh, Sarah.'

I bite my lip. 'But it's not that,' I manage to say. 'She said it was her. She knew, I'm sure she did, and she took the blame for me willingly. Why would anyone do that?'

We stare at each other, eyes wet. David gets up and crosses the room in a moment, wraps his arms around me and holds me tight. He strokes my hair and sighs. 'Sarah.'

I cling to him, sobbing now.

He hugged me like this when we were children and I rowed with my new parents, time after time. My perfect big brother, their own flesh and blood, always their golden boy. He hugged me like this when I told him I was pregnant and too proud to let our parents help. He was the one who set me up here, rent-free, and quietly helped with bills. He even agreed to my conditions, keeping it all secret from them – even from Ella, when she came along.

I manage to say now, sobbing into his shirt. 'What if it's true? What if it's really her? What if she came looking for me, after all these years, and I did that to her?'

I think of all the things I said, of the way she looked at me the time she asked me to join them for dinner and I said no. Her face was so hurt, so crestfallen.

I sob: 'I was so mean to her. I called her a bag lady. A nothing. What must she have been through to end up like that? Down and out. She tried to reach out to me and I pushed her away. She must hate me.'

He gives me a squeeze and says into my hair: 'If she is your mum, she'll still love you, Sarah.'

'But why didn't she tell me?'

'Maybe she was frightened. Frightened you'd be ashamed of her.' He sighs. 'Anyway, you don't know it's true yet, do you? The next thing we need to do is find out.'

*

We tell Ella it's a special holiday, a weekend away. I settle her in the back of the car and David drives us late on Friday, after dinner. Ella's eyes blur as she watches the lights streak past and is lulled by the steady vibrations of the engine. By the time we reach the motorway, she's asleep.

The M1 is thick with traffic and we sit for too long in stop-start lanes, snaking our way through road works. I fidget and squirm in my seat, trying to get comfortable.

Now and then, David says: 'It's all right, Sarah. Calm down.'

He reaches for me and squeezes my hand. I glance sideways at him, consider his profile. He's so loving, so kind. He works so hard, and spends too much time and energy looking after The Parents, looking after me. He deserves better than that. He deserves a family of his own.

'I like Becca a lot.' I hesitate. I'm not sure he even wants me to talk about her. He's a very private man. 'She's really special.'

He keeps his eyes on the road. After a moment, he just says: 'I think so, too.'

I don't answer, just squeeze his hand back.

Gradually, as we drive, the traffic thins around us and there's a sense of urban England falling away and of the countryside opening out at our feet. I peer through the darkness at fields and hedges, then the raw, rolling wildness of the Pennine Hills. The wind buffets the car and David grips the wheel to hold it steady on the road. Behind, buckled into the back, Ella sleeps, her head lolling and mouth open.

'Nearly there.'

We run out of motorway at Leeds and David navigates his way over flyovers and across multi-lane roundabouts. It's late and the city is hushed. The streets are almost deserted, shops in darkness. Here and there, light spills out onto the pavements through pub windows and restaurant fronts while couples, coats wrapped tightly around their bodies, arms entwined, shoulders hunched against the cold, scurry past.

He picks up the road out of the city, still heading north and, within minutes, the houses and factories start to disappear. I look out over dry-stone walls to field upon field, then open countryside and a dark, silent landscape of distant hills.

He gives me a quick sideways glance. 'Doing OK?'

I can't answer. I can't describe what I feel. I don't remember it, of course. I was too young. And yet something stirs in me.

Something opens, responding to this vast, broad landscape. Some part of me feels as if I'm coming home at last.

The next morning, in the hotel, David and Ella take time discussing the merits of sausages and fried bread, scrambled and poached eggs. They barely know each other but they're both delighted. I look at their heads, bent close together as they spell out the words on the breakfast menu.

She makes a silly mistake and he pretends to tweak her nose and she giggles.

I've barely slept. I can't face food, just coffee.

David glances across at me as I sit in silence, gnawing at my nails. Sick to the core. Waiting.

After breakfast, we get in the car and go in search of the address. I've said very little to Ella and she whines for a while, asking where we're going, what we're doing today, then finally falls silent, picking up on the darkness of my mood.

My stomach is ice. David turns into a narrow residential road and as I see the street name as we swing past it my throat constricts. The same street name I saw printed on the court papers. The same street name I wrote and rewrote on several envelopes before I was satisfied and dared to post my letter. Someone came here, nearly six years ago, and delivered it. Pushed it through a letter box and heard it strike the mat inside.

David drives slowly, counting down the numbers. It's part of a suburban housing estate, unremarkable, all cul-de-sacs and front gardens, side garages with private drives. We reach number thirty-seven. A small house. Semi-detached. The garden is tidy. The window sills need fresh paint.

David parks outside. I look at the bay window. The lower half is concealed behind semi-transparent curtains. I wonder if they're looking out, watching, judging me.

'Ready?' David's eyes study my face. 'It's twenty-five past nine.'

Ella is already undoing her seatbelt, kicking the back of my seat as she scrambles to escape from the car.

A man of about thirty opens the door. A shabby, weekend sweater and jeans. He looks nervous. His hand scrapes back his hair as he looks us over.

'Hello. I'm Jeremy. You found us OK?' He smiles down at Ella as if he doesn't know how to talk to her. 'Hi, Ella. I'm your mummy's cousin. Anyway, come in.'

We process through the hall and into the sitting room.

'This is my dad,' Jeremy says. 'Your uncle. Uncle Tom. Dad, Charley's here. And Ella.'

An older man of perhaps sixty, greying now and slightly stooped, nods at us from a chair. He makes no move to get up and greet us. He doesn't smile, just stares at me.

'You remind me of Christy at your age,' he says at last. 'My wife. You've got her eyes. They were a lot alike, Christy and John, your father.'

David, steady at my elbow, steers me out again to the small kitchen at the back where Jeremy is making tea. As we join him, Jeremy pulls out chairs and sets a packet of chocolate biscuits on the table. Ella looks at me and takes one when I nod. She busies herself with licking off the chocolate as we talk.

'Don't mind Dad.' Jeremy flushes, awkward with embarrassment. 'Mum never liked to talk about Aunt Maddy and what happened to her brother… I mean, to your dad. I think she never really got over the fact he—' he pauses, gives Ella a quick anxious look, and lowers his voice, 'he took his own life.' He swallows. 'I'm sorry. This must all be a bit of a shock.'

I can't speak. It all feels unreal, being here in this small suburban house with people who knew my real parents, who knew me in my first life as Charley. My own flesh and blood.

'We hardly saw Aunt Maddy – your mother – when we were growing up. I only met her again last year. She came to Mum's funeral. That's when I gave her your letter, you see. With your address on. I found it in Mum's desk.' He gives a short cough. 'I hope I didn't do the wrong thing.'

He reaches down to the chair beside him and lifts a box onto the table. The packets of photographs are dusty and jumbled.

'Mum always said she'd sort them out. Put them into albums.'

He picks up a paper packet from the top and pulls out the photos. Two children, a boy and a girl, both about four years old, stand on the beach in sunshine, wearing matching straw hats. They have the same deep brown eyes. My eyes. Ella's eyes. The boy is grinning widely, excited, energised, holding his sister's hand.

Jeremy hands it to me. 'I don't remember Uncle John much, I'm afraid. Your dad. He came to see us a few times when we were small. I remember him charging up and down the park, playing football. He was good fun. Bit of a joker. But I was only, I don't know, five or six when he died.'

He stirs the pot and pours tea. I sit there, in the dingy kitchen, looking at this picture of the past, the image of the father I can barely remember. I lift my eyes and look out at the back garden with its miniature greenhouse and crazy-paving path and neatly tended flowerbeds and I try to imagine this family, my aunt and uncle and cousins, living out their ordinary lives here, all this time.

Jeremy hands out mugs and sits down with us. Ella sucks on the remains of her biscuit, chocolate melting around her mouth, swinging her legs and looking out at the garden.

'So,' he says, 'what can I tell you about Aunt Maddy?' His hand rakes again through his hair, his eyes anxious. 'I've pieced together what I could. Where do we begin?'

*

Later, when he's told me everything he knows, Jeremy comes with us in the car. He takes us round. He points out the small estate of old factories, all converted to quirky flats more than thirty years ago, including the candle works where we once lived, when my father was still alive and I was a little girl, younger than Ella. He shows me the school where my mother once taught English. Where I might have studied myself, in another life.

We sit for a while at the back of the church where his mum and dad were married. My mum was a bridesmaid, he said. My dad was an usher. He's seen the photos. His mother's funeral was here, too. The last time he saw Maddy. That's when he gave her my letter, the letter which must have prompted her to come to London, to seek me out.

Ella's restless. She's bored and tired of being shut inside the car, of being told to behave and listen in silence while grown-ups talk. In the graveyard, she runs off after a while and hides from us in the trees and I scold her for being disobedient.

I'm not sure Jeremy wants to show me anything more. David looks at his watch and says maybe Ella needs some time to play now, a chance to let off steam. We can always come again tomorrow, before we return to London.

But I don't listen. I want to see it now. I want to visit the spot where my father took his life and left us both, the point at which time split and we were sent careering down the wrong path, the path that changed everything for us both, my mother and me.

The men exchange a quick glance, then Jeremy shrugs and we all pile back into the car, Ella cross and protesting, and head for the railway tracks.

MADDY

I drink what I can find. Here and there. Ways and means.

The hit's greater when it's been a while. The abyss is deeper than I remember. I'm going down, way down, so far I'll never rise again. That's best. I'm numb, mostly. Head blurred. It's bad this time.

At night, I sleep where I can. Under bridges. In derelict barns. Against walls. Doesn't much matter. I'm home again. *In my end is my beginning*. Something like that.

During the day, I walk, mostly. I come down to the tracks, searching for John, waiting for him to call me to him. It's almost time, I feel it. Nothing else matters now. I'm done. Done and dusted. *Dust to dust.*

I'm almost there. Almost home. *I'm coming, John, my love. Coming as soon as you call.*

His sobbing stays with me, everywhere. Louder now than it has ever been. It leads me today to the railway tunnel, the one just before the fatal bend where he lay down and waited for death to come. The tunnel is mouldy inside. Smells like a cellar. Must and damp earth.

I pick my way along the tracks, staggering over loose rocks. An old boy slept down here last night. I heard him shuffling, crying out in the darkness, in his dreams. No sign of him now.

The toes of my old shoes kick up fragments of rock in the half-light and send them spinning. Weeds sprout, slippery, between the rails. *Born to blush unseen. Waste its sweetness.* Who was that? I don't know any more. Don't even care.

I hear him, up ahead. My John, calling me. Calling me to him at last. I quicken my pace. My hands graze the brickwork. Old bricks. Victorian. I think of Mick and almost laugh. *Back to bricks*, he used to say. *Go back to bricks, Maddy, if you get the chance*. Well, I have, my friend. Here I go.

I'm partway through when the rails start to hum. A train's coming. I hurry, panicked now despite my need to reach John. Not yet. Not quite. Not like this. Preservation. *Preserves. Jam*. I'll be jam in a minute if I don't get a move on. Come on, Maddy. You know this place. You came here before, remember? Drunk as a skunk and stinking like one, looking for John, to turn back time and save him. I was young then. A long time ago.

I press forward, fleeing the oncoming train. I'm too far into the tunnel now to get back out the way I came, to get out in time. The darkness presses in around me. Here and there, in the depth of the tunnel, there are shallow archways. I remember them. Cubby holes. Invisible spaces, niches for living statues, set back in the brickwork. For engineers to hide in, maybe.

I reach one now and press myself clumsily inside. Back against the brick. Hold my breath. Wait. My eyes spangle in the darkness. There's an animal stink. Fox dirt maybe, or a dying rat. I'll fit in nicely here, I think, when I rot. *Those are pearls that were his eyes*.

Just in time. A train's whistle, sharp and close. A flash, blinding. It explodes into the tunnel. A cacophony of rattling and screeching, sparks, orange stabs of light, a rush of wind so fierce it blows me back against the stone, cracking my skull on the brick. I shake, too afraid to breathe, fighting for life.

Then it's gone, leaving a flurry of empty air. Leaving me gasping, limp, sinking to the ground, reaching again for the bottle, for another nip.

What were you thinking, when you laid down your life, there on those rails? What were you thinking, my love?

The weeping in my head is deafening. John is here, just ahead of me. Just beyond. His face swims in and out of view as I struggle to reach him. I'm starting to forget his face. After all this time, it blurs and distorts as I strain for it.

Oh, John. I'm sorry. His eyes are puffed and blotchy and he's shaking his head, his eyes full of sadness. He doesn't speak but I hear his voice. *Oh Maddy*, he seems to say. *Hurry*.

I pull myself upright again, open my eyes and stumble forward along the wall, dragging my arm, scraping the knuckles raw on the crumbling stone. He's just ahead, beyond the tunnel, just a little out of sight, there on the tracks, just as I imagined him. If I hurry, I won't be too late. I can warn him. Save him. It's not too late. It's just a different time. We can still be together, still have our life.

And then, as I round the curve, closing in on the far end of the tunnel, I see her.

My little girl, glowing with light, standing there on the track. She's a solid, gleaming figure in the brightness of the tunnel mouth. I lift my hand to wave to her but she can't see me. I'm shrouded in darkness.

She's a small thing, delicate, her coat padded and zipped up against the cold. Her hair is neat, divided into thin plaits. Charley. Oh, that I can come out of this tunnel, out of the blackness and live it all again, with John at my side, with you still a child, both of you still mine. Don't you know how different I'd be for you, my love? How different everything would be.

She stops peering into the tunnel and turns and starts to trot away, jumping from one wooden sleeper to the next, hopping down the track. Her backpack rises and falls on her back as she bounces. Her bearing is erect and purposeful and her jauntiness makes my heart ache.

I try to shout but no sound comes. I am slow and lumpen and she is too far ahead, steadily opening the distance between the two of us with every leap. John's weeping is loud in my ears and I try to say to him: *I won't let her go this time, John. I'll never let her out of my sight. Don't cry. I'll do better this time.*

I hurry out of the tunnel at last and race after her, clumsy, tripping and slipping on slime and moss. I splash through filth, soaking my flapping shoes. The rails are again humming and I'm hurtling now, trying to reach her, feeling the warning down the track, frightened beyond thought. Behind me, I sense the train drawing closer, hearing it rattle and shudder down the line, the sharp blast of the whistle as it approaches the tunnel.

'Charley!' I scream at her, my arms waving high, lunging for her.

She turns at last and I see her face, those big eyes, John's eyes, fixed on me. Terrified. Transfixed.

I stagger forwards and throw myself at her, knocking her sideways off the rails, trying to curl my body around her tiny frame.

Even as we fall clear of the track, striking the ground hard, the train speeds past us both, wheels spraying sparks as the driver sees us at last and tries desperately to brake in an explosion of sound and air and colour.

Then silence. Nothing and again nothing. He's gone. The sobbing has ended. John is quiet at last.

A distant voice, high up on the embankment, starts to scream. Hysterical. Charley's voice, here and now, adult, screeching from the ridge above: 'Ella! Ella!'

Not Charley at all, here on the tracks, alive and clinging to me. Not my daughter but hers.

'Ella!'

She hurls herself down the slope towards us both.

And then she's here, on the ground with us, throwing herself on her daughter, crying, seeing her safe and whole, even as I wrap my arms around them both, around my child and my child's child, drawing them to me at last.

MADDY

One Year Later

Time and I are back in step now. *Trip, trap, hurry, scurry*. Along the pavement, down the high street, over the crossing to the beat of the electronic beep, beep, beep. Quick, purposeful strides. Places to go. Things to do. No time to lose.

I arrive slightly early, as always. Here I stand, smart and sensible, waiting at the school gates. My hair is short and tidy. My clothes are clean, if a little odd. My lace-up shoes are practical. One or two mothers nod hello, then turn their backs on me to continue their murmuring chat.

I don't mind. I'm not one of them. I never was, never have been, whoever the other people were. That's just how it is. I'm accustomed.

Then the main door opens and the children tumble out, hair flying, feet kicking, bags swinging, racing over the playground to find us. Ella reaches me first and I scoop her up, hug her to me hard, my beautiful girl, and then Rosie, catching up, bangs into us both, arms wide, group hug.

We set off, three of us speaking all at once.

'How was school?'

'Guess what Miss Hardcastle said?'

'Tell a story!'

They bounce and pull on either side of me, tugging at my hands.

'D'you know…?'

'What did you get for your spellings?'

'I'm hungry.'

On the high street, we pass the cash machine where Becca left her money in the rain all that time ago. The doorway where I sagged, surrounded by dirty plastic bags, head aching, heart heavy and watched them. Now I flow on past, part of the stream.

Homeless people don't collect children from school. It isn't possible. But I'm an officially recognised grandma now. My name is typed on the school list. I'm somebody.

We slow down as we pass the broad shop windows of Jason's and peer in at the shoes on display. For a while, we play: 'If you had to have one pair, which pair would you have?'

Rosie goes for the red stilettos. Ella wants the cowboy boots with heels.

Then Charley emerges from the depth of the shadows inside and the shop bell jangles as she opens the door and peers out.

'Well, look who's here!' She smiles, then shakes her head. 'I can't chat. We're busy.'

'Oh, Mum!' Ella pulls a face.

'Have a lovely sleepover.' She reaches down and kisses her daughter on the top of the head, then looks across at me. 'See you later.'

And she's gone.

'Come on then.' I shoulder their bags, take their hands again and we set off, more slowly now, threading our way as a clumsy threesome down the pavement.

Charley's lucky she's still got a job at all and she knows it. David saved her. He hired a lawyer and they made long lists of the shops she'd robbed, the goods she'd stolen. He paid them all back, item by item, for their losses. I sat with her as she wrote out dozens of statements and apologies and admissions of guilt and trudged from one store to another, making her confessions.

In the end, they all agreed not to prosecute. She takes after her father. They fly too close to the sun.

'Can we bake a cake when we get home? Pleeeeease?'

I shake my head. 'I can't stay that long, sweetheart. Not today. I've got things to do.'

They run ahead of me up the communal stairs and I follow them by sound, hear them bang on the flat door.

By the time I catch up, they're both in the kitchen with Becca, chattering. I sit heavily in a chair, getting my breath back. Becca is still in her coat as she moves rapidly from table to cupboard to fridge and unpacks the shopping.

'And guess where he's taking you!'

Rosie says: 'China?'

'Not China! That's practically the other side of the world. Somewhere with a special tower.'

'I know!' Ella bounces on the balls of her feet, excited. 'Pisa!'

'Paris!' Becca says. 'For a whole weekend! Isn't that amazing?'

'Yay!' The girls career around the table, arms outstretched. 'Aeroplane!'

Becca smiles, watching them. 'Maybe. Or it might be by car.'

I manage to ask: 'What's this?'

Becca raises her eyebrows at me from across the kitchen, two cartons of orange juice in her hands.

'Mark called this morning. He's offered to take all three of them to Paris just after Easter. Rosie and Alex, and Ella's invited, too.' She gives me a meaningful look. 'Says he wants them to spend time with his new friend.' She pauses, checking to make sure the girls aren't watching, then mouths: '*Girlfriend*.'

I nod, my eyes still on hers. He's moving on at last, then. Good. It's time. 'That sounds positive.'

'I think so.' She puts the orange juice in the fridge and the door smacks shut. The girls run off screaming together towards the sitting room and, once they've left and the noise has died, she adds: 'He sounded relaxed. Happy.'

'Thank the good Lord for that.'

I watch her as she moves around the kitchen and I read her movements. She's tired, I can see that. She's home later than I expected. Must have been a busy lunch shift at Jane's and a lot to replenish for the evening team. She works hard, especially now Dennis has finally announced plans to retire. She'll be in charge of the kitchen by the end of the year.

But there's a lightness in her face, in her shoulders. She's pleased for Mark then, as I thought she would be. He learned to stop pestering her, in the end. Seeing her with David forced him to realise there was no going back. But it's been a painful process. Maybe, if he's finally met someone new, she can let go of her guilt. Maybe she and David will even press ahead with their own plans and get a bigger place, together.

Rosie and Alex keep pestering them to do it. They're desperate for their own bedrooms. Rosie wants room to display her pony collection and space for Ella to sleep alongside her when she stays over. Alex needs a proper desk with room for his laptop. He's working hard at school and excited, most of all, about his computer science class and the chance to design his own games.

Becca goes through to join the girls in the sitting room and I say goodbye, leaving them sorting out Ella's bedding and arguing about who'll sleep where tonight.

On my way home, I dash to the supermarket. A middle-aged woman in a grey coat and green woolly hat is sitting outside against the wall, close to the taxi rank. Her legs stick straight out into the path of passers-by. Thick tights, ripped down the seam.

Swollen ankles. The smell reaches for me. Stale whisky and urine and sour breath. Her eyes are glazed. Someone must have given her enough cash for a bottle of the hard stuff.

The supermarket is bright with noise and light. I take care of my money. I haven't much to spend but it's a joy to walk down an aisle and make choices, knowing I have cash in my pocket and a kitchen where I can cook, however small. Normal life is still extraordinary to me.

The only place I never stray is the drinks aisle. Best not. Too much temptation. Charley and I both. We made a deal, when I came back to London to be near them, a pact with each other for Ella's sake. No more alcohol. *Never, never, never, never, never.*

Afterwards, shopping bags bulging, I go back to the prostrate woman and crouch beside her to hand over the sandwiches I've bought, the packet of biscuits and the bottle of water.

She blinks and struggles to focus on me. 'Thanking you. Very kind.'

I say, pointing to the food: 'You should eat something. You'll feel better.'

She raises her voice and a sudden volley of tuneless singing erupts into the street. I can't make out the words. I dip my hand into my pocket and show her one of our printed cards.

'You can get a hot meal here, three times a week, see?' I point to the address. She smiles up into my face, oblivious. 'I work there, in the back office. They're all right. They'll help you find a place to sleep. Get you off the street.'

She shakes her head. 'Oh, I don't think so, darling. Don't like those places. Dirty, most of them.'

I know. I remember. 'Well, keep the card, will you? Look, I'm putting it in your pocket. Try to eat.'

When I look back from the corner of the road, she's still singing, her hands high as she conducts an invisible orchestra. Shoppers step off the pavement, eyes forward, to avoid her. I make a mental note to tell the outreach team about her tomorrow. They'll come by and see what they can offer.

I'm still thinking about her as I put the key in the lock of the main door and climb the stairs to the bedsit. It's David's bedsit really, but I pay him what little I can.

Inside, I put the kettle on, unlace my shoes and place them side by side on the hall mat and go through the shopping. Not much, truth be told. Not much for – I count again on my fingers – Charley, David, his parents and me – for five people. I frown, considering. His mother might bring a pudding or a cake. She did at Christmas. David favours fancy chocolates and flowers.

The kettle boils and I make myself tea in my second-hand teapot and pour it into one of the mismatched bone china cups and saucers. Soon I'll get out the chopping board and think about cooking. But for now, for a moment, I sit quietly in the stillness and savour my hot drink.

I look around the tiny kitchen. At the girls' drawings and paintings, stuck with magnets to the front of the fridge. At the small shelf of second-hand books, the personal library I'm slowly rebuilding, piece by precious piece. At the kitchen clock, my house-warming present from Becca and David. And at the photograph framed there in the corner of a brother and sister, bright-eyed and full of life, holding hands on a holiday beach, matching straw hats on their heads. John and his twin sister, Christy. My John. The love of my life.

Soon, the doorbell will ring and Charley will be there, my wonderful daughter, shop-weary but ready to help. She'll set down her bag and wash her hands and put on an apron and join me at the kitchen table, drinking tea and peeling and chopping and stirring.

I try not to fuss her but I take sideways glances now and then when she's talking, her hands busy, chatting about Jason's or about Ella. I love to watch her. I see John there. He's always with us, peaceful now, happy for us both that, despite all that happened, all the wrong we did, we're together again at last. The love keeps stretching.

The bedsit will be overwhelmed by five adults but it's neutral space and Charley needs to sit down here with her adoptive parents every month or so – I insist on it. I have a lot to thank them for, and David too, and so does she. It's a long journey, recovery. But we're taking it together, one step at a time.

I finish my tea and stir myself back into motion, get to my feet, rummage for a knife to start on the carrots and beans.

My waiting days are over. My lost child is found. My life can begin again.

A LETTER FROM JILL

I want to say a huge thank you for choosing to read *Invisible Girl.* If you enjoyed it and want to keep up to date with all my latest releases, just sign up at the following link. Your email address will never be shared and you can unsubscribe at any time.

www.bookouture.com/jill-childs

Would you give a stranger shelter in your home?

In London today, it's impossible to avoid the homeless. On my high street, on my walk to and from work, outside railway and tube stations, people – men and women, old and young – are visible in shop doorways and dark corners, lying huddled inside sleeping bags or under blankets.

Recently, a man started living on the pavement outside a disused restaurant at the end of my own suburban street. We all worry about him. He feels like 'our' homeless person and we feel responsible. Some neighbours give him food. Some sit and chat with him. Others have called social services in the hope he'll get help. What else can we do?

One of my five-year-olds, a girl rather like Rosie, tugged at my hand one day as I was hurrying her past an unkempt homeless woman and pointed to her.

'That lady hasn't got a home,' she said. 'Why doesn't she come and live with us? We've got room.'

My answer – some excuse – made me feel ashamed. At the age of five, it's hard to understand how complex adult problems can be but her solution seemed so simple and touching in its kindness.

The incident stayed with me. What might happen, I wondered, if someone did invite a homeless woman into their lives, a woman with a complicated history and multiple problems? And what if that woman was also feisty and well-educated – and was sleeping in that particular street, in that particular suburb not by chance but for a reason?

It was out of these thoughts that *Invisible Girl* was born.

I hope you loved *Invisible Girl.* If you did, I would be very grateful if you could write a review. I'd love to hear what you think, and it makes such a difference in helping new readers discover my books for the first time.

I love hearing from my readers. You can get in touch on my Facebook page or on Twitter. Thank you!

All best wishes to you and yours,
Jill

jill.childs.71

@author_jill

ACKNOWLEDGEMENTS

Thank you to my wonderful editor, Kathryn Taussig, and all the team at Bookouture.

Thank you to my brilliant agent, Judith Murdoch, the best in the business.

Thank you, as always, to my family for all their love and support.

Made in the USA
Middletown, DE
07 August 2021